The Great Free Enterprise Gambit

New Years' Eve
Dec. - 2000

To Barbara + Anna -
Happy New Year, of
course.

Jim Bean

Other books by James Baar

The Careful Voter's Dictionary of Language Pollution
(Understanding Willietalk and Other Spinspeak)

Polaris! (coauthor)

Combat Missileman (coauthor)

The Great Free Enterprise Gambit

by James Baar

The Great Free Enterprise Gambit

First soft-cover edition 2000

First Internet edition 2000 (www.1stboooks.com)

First published (Houghton Mifflin) 1980

Copyright © 1980, 2000 by James Baar

Library of Congress Cataloguing in Publication Data

Baar, James, date
The great free enterprise gambit.
     I. Title.
PZr.B1113Gr [PS3552.A15] 813' .5'4 79-25889
ISBN 1-58721-132-7

ABOUT THE BOOK

This wild and satiric tale of big business and sleazy political derring-do has been called one of the funniest business novels ever written.

International Coagulants, a conglomerate corporate octopus, is bleeding around the world from massively poor business decisions. But a cast of questionable characters are determined to save it for a variety of questionable reasons even as they undercut each other for control. The date: the late '70s. It could be this morning.

J. Wigglesworth ("Wiggy") Pratt, IC's CEO, is a thirsty "Roman senator with silver hair, great dignity and blue but somewhat fishy eyes." He tries to save the company with a series of smarmy new ventures and a secret deal with Major Ibn Mamoud, elegant Levantine representative of the Sheik of Sharm who owns Yankee Properties, Inc.

Meantime, Ward Winchester Read, Wiggy's arch rival who looks like a cross between Jack Kennedy and a frustrated battle tank commander, plots a takeover from exile in a plush non-person suite in the IC Tower in New York.

Others with key roles are the power hungry Senator Jefferson Jennings Bryan of the great state of Louisiana; a sinister ex-CIA operative and master of disguise; a Mexican Zapotec Indian oil billionaire named Joe the X; and Gaston Edsel, a former fork-lift truck operator elected to Congress by a fluke, elected Vice President in error and elevated to the White House when his running mate resigned after being exposed as an unemployed summer stock impersonator of presidents.

There are multiple plots, slippery maneuvers, betrayals and stumblebum connivings all swimming in a thick marinade of spinspeak and cant. The IC Tower itself is besieged by a private IC army of social dropouts recruited under a government contract to serve as peacekeepers in Third World countries. The stock market swings insanely, folly is loosed and the world wanders toward cataclysm. A final surprise resolution comes decked in yards of euphemism and offers at least a visionette for tomorrow.

Preface to First Edition

The resemblance of any of the following characters and events to the real world is both coincidental and absurd. Obviously, the converse could only mean that collapse of tho system is imminent.

Preface to First Softcover and First Internet Edition

Ditto.

Also a cautionary note of possible interest to natural survivors: The action in this story takes place in the late 1970's. Even a casual glance at the world of the New Improved Millennium would suggest that much of what takes place in this absurd fictional past clearly recalls the old saw that life imitates art.

Ward Winchester Read.

There was a name to contemplate. Or should have been.

He had everything in just the right amounts. Or, at least, many would say he did.

Appearance: In youth, a blond hero escaped from an old Maxwell Parrish cover. Particularly in uniform. In middle age, a combination of John F. Kennedy and Dean Acheson.

Education: St. Mark's (for Waspy polish), Dartmouth (for skiing and drinking), Sloan (for seriousness and reverse snobbery).

Family: His mother was a lateral descendant of Increase Mather; his father, of Light Horse Harry Lee.

Money: Never the crudity of too much; always the balm of enough.

Career: Incandescent. A corporate wunderkind. Subsequently, everyone's man to watch; secretly to hate; publicly to court.

Then, suddenly, incredibly, in his mid-fifties, everything fell apart: his career; his family; his trust fund. And now he sat on the sidelines of the increasingly tacky last quarter of the American Century. He was not on the field; he was barely on the bench.

But, intuitively, he knew there would be more glories to come. He had to wait for his moment. He had to be extremely careful; to watch; to be ready; worst of all, to be patient. The pain was excruciating.

In an heroic leap of faith, he sustained himself with a simple vignette that he carried about in a secret corner of his mind: surely, surely there would be a time when glowing opportunity would beckon; when princely fortunes would be at stake; corporate empires would be near disaster; nations, possibly whole civilizations, would be in jeopardy. Oil, the dollar, the yen, six hours of commercial television a day for the average family, the golden expense-account meal ticket, the unemployment check mailed to the Florida beaches, corporate Easter baskets burgeoning with executive perks, all. . . all would hang over the abyss. And he, Ward Winchester Read, would step confidently from his Mercedes 6oo into the waiting TV lights to save the day.

Let the bells of Harvard Business School ring out in hope and joy. Such a time was near.

Spring in Manhattan.

Date: Any year now. Time: 9 A.M.

Muggy weather. Pervasive smog. Building and automobile lights burn filmily through the semidarkness.

A million or so people hurtle frenetically about the midtown streets. Traffic on the Avenue of the Americas does not move. Possibly it will never move again.

In grubby concrete Grecian urns on the curb between Fifty-fifth and Fifty-sixth streets six spavined trees try to bud. They will fail. The all-polymer Early American pine façade of the world headquarters building of International Coagulants permanently shields them from any nutritional sunlight that might penetrate to street level.

But the sun is shining.

Eighty-eight floors up from the windows of the International Coagulants Tower spring sunshine can be seen everywhere. It lights the great, blue sky over New York. It gleams through the windows, bouncing off white, fat clouds. It sparkles off the blue metal boxcars of air-conditioning equipment crowning the tops of the other Manhattan towers that pierce skyward through the gray sea of smog.

J. Wigglesworth (Wiggy) Pratt, chairman and chief executive officer of International Coagulants, stands somewhat unsteadily at one of the great windows in the foyer outside the IC Tower's World Conference Hall and momentarily looks at the view. Wiggy is a sixty-two-year-old model of a business statesman: With the benefit of only one jowls and one eyelids adjustment, his profile is as well formed and clean cut as the day he left Princeton; his silky, white hair is perfectly parted and combed; his skin, except for a few telltale red lines, is slightly tanned; his tall frame is lean and yachty. As he wrenches himself away from the window, he thinks of his condominium on Aruba, sighs in-

3

wardly, and somewhat unsteadily resumes his heavy burdens.

In fact, those burdens this morning are particularly heavy. In not more than five minutes he must talk to the business press. He does not like to do this anytime, and today he hates the idea. But, unfortunately, there have been problems. In an up market, IC stock has moved downward with painful consistency. The usual confidential phone calls to security analysts have had no effect. Bankers in such places as Frankfurt and Zurich have made unkind remarks. A number of pension fund executives have also been less than pleasant. Wiggy feels a need to renew general confidence among what the IC Public Affairs Department refers to as his many publics.

As an initial step toward renewing confidence, he steps quickly from the window into a private washroom and grants himself an extra quarter-tumbler of Scotch. Then, adjusting his already impeccable tie, he walks briskly into the IC World Conference Hall.

About two dozen business writers are gathered there. They have been sipping coffee and eating pastries. The coffee is served in Limoges-type cups made from reprocessed soft drink bottles by the IC Fine Housewares Department. The pastry is from House of Buns, an IC fast-food franchise chain.

The business writers sit in a three-row semicircle in plush oversized conference chairs upholstered in a bright orange —the IC color. Some of the writers dress like bankers and carry pocket calculators, gold pencils, and attaché cases. They assume the attitude of senior loan officers. Some are rumpled and openly pugnacious. A few in business gray prepare to fawn nervously in hopes of future employment. All but the latter smell trouble and happily anticipate claiming major space in their publications for particularly nasty stories.

At the base of the semicircle of chairs is a small, raised platform with a table. On the left side of the table sits Orrin Boon, IC senior vice president and chief financial officer.

He has the face of an aging teen-ager but is devoid of all hair. He could be a moonman in a late afternoon TV repeat movie. At the right end of the table sits T. J. Lightmeade, executive vice president and twice-rejected heir apparent. He is a lawyer. He looks kind and avuncular. He isn't. Wiggy sits in the middle, with great dignity. He is a Roman senator with silver hair and blue but somewhat fishy eyes.

Directly behind Wiggy sits Leslie Gross, vice president of corporate information. He is pleasantly pudgy and very jolly. He is also almost totally incompetent. Leslie has on his lap a large, orange notebook. He always refers to it as "the Bible" and winks confidingly when he says it. The notebook contains carefully designed responses to hundreds of questions that he suspects may be asked. They seldom are. Or, if asked, the answers are seldom located in time.

"Thank you so much for joining us this morning," Wiggy begins and beams his board-of-directors smile. "Always a pleasure to meet with you. I hope everyone has had some of Leslie's famous Danish pastry and coffee."

"No goddamn cheese Danish," a writer (rumpled variety) says loudly to his neighbor near the back row. "Wait'll they see my story."

General laughter. Les joins in enthusiastically, introducing a wisp of idiocy. Wiggy smiles automatically and goes on.

"We want to keep things as informal as possible. I have a few words to say. Then we'll take questions."

He then introduces "Or" Boon as one of big business's "dazzling financial wizards" and "Tommy" Lightmeade as "our ambassador extraordinary." Little anecdotes made up by Les to demonstrate human frailty at high corporate levels are offered on each. The job seekers and Les chuckle a lot.

Wiggy adjusts half glasses on his beautiful nose and begins to read from a script.

"Our meeting today is part of our new policy of helping you gentlemen follow our growth and our developing

5

business. After all, when you have a twenty-billion-dollar company like International Coagulants, even we who are so close to it have some trouble keeping on top of everything."

General snickers. Les laughs. Or Boon winces. Tommy Lightmeade smiles diplomatically.

"As you know from our quarterly report yesterday, earnings are indeed rather down. Twenty percent from the first quarter; twenty-five percent from the same period last year. But numbers, gentlemen, plain numbers just do not tell the story. Frankly, to put it another way, the stories that some papers carried this morning do not tell the story either.

"For example, we have had in the last few months some very serious nonrecurring costs. Primarily, these involve the selling and writing off of our chemical car business to the Japanese trading group, Mishisawa, for ten cents on the dollar. We still feel that liquid hydrogen has great promise as an automobile propellant; but after thorough analysis, this is not for the near term.

"Another nonrecurring cost involves the damage claims resulting from class action suits filed against our Major Leisure Division. As you know, these involved our Totalpower Sunlamppe™ which now has been withdrawn voluntarily from the market. Please keep in mind that we withdrew this product from the market without prejudice. We felt that it was a fine product. It is apparently true that certain white mice, when subjected to intense dosages from a Totalpower Sunlamppe, developed skin cancer and some developed convulsions. But no direct link has ever been proven. And no such cases ever developed in human beings. Despite this lack of clear evidence, one hundred million dollars in damages have been awarded by lower courts. But we are continuing to appeal. When these awards are reversed —and we are quite confident they will be — then this will have a most favorable effect on earnings

6

"Finally, our quarter earnings picture in no way properly reflects outstanding growth and new developments of International Coagulants in a number of important areas. One of these is in our Grocery and Gourmet Foods Division. Within the last six months we have introduced a new pet food product — Albeef™ — that has become the country's number-one seller. Albeef actually is a spin-off product from our Outer Space Division. It is a highly nutritious, absolutely pure meat food grown under laboratory conditions. And, I am happy to report, American pets love it.

"At the same time IC is branching out into a number of areas important to the future of mankind. I can disclose two here today. First, our Goodtimes Land Division has acquired one hundred-year leases to six Pacific islands in the Marianas and will build there complete vacationlands incorporating literally dozens of the newest and most exciting products and developments from our laboratories. And each island will be customized for a different segment of the vacation market. These new Vacationlands will be ready just in time to capitalize on the four-day workweek and the SST, in which we still have great faith.

"The other exciting new development I will disclose today comes from our New Life Styles Division. This is essentially a spin-off from our work with the Administration in Washington in retraining the disadvantaged. As you may recall, we ran a training center in Idaho called New Life City. Well, at first, the results at NLC were very unimpressive. Frankly, the inmates appeared to be untrainable for any known useful occupation. But then we hit upon the idea of employing these basically fine people as security forces in some of the less privileged countries of the world on a lend-lease basis. We have now developed several prototype units, and I am happy to report that two of these units are fulfilling our full expectations for important clients in Latin America and Africa. As you might expect, this is a highly profitable service business.

"And now gentlemen we will be happy to answer any questions.

Thirty minutes and twelve questions later the press departed. They looked a lot happier than when they arrived. There was much jolliness when everyone shook hands.

"You were great," Leslie told Wiggy afterwards. "You were all great," he said again, taking in Or Boon and Tommy Lightmeade.

"I hope so," Wiggy said, and nothing in his voice inspired much hope. "I didn't like some of those questions about Albeef and the Goodtimes Land program. I think a lot of those S.O.B.'s have it in for us."

"Don't worry, Wiggy," Leslie said. "That's just the press. We can handle them. Believe me, I know those guys."

"Somebody ought to cut a couple of those bastards off at the pockets," Tommy Lightmeade said. "How much advertising do we run in some of those papers?"

"Not much," Wiggy said.

"Well, we might."

"Don't worry," Leslie said. "Believe me, you guys were great."

"I hope so," Wiggy said and looked more worried. Or Boon said nothing. But his eyes looked very cold.

A headline on the front page of the *Washington Star* that afternoon said:

IC RENTS MERCENARY TROOPS
TO LATIN AMERICAN DICTATOR

The story went on to report that the State Department and the White House had no immediate comment. However, the chairman of a House subcommittee disclosed that the State Department had granted IC an export license for "security service programs" for three Latin American cities and an unidentified African developer.

The wire services played up the plan to develop the Marianas. All wires picked up a statement J. Wigglesworth Pratt had made in response to a question about the U.S. Navy's activities in that part of the Pacific:

Our lease is from the Navy, and of course the Navy would retain certain rights in time of national emergency.

As for the Japanese, I don't see that they have any rights there. My understanding is that the islands belong under mandate to the United States by right of conquest.

The State Department and the White House were reported to have no immediate comment. A Tokyo dispatch reported student riots in front of the U.S. Embassy.

The New York financial press preferred to feature Albeef —particularly its high sales volume.

A lead story prepared for the following day's issue of the *Wall Street Journal* and carried that afternoon on the Dow Jones broad tape reported:

Mr. Pratt denied reports that more than fifty percent of all Albeef sales in the last six months were to the U.S. Army for distribution to Vietnamese refugees. Moreover, he denied any knowledge of recent stories in *Le Monde* that black-market speculation in Albeef shipments had made Albeef cans a major medium of exchange in Angola and India.

"Albeef is pet food," he said. "We sell it as pet food. But it certainly is good and wholesome. I'm sure if properly prepared it could be quite delicious."

Asked if he would eat it, he said:

"Well, why not?"

The Defense Department had no immediate comment.

More than six million shares of IC stock were traded on the New York Stock Exchange by the closing bell. Transactions in IC stock ran up to twenty-five minutes late on the tape as major blocs were dumped and independent traders scrambled to follow.

IC finally closed at 50— down 12.

*   *

The following morning was a public relations nightmare for Leslie Gross.

Beginning at 8:00 A.M., he sat in his office, which at happier times he referred to as "desk central," and talked continuously on a bank of telephones. At no time were there fewer than four calls backed up. He broke off talking only to take an occasional bite of a Dietquik™ roll from the House of Buns. He was undergoing a saturation attack.

Time wanted more on Albeef. *Newsweek* planned a major story on the Marianas.

Business Week wanted more on IC's sinking stock. Then came a rolling wave of new calls from major dailies and the networks.

"They're not mercenaries," Leslie said for the fifth time to his latest torturer, a syndicated columnist and TV

10

commentator named Harvey Catoni.

"Call them any damn thing you want," Catoni said. "You still haven't answered the question. How many of these retreaded spade killers do you have on the payroll?"

"Disadvantaged trainees," Leslie said, slipping down in his chair.

"Sure, but how many?"

"I'm not in a position to say. They were trained on a government contract. It's classified."

"Bull. Does the government know that you've shipped these gunslingers to Bolivia to help crush a revolution?"

"We have no knowledge of any police actions of that sort," Leslie said, slipping further in his chair.

"What do you think they're doing down there?"

"They guard public buildings and direct traffic."

"With mortars and tanks?"

"We have no knowledge of that," Leslie said, his head barely visible above the desk.

J. Wigglesworth Pratt called him at 10:30. For midmorning he sounded unusually crisp.

"Four members of the Board have already phoned this morning," Wiggy said. "What can I tell them? What are you doing? How could you let this happen?"

"Don't worry," Leslie said. "Tell them not to worry."

"But what are you doing about it?"

"We're right on top of it. Don't worry. We've already made tremendous progress."

"You have? When do we see it?"

"You have. You should have seen the stuff they were going to print before we got to them."

"It was worse?"

"You bet. It was disastrous. There's just no trusting those guys. Fortunately, we got them to drop some of the really bad stuff. And we're not through yet. We're right on top of it. Don't worry. "

"Thank God. I'll call the board members."

"Don't promise them too much. After all, there is just so much even the top PR guys in the country can do In a situation like this."

"What should I tell them?"

"Tell them the truth. Tell them it was a 'save.'"

4

The full delightful enormity of the situation was not at all clear to Ward Winchester Read as he began his daily pre-breakfast jog through Central Park that morning at six o'clock.

He already had seen the *New York Times*. His immediate reaction was fully predictable:

"Goddamn jackass," he said. But then he dismissed the matter as merely another bit of Wigglesworth bumble — a malaise with which he had been contending for years. As he jogged through the cool April air along the empty path, he hummed in his head excerpts from his favorite record, "Four Centuries of Fanfares." He did not want to think about Wigglesworth and IC. He wanted to feel only the pleasant narcosis of music and physical exercise. It made the world seem almost right again and full of promise. However, he could not avoid noticing in the grass along the path the leavings of a typical night in Central Park: broken muscatel bottles still encased in paper bags; bits of tire chain and rope; crushed beer cans; smashed bushes; shreds of clothes; gnawed Kentucky Fried Chicken bones; soiled Big Mac boxes. He was once more reminded that the world machine was running amuck. And the thought of a world amuck, of course, reminded him immediately of J. Wigglesworth Pratt.

At one point he had been Wiggy's golden boy, a magical savior who could be dispatched from business disaster to business disaster where he would shortly make all well. Wiggy treasured him. Many others feared and hated him. Ward had reveled in the role.

He knew he was truly a very special type. He had fought as a tank commander with Patton's Third Army through France from St. Lo to the Rhine and emerged from World War II as one of the army's youngest and most decorated majors. He had moved smartly through

Dartmouth and Sloan with honors that he achieved without visible effort; joined IC and jumped almost immediately to a fast career track; rose rapidly and became the man to put in charge of trouble.

He recalled sourly three occasions when he had — as he liked to put it these days — saved Wiggy's ungrateful ass. There was the time when Wiggy, as executive vice president, had bought a fire engine company which turned out to be almost bankrupt and IC had to recall one hundred thousand feet of leaky hoses. Then there was the unpleasantness when the IC Plastics Division was about to be expropriated by Mexico. And no one could forget when Wiggy, as vice president for Asia, had·arranged a Laurel and Hardy coup to remove an amazingly greedy southeast Asian dictator. Ward had personally helped Wiggy escape to Tokyo in a Chinese junk loaded with scrap trolley tracks and five hundred prints of an oriental porno flick called *The Yangtze Girls on the Beach.*

But finally the magic failed.

Two years ago Wiggy had made Ward general manager of IC's increasingly dubious entry into the international oil business. IC was one of the world's largest buyers of petrochemicals. When a principal IC supplier, Royal Yemen Oil Ltd., desperately needed cash for new exploration in the Persian Gulf, Wiggy saw an opportunity to control his oil supply and possibly expand the Seven Sisters to eight. He bought 51 percent.

Ward had performed his usual act: He remembered gleefully how he ordered complete reorganization of Royal Yemen; teams of accountants and MBAs swarmed into the Middle East; hundreds of Royal Yemen managers — mostly Frenchmen and Englishmen, a few ex-Nazis, a very few Yemenites — disappeared without a trace; whole buildings full of offices done in late Corporate Imperial were thrown on the market; an aggressive new distribution system of independent YEMMO gas stations was started in the United States.

There was early success. But it was ill starred.

14

Royal Yemen's old wells ran dry. Its new wells remained drier. Meantime, the Seven Sisters, in a burst of good fellowship, drove the new YEMMO stations to the wall. And the local employees in Yemen continued to steal with both hands despite the local custom of removing those hands with scimitars. Soon there was no oil. Royal Yemen became the first company participating in the Great Arabian Oil Rush to turn on the faucet and have sand run out.

IC finally sold the venture at three cents on the dollar. Ward came home. He was fully credited in the business press with one of the largest losses in U.S. business history. Wiggy saw to that.

Unfortunately for Ward, his private life had not gone well either of late.

His twenty-year-old daughter, Hopey, currently lived with a handsome Chicano in a van featuring a Louis XIV bed and a ceiling mirror. They supported themselves on occasional extortions from Ward and by selling sand-cast candles in rural flea markets.

"Daddy," he vividly remembered Hopey saying, "meet Diego. You two have a lot in common. Isn't he beautiful?"

His son, Winchester Lee Truett Read, checked gas meters in Chicago and was a follower of a Zen guru from Huntsville, Alabama.

"The Path is the Way," Win told Ward when they last met to discuss Win's need for a large loan to enter the guru's commune, a run-down Victorian heap called "The Shaggy Balloon." Win also offered Ward a funny-looking cigarette.

Ward's wife, Winnie, had divorced him to marry the president of Air Yemen, an ex-Luftwaffe pilot and Austrian ski instructor.

"Franzi understands me," she told him in the bar at the Beirut Hilton. "We take hot baths."

And his "Friend at Chase" had just informed him in the friendliest way that the futures market was more fickle than had been expected.

"Pork bellies," the Friend said, "just aren't doing what we had hoped."

Life, Ward thought unhappily as he jogged on, had become a dull and disappointing round indeed. Each morning he rose early in his small apartment on Central Park West; jogged in the park; and went to his office in the IC Tower where he did nothing until dinner. Because of his sizable holding of IC options he knew he could not even quit. He could only sit in his large office where no phone rang and wait in vain for corporate remission of sins and reassignment. Or the opportunity he longed for and felt must come.

On this particular morning, soon after entering the park, he jogged toward the zoo. He hoped that he would meet his sometime jogging companion, Suzuki Utagawa, who might have some inside information on market reaction to developments at IC. Suzuki, a failed kamikaze pilot turned money manager, was the chief genius behind what he nostalgically named the Iwo Jima Venture Fund. He also was a black belt karate expert. Usually, when Suzuki jogged, he made a point of running through the woods near the zoo. There, with any luck, he would be immediately attacked by muggers whom he would cheerfully club to the ground with the edge of his outsized hands.

"All take many chances in this world," he would say. "Those fellows make bad selection."

As Ward rounded the Sea Lion Pool, he saw Suzuki sitting on a bench and wrapping his left hand in a handkerchief.

"Little cut," Suzuki said, greeting Ward with a toothy smile. "Faggy blastad wore a neckchain."

Ward sat down next to him, overshadowing the square little man with his large frame. Two sea lions propped their chins on the edge of the pool and watched them.

"What's new?" Ward asked.

"Bad turn for you fellows," Suzuki said. "We dumped IC late yesterday. Plenty follow today."

Ward felt his stomach jump with glee. Suzuki never

16

dumped stock until he was certain that everyone else was nearing the edge of the falls.

"Overreaction," Ward said blandly. "We're basically sound."

"That's what they told me when I took off on my kamikaze mission in forty-five."

"What did you do?"

"I slapped on extra fuel tanks, dlopped my bombs in the Sea of Japan, and landed in Hong Kong in time to take part in peace celeblation."

Ward jogged out of the park shortly after seven o'clock and crossed Fifty-ninth Street to his apartment building. He again saw the *Times* headline:

DOW DROP PACED BY IC

"Jackass," he said happily to no one in particular. "Fucking jackass." And he dared for the first time in months to blow gently on his banked fires of hope.

5

Sally Laurence, executive secretary to Tommy Lightmeade, sat at her desk in the IC Tower and, with a deadpan expression, worked on arrangements for the annual IC management meeting.

In less than one week, IC top management would gather from throughout the earth for what was essentially an annual rite of renewal of the true faith — an abiding belief in the perpetuity of IC and, they hoped, themselves. As always, this secular conclave of cardinals of the true corporate church would be held at a famous hostelry. Such posh surroundings would soothe worldly cares; make possible the reestablishment of the warm camaraderie that only a group sewn with mutual and usually well-founded hate, envy, and distrust can feel; and isolate the august group from the rude eyes of the consuming *fellaheen* of the land. The chosen hostelry this year was the Greenbrier at White Sulphur Springs, West Virginia.

Tommy Lightmeade, assuming an ambassadorial air reminiscent of the Court of Vienna, was in charge of such gatherings. Because of these heavy duties, the irreverent on occasion referred to him as His Majesty's Master of the Games. However, the role gave him great power.

It was he who decided the central themes to be discussed (self-serving to Tommy, embarrassing to the speaker, or dull and therefore career inhibiting). It was he who decided which executives would speak and at what time (early morning, prime, fringe). It was he who even decided such critical minutiae as where executives could sit (honorifically close to the throne or stigmatizingly distant); where their rooms were located (main building, annex, motel off the grounds); and which golfing foursome (captains and kings, rising stars, has-beens) they would join during the allotted fun periods.

Moreover, he brought a special talent for dramatics to

the event. One year, when IC was in a particularly expansive mood, Tommy held a sneak preview of the movie *How the West Was Won* and had buttons and placards emblazoned with the theme "Manifest Your Destiny." Another year, when IC's sales were particularly unsatisfactory, he ordered an original musical written around the theme song "Diamonds Are a Girl's Best Friend" and imported a cast of London stars to perform it. The buttons and placards that year said "Sell One for Wiggy."

But all such arrangements were moved aside on this morning. The particular arrangement on which Sally Laurence labored was the retyping of Tommy's introductory speech for the meeting. At 9:05 Jack Tollhouse, Tommy's favorite speechwriter, had personally delivered to her a draft of major revisions. These had been made imperative by the developments of the last twenty-four hours.

Normally, Jack liked to deliver speech drafts personally to Sally Laurence. She had lovely blonde hair; a lovely profile; a lovely physiognomy; and a lovely cynical turn of mind. But his arrival at 9:05 made it clear that he had more on his mind than idle office ogling.

"Get this to him as fast as possible," Jack said. "He's in pain."

"I think he's beyond pain," she said and began to type:

We are gathered at a critical time when certain elements in the financial community and the business press are taking a far too negative view of recent developments.

As fellow members of management, as shareholders, as veteran ICers, you do not need to be told that this unwarranted negativism which is being spread by our competitors and a few malcontents must be dispelled.

We must rally our great strength. We must renew the IC spirit. We must gird our corporate ship for battle. To do this, we will marshal all of our worldwide capabilities in a new corporatewide program. I have called it OPERATION INTEGRITY.

Sally stopped typing.

"How do you gird a ship?" she asked.

"Have a drink with me tonight and I'll demonstrate," Jack said.

This would not be difficult to arrange because for the last three months they had shared an apartment most weekends.

*   *

Mayhew Stark did three things that morning after reading the *New York Times* on the terrace of his Manhattan duplex apartment.

He called his broker and told him to sell ten thousand shares of IC short

He dictated the lead of his financial newsletter, the *Specialists' Insider:*

Look for early interest by at least three congressional committees and the SEC into Wiggy Pratt's many problems at IC.

He telephoned Parke Bernet and put in a substantial bid on a K'ang Hsi porcelain bowl.

*   *

Shortly before 1 P.M. Paris time, Major Ibn Mamoud of Jedda, Sandhurst, and the Waldorf Towers waited in the lobby of the Plaza Athénée for his American business associate, Mr. Marvin Ikworth.

The major sat on a Louis XV sofa, sipped a wine glass full of orange juice and vodka, and carefully read *Le Monde.* An Agence France Presse story datelined New York was in general agreement with what he had already

21

read in the *International Herald Tribune.* It was very heartening.

Only yesterday he had met with his good client, His Gracious Highness, the Sheik of Sharm. They sat on a pile of priceless carpets in a long, white room in an old fort overlooking a harbor. The harbor itself was jammed with oil derricks and tankers. Conversation was considerably inhibited by the thumping noise of oil pumps. The sheik, a bearded former desert bandit with sad, half-closed, brown eyes, sipped icky coffee.

"Good falcons," he said. "They are increasingly hard to obtain."

"A pity," the major said. "The times are bad indeed."

"I have six sons at Le Rosey in Switzerland," the sheik said. "They are not interested in falcons."

"The young," the major said and shrugged. "What can you do with them?"

The sheik nodded in agreement and began to pare his nails with a jeweled dagger.

"Truly, it is a bad time, Mamoud," he said. "Tell me of your progress."

"Things have gone very well, Your Highness," the Major said, glancing briefly at some papers. "We have acquired a steel mill in Silesia, three hotels in Venice plus a vaporetto line, a majority interest in the Bonnie Dew Scotch distillery, and a chain of French fast-food restaurants called Le Quik."

"Trifles," the sheik said. "Less than one day's production. When do you start buying something big?"

"There are some things in America that we are working on, of course, but we must move with caution. The Americans are so sensitive these days."

The sheik nodded and replaced his dagger in a sheath hanging from his sash.

"Something like Boeing would be gratifying," he said.

"We have something even better in mind. But, as I have heard you say, the race goes to the camel with the big hump and the soft foot. I am afraid it loses something in translation."

"Remember that it is written that the burning sands bring messages from heaven when they blow against the tent flap. When can we expect to hear good news?"

"I leave for Paris immediately to meet with our business associate from America."

"Allah is kind."

The major contentedly took another sip of his screwdriver and admiringly watched a tall French girl fiddle with the low-cut front of her wispy Dior dress.

The business associate for whom the major waited was the president and chief executive officer of Yankee Properties, Inc., operator of a chain of budget motor hotels in Florida. Yankee Properties also had controlling interest in a ski resort in Denver, a solid waste collection service in Houston, and an artificial lemon-flavor soft drink plant (Trulemon) in Tampa. The major was owner of record of 98 percent of Yankee Properties stock. The beneficial owner was a very important personage in Sharm.

Marvin Ikworth, of Queens, City College, and Miami, bustled into the lobby, sat on the puffy damask cushion next to the major, and ordered a martini. Together they looked like a matched set: both short, both dark, both elegantly Levantine, both dressed in very expensive, very dark, very chalk-striped suits made in London.

"You have read the papers, of course?" the major asked.

Marvin smacked his lips and rolled his eyes in response.

"Bloody fine. We shall have a splendid lunch and then ring up our friend, Mr. Wiggy Pratt. I should think he is about ready to talk some more."

*   *

Senator Jefferson Jennings (J-J) Bryan — Democratic statesman from the great state of Louisiana, fourth cousin of America's Great Commoner, and, not incidentally,

23

chairman of the great Joint Congressional Committee on National Oversight — smiled the confident smile of the proverbial Christian who had just drawn his fourth ace.

Only last week he had quietly agreed to the pleadings of his most dedicated and indebted supporters to challenge the President in the forthcoming primary elections. But he had admonished the enthusiasts closest to him that this time he needed a truly major issue. Charges of malfeasance and sexual aberration among presidential appointees, personal peculation among the habitués of the White House, and mere outrageous bumbling in foreign and domestic affairs were a waste of prime time. The public these days required much more startling accusations to divert them from the abominations of day-to-day living. Only the rawest meat would prove amusing. J-J would have to wait for developments. And now a gift had appeared at hand.

As J-J read of IC's problems, he literally gurgled. He saw the scenario clearly. Since the unseemly corporate disasters of the 1960s and early 1970s, no Administration could allow a major corporation to fail without jeopardizing the national economy and the social fabric. And IC was much more than a major corporation—it was a corporate state; an integral part of the world economic system; an ally of nations; the direct and indirect employer of millions; a master of middling Maos and dusky Mussolinis.

Locked, as luck would have it, in the Joint Committee's files were numerous undisclosed reports left over from previous investigations. Included in this mother lode of unused material merely awaiting its time on camera were reports of covert IC activities from Zaire to Tashkent to Singapore. There were reports laced with enough greasy deeds and late-night derring-do to make millionaires of a half dozen investigative reporters and carrying the potential of bringing down any Administration that had to involve itself.

Surely IC was moving toward some terrible cataclysm. Just as surely the Administration would have to come to

IC's aid. And when that happened, Jefferson Jennings Bryan and his Joint Committee would be there. No true patriot could do less.

*   *

Archibald Kennedy, the beautifully graying IC vice president and area manager of Southern Europe and the African Littoral (SEAL), finished his oeufs brouillé. He ate breakfast as usual in the glass-enclosed patio of his home outside Milano — a white stucco eighteenth-century villa with a Palladian façade and an orange shingled roof. There was also a small fountain in the middle of a circular front drive, but, as with most such things in Italy, it had ceased to function.

To Archibald the world felt extraordinarily good. But then it usually did. It was the way that he had ordered his life. Placid day followed placid day. Despite his title, he had few real responsibilities other than to perfume the air of various European cities from Madrid to Istanbul with his presence.

The many boring details of assuring adequate arrangements for visiting IC executives were handled by his staff of nationals.

Meantime, he busied himself with customer golf, customer lunch, customer dinner, customer concerts, and customer theater. Or he followed the same round with government officials and persons of importance. Or, when neither customers nor officials nor persons of importance were available, he practiced by himself.

Conversation during these happy days and nights was always worldly, gossipy, and witty. Business never needed to be mentioned. Actual IC business was pursued aggressively by others who did not report to Archibald but to distant corporate barons. They worried about such grubby matters as profit-and-loss statements. Archibald worried only about relations.

For example, on this particular day, at midmorning, he had to escort the wife of an American steel executive and the Contessa di Sforza-Palma to Bulgari's to buy a bit of jewelry; then he had to lunch at the Principe e Savoia with a banker from Stuttgart to discuss the banker's interest in belonging to an exclusive club in Rome; that afternoon he had a break in his schedule and planned to squeeze in nine holes of golf; and that evening he and his wife would entertain a group of IC stateside executives at La Scala and dinner.

The last item was obviously the most important. Archibald's entire position was based on the maintenance of good relations within the constantly shifting lines of political power of the IC establishment. Extraordinary finesse was required. Contacts needed to be nourished, cut off, reestablished in an endless cycle, as executives moved in and out of favor or emerged from the provinces of corporate empire. When new people were moving into position, great activity was required. Many meetings "on the situation" were held. Many reports filled with inside information— a mélange of rumor and translations from local newspapers — were written. Many errands, involving such matters as vineyard tours, scarce theater tickets, questionable art and antiques, and friendly ladies (or boys, as tastes ran), were performed.

On the other hand, sometimes Archibald found it best to become invisible. Usually this occurred when someone in New York was seeking the high road to corporate canonization by assuming the role that is the holy of holies, the cost-cutter. During such periodic vendettas, Archibald would literally cut off communications and disappear. Anyone asking his whereabouts was told that he was engaged in the most delicate discussions in Libya or possibly with Party and Apparat officials in Sofia and Bucharest. Meantime, most of the staff in Milano also left the country on sick leave or to attend funerals. Should anyone arrive from the States on a survey mission, he would find only a few secretaries and an accountant whose language capabilities did not go beyond a brand of Italian spoken only in the more remote parts of the Po Valley.

Accordingly, obtaining corporate intelligence in a timely manner had a very high priority. Direct contact with reliable sources by phone and in person was essential. In this regard, Archibald's dinner party that evening could be particularly useful. Possibly he could learn the true seriousness of the recent alarming news reports from New York. Possibly he could learn whether any unpleasant executive shifts were planned. Then he could decide whether it would be best to attend the IC management conference at White Sulphur Springs or rush to urgent and potentially imminent secret meetings somewhere in Morocco.

But all that was for later. For now, the sun shone beyond his villa on the distant peaks of the Italian Alps; his second cup of coffee was excellent; and the moment arrived to be driven to his office in his well-polished, dark green Mercedes 450.

6

Wiggy sat in his office and pondered his situation.

The office was the size of a cozy indoor football field. On either side of the door, which opened by push button and slid silently into the wall, there were seemingly endless bookcases and occasional chairs where no one had ever been known to sit or read. On the right hand of anyone entering was a clutch of huge, comfortable chairs and couches for informal conversation; then a small bar with barstools upholstered in the tartan of some obscure bandit clan; then a clutch of elegant antique French chairs. Across the expanse of space was an endless row of richly draped windows and small tables displaying a variety of English and German antique porcelains. At the end of the room, in front of a huge Flemish tapestry, was an aircraft carrier of a desk handicrafted of glass and steel. The tapestry depicted distracted ladies, knights with bulging codpieces, flunkies, large-bottomed horses, and a couple of coy unicorns readying themselves eternally for the chase.

Behind the desk, of course, sat Wiggy, staring somewhat blankly at a row of buttons that could connect him instantly by phone with the farthest reaches of corporate empire. On the desk was an empty glass. Inside his head plans of momentous import took shape.

For despite what Ward Winchester Read in anger and frustration might think, Wiggy was no jackass. Bored, aging, tired: yes. Alcoholic: sure. Irresponsible: no question. Only moderately intelligent: a fair estimate. Greedy: absolutely. Lucky: unbelievably so. But he was not a jackass.

With enormous care, Wiggy rose from his desk, walked to the bar for a refill, and unsteadily returned to his desk. This was no ordinary day. He deserved a few little pick-me ups. No one really appreciated the great burdens that he carried. Being the top man at IC was increasingly no all-day picnic. And it was not as if he had carefully planned it all. Somehow he had merely blundered onward through a swamp of screw-ups and great office had found him out.

Wiggy was one of those steady, stalwart fellows who, by luck and occasional flashes of cunning, had slowly but certainly risen to leadership. Far brighter, flashier chaps had long since crashed and burned spectacularly; or somehow blazed brilliantly like the stars that they were and then disappeared into the numerous special corporate oblivions maintained at shareholders' expense.

Meantime, Wiggy had plodded — or, more appropriately, drifted — to the upper reaches of IC management. Finally, his coronation became almost an obvious afterthought. He was each baron's least offensive candidate. And not the worst of his charms — some cynics said the only one — was that he was one of the few survivors, along with Tommy Lightmeade, of the early days when the empire was still young. Today few other than Wiggy even remembered those times.

IC had been founded in a broth of innocence, mendacity, guile, and good old American know-how in the first years of the twentieth century.

As in so many great business enterprises, first came genius. In this case, the genius was an immigrant German pharmacist from the cuckoo-clock village of Heppenheim. His name was Heinrich Volksblatt. His great discovery was a flour paste-like substance of the consistency of Elmer's glue. When spread on an open wound, it prevented excessive hemorrhaging. Back in Heppenheim, Heinrich called his miracle drug Haltblut. After he immigrated to Camden, New Jersey, and hung out a mortar and pestle sign, he renamed his invention Bleed-no-more.

Except in the immediate environs of Camden, Bleed-no-more was not an overwhelming success. But, at the advent of World War I, Heinrich sold his patent to an itinerant government bond salesman and business visionary named Wingate Cotton, a gifted talker who claimed direct descent from old New England, Southern, and — sometimes — Seneca Indian stock.

International Coagulants was born. Wingate sold Bleed-no-more to the French and the Germans. He sold it to the Russians and the Austrians. He sold it to the English, the Italians, the Bedouins, and, finally, to the Americans. A few still remember how Wingate used to stand in the cold at Thirtieth Street Station in Philadelphia and personally sell Bleed no more to recruits as they boarded trains bound for the training camps and the Argonne.

For four years the assorted combatants could not get enough of the stuff. Meantime, Heinrich went to work for IC as the director of its first research laboratory. It was located in his kitchen in Camden, a historic site now open to the public daily except Christmas and much celebrated in corporate brochures.

By 1919 IC had made millions and Wingate had retired to Cannes. But IC now had a marketing problem caused primarily by the Versailles Treaty. Then, in that moment of commercial darkness, Heinrich's laboratory produced the first of its wonders: Heinrich had discovered that the Bleed-no-more formula had almost infinite possibilities.

First he developed a new method for rapidly hardening cement. From there he moved onward through the 1930s to quick-dry blacktop, plastic toys, cake mixes, and gelatin desserts. And, during World War II, IC developed for the Navy a superhot napalm called "Well Done"; for the Army, a multiuse material for waterproof sandwich packs and contraceptives.

After the Second War, IC grew both horizontally and vertically in all of its various businesses. A cornucopia of products and enterprises resulted, until IC's product lines ranged from America's favorite artificial bone china — Limogeware — to IC's most important invention — the secret epoxy substrate that made the neutron bomb possible.

Wiggy, who had known Heinrich personally, attended

his funeral at the First Lutheran Church in Camden. He often recalled at company dinners and meetings how Heinrich had appeared laid out in the church, wearing one of IC's first forty-year tie clips.

"He looked like a man who had come to rest after completing his mission," Wiggy said. "But even then products like Limogeware and the neutron bomb were still a dream."

Even Tommy Lightmeade had been impressed. It was the kind of grand thing he liked to say. Wiggy knew, of course, that Tommy should probably have been president of IC. So should a lot of other people who were no longer around. But it had been Wiggy who was chosen. And he rose to the opportunity in his fashion.

During the first years of Wiggy's presidency, IC had not done too badly. To a great extent, an organization the size of IC has a forward movement that will continue if left to itself. Wiggy was very capable of meeting such a challenge.

Internally he did almost nothing. It was his specialty. And externally the world economy was good.

Meantime, one by one the more talented executives who might have been selected instead of Wiggy drifted away to run other companies. That, of course, was a blessing. Nothing made Wiggy more uncomfortable than a lot of smart asses sitting around suggesting things for him to do. Also, he found in Tommy Lightmeade a great comfort. As chief operating officer Tommy was willing to assume all grubby administrative details. Wiggy was delighted to let him. Tommy had no vision, but he had an immense hunger for paper and a talent for constructing huge bureaucracies to handle it. He combined this with an equally great talent for a style that might be called Imperial Conglomerate.

Under Tommy corporate staffs multiplied like amoebas in a warm, lambent pool. A hundred did what was once done by ten, until the day when a thousand took the place of the hundred. Buildings, limousines, jet aircraft, yachts, antiques, and paintings spilled over each other to meet the growing needs of the expanding staff groups. And everywhere an increasing self-generated sea of paper, corporate meetings, and surveys fed the urgent need to keep everyone busy and multiplying further. No one questioned the cost. Everyone was having too much fun.

Through all of this Wiggy moved happily. Much of his time was taken up serving on external boards and committees. When on occasion he appeared at IC, rather than tamper with the machinery he devoted considerable effort to increasing his personal wealth through the invention of executive benefits in new forms of incentive compensation, bonuses, delayed stock options, phantom stock, and other ingenious plans. All, of course, were devised to keep these executives working hard for IC or at least alert and present — Wiggy most of all.

His chief ally in these internal activities was Or Boon, a financial executive of rare talent who possessed the peculative instinct of a Willie Sutton. For example, it was Or who devised an incentive plan — later called unique in industry — under which only the stock of the company's six top executives was split, while retaining full market value. It was also Or who, through his able handling of the company's books, was able for so long to protect Wiggy — not to mention the shareholders — from worry about the company's growing financial problems.

But, despite Or's thoughtfulness, Wiggy in the last year had increasingly pondered little else. As disaster followed disaster, the financial problems had become most unsettling. But no one other than Wiggy, Tommy, and Or knew how unsettling.

IC sales for the current fiscal year were expected to be $20 billion. IC earnings for the same period, barring a series of miracles, would be nonexistent. Leslie Gross, despite his occasional trouble with long division, had been sent into the streets to forecast strong third and fourth quarters. But that was merely a delaying action concocted by Or Boon. The action was necessary because there might never be a third or fourth quarter. IC was rapidly running out of cash. The immense drain caused by Tommy's spending plus the Royal Yemen disaster and subsequent catastrophes had wiped out reserves and all usual sources of short-term credit. IC already had immense long-term debts and the possibility of increasing them was considered to be almost zero.

Most of this did not show up in the company's publicly disclosed financial data —an accomplishment due to Or Boon's great finesse both in creative accounting and in convincing IC's independent auditors of the correctness of his dynamic bookkeeping. But the crunch now was fast coming. IC had a worldwide biweekly payroll of $100 million. It probably would not be able to make that payroll at the end of the current month. If it did, it certainly would not make the next one.

"Three weeks at best," Or Boon told Wiggy and Tommy only a day ago. "Three weeks unless we find the money."

"The government will never permit it," Tommy said. "This great American enterprise cannot be allowed to fail."

"Of course," Wiggy said. "Never."

Or stared at both of them.

"Three weeks," he said.

"Well," Wiggy said, "we have the feeler from Yankee Properties."

"Never," Tommy said. "Impossible."

Or shrugged.

"Three weeks," he said.

Now Wiggy looked at a small pad on his desk. On it he had jotted his current personal net worth. At current market value it was $60 million. That represented a lot of houses, cars, and boats, to mention three items close to Wiggy's heart. But if IC could not meet its payroll, that $60 million, in the resulting corporate debacle, would be worth about one ferry ride. Wiggy found the thought unpleasant.

He rose from his desk again, walked across his office to the bar, poured a tumbler half full of Scotch, and sipped it generously. Then he instructed his secretary to return

34

Major Mamoud's call from Paris. Marvin Ikworth might not be a bad chap on the Board after all.

7

World in Brief— One
(Wednesday P.M., EST)

In Sally Laurence's apartment off East Eighty-fourth Street the TV tube came alive with the seated, four-inch-high figures of Martin Dasher and Betsy Poke. A cacophony of French horns and drum beats batters the air. A wall-size screen behind them flashes the exciting words "Your Evening News." And the camera zooms in on the two most popular anchorpersons in all America: Martin — a macho, graying blond poster with deep suntan; Betsy — a cuddly pastiche of hair, teeth, and legs.

"Hi ho there, Betsy. It's a beautiful night here in New York."

"Hi ho to you, Martin. It certainly is. And you know tonight we have a first-time-ever interview with former King Beowulf of Crete and his lovely new bride, cousin of the Dalai Lama and the talk of last season at Cap d'Antibes."

"Yes, Betsy, and we're going to try to get through by satellite to our roving correspondent, Paolo St. John, who will be talking to the man in the street in Kazak. And there'll be Jim Jump and the weather. And Red Bash telling us about that big hockey game in Philadelphia. And lots more."

"But first you have the headline stories for us, right, Martin?"

"Right, Betsy. The news this evening is not too good."

Sally Laurence watched from a stool at her kitchen counterbar—room-divider. Jack Tollhouse lounged on a couch in front of the TV set. Both held gin and tonics.

"Let's go out to dinner," Sally said.

"Let's wait and see if there is anything on IC," Jack said.

"Fantastic dedication."

"Sick curiosity."

"In Detroit, the lights are still out," Martin Dasher said, his voice somewhat upbeat.

On the screen, the black smoky streets of downtown Detroit appear. Dim figures hustle in and out of broken store windows. Fire trucks, police cruisers, and partly dismantled cars jam an intersection.

"Looting slackened during the afternoon but new looters are back in force. Network riot correspondent Joe Garden talked to some of them only a few minutes ago."

Fade to Joe Garden and two fat black men carrying a pink washbowl, three mink coats, and a stuffed moose head.

'Why are you fellows doing this?" Joe asks amiably.

"We're hungry, man. You blind?"

"Honkie fucker."

Fade to the lighted dome of the Capitol.

"In Washington, President Edsel's latest tax reform bill is in big trouble. This will be the first real test of Administration strength in the Senate since defeat of the President's plan to cut government spending by reducing the number of federal employees scheduled to be added to the federal payroll this year."

Fade again to a blazing, wrecked Exxon station outside of San Diego.

"Gas-hungry motorists are waiting impatiently again around the clock in long lines at southern California gas stations. At one station outside of San Diego a housewife wearing pink plastic rollers in her hair went berserk when she was informed after waiting seven hours that she had missed the even day. Roaring away from the station with only a quarter gallon of gas remaining in her tank, she returned moments later at ninety miles an hour and drove her car into the pumps. The crash created a fireball that could be seen from the decks of a fleet of tankers loitering ten miles off the coast.

"The martyred woman — identified by police as Mrs. Wanda Pawtucket of Redondo Beach — is already being

38

called Our Lady of the Pumps. The governor of California will head an official delegation tomorrow at a special memorial service at the Shrine of the Heavenly Highway, a new drive-in church in Malibu."

Sally studied Jack Tollhouse's abstracted, youngish face and decided that beneath the fine features it was definitely weak. Originally she had thought otherwise. He looked beautifully perfect in gray flannels and Harris tweed jackets.

He was bright, amusing, well-bred, educated, and sexually agile. But the longer she knew him, the more certain she became that somehow at around the age of eighteen his development had become arrested.

He was thirty-five and had never married. He simply moved from girl to girl as once he had changed dates at Deerfield and Amherst, where he first became known affectionately by his chums as Cookie. Anytime he came up against a relationship leading toward a commitment longer than a two-week vacation, he temporized and ran. Meantime the sport of the chase apparently never palled.

At IC she had seen this mental set show up in other ways. He was an accomplished writer and contact man with the press. His typewriter could convert Napoleon's retreat from Moscow into a brilliant tactical redeployment. He was the fun-loving, wisecracking kid brother to every newsman in town. But he had difficulty organizing his morning mail; he became physically ill at the thought of directing the activities of a mailroom clerk; and he was the victim of every unhanged felon in the Executive Office.

She took a long drink from her gin and tonic.

Fade from the Capitol dome to a battlefield crowded with blazing native huts, smashed tanks, and exploding aircraft.

"On the Sudanese border, Angolese freedom fighters led by Cuban soldiers of fortune are mounting the biggest attack to date in their drive to reestablish the government of Emperor Numba. Washington observers expressed concern today that the former French colony may fall into the Soviet orbit. But, in London, a government spokesman said Emperor Numba, who took a first at Cambridge, is a true friend of Western democracy and accepted Cuban volunteers only after Washington refused to sell him a squadron of the Pentagon's new F-22 nuclear strike bombers."

Martin Dasher's head and reassuring smile fill the screen against a backdrop photograph of the New York Stock Exchange and a giant red arrow pointing downward.

"More trouble on Wall Street. Yes, the bears still have it. The Dow Jones index plunged through two support levels to seven ten — lowest in five years. IC set the pace at the opening bell, dropping six points by noon. There was a brief rally. But it collapsed under pressure of new IC selling. That followed reports of major government investigations of the big multinational."

"Jesus Christ," said Jack Cookie Tollhouse.
"Let's go eat dinner," Sally said.
"Don't you want to see King Beowulf?"

8

Karma. Will of Allah. Fickle gods. Twenty-four hours after Wiggy talked to Major Mamoud, two casual events occurred involving Ward Winchester Read, and after that nothing would ever be the same again.

Casual Event Number One.

Ward walked into an elevator in the IC Tower and met Jocko Burr, a one-time comrade in arms and now assistant IC comptroller. Jocko had been with Ward almost until the final debacle at Royal Yemen. Then Jocko had been miraculously airlifted by the IC accounting Mafia from the collapsing fortifications just before the native hordes swarmed over the walls.

Jocko, who was known to inhale as many as six martinis at lunch, was not the strongest bookkeeper in the accounting fraternity. But he was regarded as safe and his membership card was valid and of long standing. Accordingly he was saved to muddle through another day.

On this particular morning he looked as if lunch had already taken place. His eyes were somewhat glazed; his face, pallid; his balding head, protected with a few strands of blond hair, moist. He failed to offer his normal, tentative puppy smile that said: "Please like me. I can be trusted."

"Good morning, Jocko," Ward said.

Jocko paused, obviously considering his answer.

"Hello, Ward," he said, finally.

Although they were alone, Jocko said nothing for thirty floors and then he cleared his throat. As the elevator slowed to stop at Ward's floor, Jocko wrenched out some more words.

"Ward, may I join you for some coffee later?"

"Sure, Jocko," Ward said and walked through the open elevator door. Jocko disappeared: a vision, ascending upward toward the top of the Tower and the sunshine.

Ward's office was on the fortieth floor, well below the

continuous smog line. It was a floor known throughout IC as the Isolation Ward. There, along with other executive outcasts, he awaited pardon or handsome job offers with other companies.

For some the wait was only a matter of weeks or months, and they marched off gayly to upper floors in the Tower or to the towers of IC's competitors. But for others the assignment was terminal. They awaited only early retirement. Or, in some cases, executives had actually retired directly from their desks to that Great Executive Suite in the sky. When this occurred, the standard practice was to prop them up in their chairs until after six o'clock. Then they were sent home to Rye or Westport for the last time on some late commuter train with an honor guard of two public relations trainees.

The Isolation Ward was an exquisite circle of hell that never could have been imagined by anyone so parochial as a thirteenth-century Italian. Each executive — officially referred to as an Executive Consultant on Special Assignment — had an individual suite that resembled a royal Egyptian burial vault. Everything that a captain of industry could want for his journey through the Shadow World was present. In the anteroom were expensively upholstered chairs in which no one ever nervously waited for the great man's summons. Mint but year-old copies of *Fortune* and the *Harvard Business Review* lay neatly on a large, glass coffee table. A beautiful, chic secretary — not a permanent employee but some always-changing temp from Manpower or Kelly Rent-a-Girl — sat at an empty desk before a mute executive typewriter with a fresh ribbon. An equally mute telephone call selector board at her side looked as if only a moment ago its many unlit buttons had been brightly flashing, but in all likelihood was not even connected. A bank of horizontal files lined one wall but contained only some out-of-town phone books and a Liberty scarf that the secretary planned to return to Bloomingdale's during lunchtime. A thick carpet added to the pervasive hush that prepared the infrequent visiting

42

explorer for the waxen chieftain within. The chief, of course, would be found sitting in a truly lifelike pose behind an enormous desk on which rested a single memo. The more experienced upside-down reader would note that the memo concerned either personal calls or executive parking.

"I saw him," the caller would say afterward in reverent tones. "He really looked great. You'd never know."

"Did he say what he's planning to do?"

"Not really. The usual. But the way they have him fixed up, he really looked swell."

The high point of the day came early. It was the mail. Only the arrival of the mail reassured an occupant of the Isolation Ward that anyone beyond the fortieth floor knew he was there.

Not that the mail was always that much: a few financial newsletters; a solicitation from a wirehouse about a new municipal bond fund with certain knowledge of which cities would not go bankrupt in the near future; occasionally a copy of an inconsequential memo from some sales manager whose secretary had neglected to purge the copy list; a catalogue from Brooks Brothers. But even these few shards, along with the daily phone hunt for a luncheon companion, could keep a slow reader occupied until noon.

By ten o'clock on this particular morning Ward had been through the morning papers twice and was ready for his postal fix. In fact, it was overdue and he was becoming restless. He buzzed his intercom for his secretary. Nothing happened. He buzzed again. Again no response. He testily grabbed his phone and called her. No answer. He marched across his office and looked outside the door. No one was there. And at this point he sickly recalled that no one had been there when he had arrived. Of course there was no mail. No one had delivered it. No one had gone to get it. Not even a temp had showed up.

An engulfing wave of anguish swept him. Nothing could make him feel more abandoned. To find himself a prisoner on the fortieth floor of a sealed building engulfed in smog with no mail and without even a temporary secretary at his command was too much. He had not felt so distraught since the day in the war when his tank had run out of gas two hundred yards from the last standing bridge over the Rhine. Blinded with fury, ex-tank commander Read hurled himself into an elevator and headed it downward like a submarine toward the subbasement mailroom.

Riding down he stood grimly near the door with his back to two IC managers who did not recognize him. It took a full twenty floors before he placed them as sales managers in IC's Goodtimes Division.

"It's a crazy quota," one said. "The man needs a shrink. It's just a crazy quota."

"Not to worry," the other said. "Just do the motions. He's already in the cross-hairs. Ninety days and he'll be a statistic."

"Jesus, I hope so. It's so crazy."

"Just don't be there when the office rearrangers go in with the flame throwers."

The elevator stopped at the ground floor and they walked out.

"Hey, how's that smart girl? Still at MIT?"

"She's living out west with the Navajos."

The elevator doors closed and the elevator dropped swiftly to the fourth basement. Ward immediately became more depressed. Here in the Tower's foundation there was no trace of Tommy's Corporate Imperial touch. The corridors to the Mail Room and Communications Center were lit with hospital bright neon. The cement walls were painted barracks green. The furnishings had been requisitioned from Salvation Army rejects. The decorating style was Late Lubyanka.

At the Mail Room window, Ward found no one. However, when he leaned inside, he found in the corner a bare-armed Puerto Rican attendant in a leather vest that exposed a great quantity of hair under his arms. "Juan" was printed in gold on the back of the vest. He was lip-reading the banner headline of a tabloid newspaper. It

44

said:

JACKIE 0
LOVES
AGAIN

"My name is Ward W. Read," Ward W. Read said. "I'm looking for my mail."

Juan looked at him sullenly for a full minute, got up, and danced to some music in his head toward the window.

"Hey, how you spell it?" he said.

"Read. R - e - a - d."

Juan slid a pencil and pad across the counter.

"Hey, you write it down, O.K.?"

Equipped with a slip of paper bearing the hieroglyphics of Ward's name, he danced away, reading the newspaper as he went. Five minutes later he returned, still looking at the newspaper. But at that moment the phone on the desk rang and he picked up the receiver.

"Hey, this is Juan," he said, smiled, and began talking in Spanish.

Ward paced outside the window. He tapped his fingers. He glared. Nothing helped. He was ignored. He was in agony. He paced some more. Finally Juan hung up, sat down at the desk, and opened the newspaper.

"My mail," Ward shouted at him. "I want my goddamn mail."

"Nada,"Juan said and shrugged sadly. "The box. It is empty."

Ward turned and with as much dignity as possible strode into the Communications Center. He wanted to find a supervisor. He wanted satisfaction. Something direct but simple would do, such as taking Juan outside and burying him up to the neck in an anthill with honey smeared on his head. But only two operators sat in front of TWX machines. They were busy sending cables. As Ward looked around the room wildly and helplessly, his eyes stopped abruptly at the signature on the top message of a "Sent File" clipboard.

The name was Pratt.

The message was one sentence:

"Look forward seeing you Greenbrier Tuesday."

The message was addressed to Major Ibn Mamoud, c/o Parisbanc, Paris.

"Bingo," Ward said to no one and walked to the elevator with new purpose and a nasty grin.

That, of course, was Casual Event Number Two.

9

When Ward stepped out of the elevator at his floor Jocko Burr was waiting for him. Jocko sat half buried in one of the large upholstered chairs. He was turning the pages of a four-year-old copy of *Fortune*. His face appeared more pallid than an hour earlier.

"These are pretty old magazines," he said. "You must read slowly."

"Most of my visitors live in the past," Ward said. "They find the magazine a comfort. Come in."

Jocko followed Ward into his office and collapsed into a chair again as if wounded.

"You wouldn't have some fine old gin to match your fine old magazines?"

"Aren't you running a little early? I thought you wanted coffee?"

"Not today. My doctor warns against too much coffee."

Ward took a bottle of gin and two glasses from a cabinet and poured some gin into one of them.

"I don't have any ice."

"Who asked for ice?" Jocko reached for the glass and took a gulp. His hand shook and Ward noticed that Jocko's shirt looked as if he had been wearing it for several days. Ward tentatively decided that Jocko might be just the man he needed at this moment. Then Jocko confirmed the thought.

"Ward, we're in beaucoup trouble. I shouldn't be talking to anyone. But, Christ, I've been literally living here for the last two days. I don't know anyone else I can talk to."

"You're talking to a nonperson. I don't exist. You can trust me." Ward tried to look reassuring, but Jocko was too distracted to appreciate the performance.

"You must know what's happening," he said. He took another gulp of gin and a little sloshed on his tie.

"Jocko," Ward said, "I have no idea except Wiggy does

seem to be screwing up more than usual."

"They're making me do funny things. They're making me do funny, funny things with the numbers."

"What else is new? That's your specialty."

"No, really. Not like Royal Yemen. I mean really funny things. The kind the government gets very nasty about. Ward, I don't think I can go along. You know I have my own problems. I have a nutty mother, my wife is a religious fanatic, my daughter is a nymphomaniac. I can't afford to go to Allendale."

Ward pictured in his mind a happy evening at the Burr home in Scarsdale. Lights in the fifteen-room colonial ranch with Tudor highlights plus an atrium glowed invitingly. There was young Cathy downstairs in the cellar with the gas meter reader who read the Burrs' meter at least twice a week. Old kindly Grandmother Burr was outside in the atrium spreading poisoned bread crumbs for the birds. Jocko sat in the library watching Walter Cronkite and sucking on a martini. Only his wife was missing. She was down in the Church of the Four Happy Martyrs burning incense and welcoming newcomers. Dinner would be irrelevant should it ever occur.

"O.K., tell me about it," Ward said. "Maybe I can help. Have another drink."

Jocko looked happy for the first time. His confession was simple. IC was having increasing difficulty rolling over its shortterm loans. At the same time, its revenues had been enormously underforecast. The ultimate short-term result was insufficient operating money.

Or Boon had tried to meet the problem by moving cash around the company from division to division at an increasingly frantic rate; liquidating any assets that came readily to hand; paying as few bills as possible. All over the world IC managers. were directed to seek immediate payment for any product or service no matter how small. Meantime the accountants were told to lose bills in their files for a minimum of 120 days. Back at the IC Tower, Or searched the world by phone for the remaining remote banks that might still be willing to buy fresh IC paper. As a basis for this magical exercise, he used the advantageously decorated balance sheets provided to him by that ace decorator Jocko Burr.

"Allendale," Jocko said. "They're already making up my cot."

Ward looked out the window at the swirling cloud of smog. A large bird, its sensory mechanisms apparently eaten away by chemicals in the air, crashed into the glass and dropped to the street.

"We better blow the whistle on the bastards," Ward said, trying to test Jocko's determination.

"No one will believe us," Jocko said. "And even if they do, you know what happens. We'll be pariahs. No one would hire us to clean the latrines. We'll be freaks. Degenerate kids will point at us in the streets."

"Do you know Major Mamoud?"

"Oh, Christ. The Arab bagman."

"Our very boy. Wiggy wants to talk to him."

They looked at each other with complete understanding. Every American executive who ever tried to peddle even a bottle of mouthwash in the Middle East knew the major. He was at the center of a thousand deals: ten thousand trucks for an emirate with a population of ten thousand; a fully furnished hospital including soft-drink machines and a point-of-sale billing system; a matched set of steel mills; a boatload of rifles with a complete set of maps of downtown Tel Aviv; a fleet of 747s for a sheik's personal use. All in a week's work. And always for cash.

Unfortunately, many of Mamoud's deals had flaws. The trucks died in the desert for lack of spare parts. The hospitals remained empty for lack of electricity. Rifles and aircraft blew up with frightening regularity. But such mishaps only increased Mamoud's business. He was a buyer and seller who had convinced everyone that he could always buy and sell at the very best price — often simultaneously for both buyers and sellers. And if the buyer of stalled trucks needed spare parts it was only a matter of time before he would arrange to obtain those too.

Wiggy obviously was going to try to solve his cash problems by selling a major part of IC to the oil bandits. If desperate enough, he might even try to sell control.

"Jocko, we'll go to the Board. We'll turn the whole thing around."

"What about us? What about us?"

"Hell," Ward said, beaming. "Our price is command."

"Oh shit, oh dear," Jocko said and reached for the gin.

10

Upstairs it was presentation time in the Tower.

The CEO Conference Room — known to the irreverent as the Womb Room — was dominated by an outsized glass and chrome table, an IC-orange carpet, and a huge rear-projection screen. The room was windowless, totally soundproof, and totally devoid of telephones. Once inside, the occupants were cut off from the known world, a condition felt to be salubrious for heavy cerebration.

Wiggy sat at the head of the table, flanked by Tommy Lightmeade and Or Boon. A dozen high-level arms bearers, note takers, and specie trimmers from the Executive Office staff filled up the rest of the table's spacecraft seats. Along one wall sat the victims summoned to make the presentations. They, in turn, had arrayed in front of them small mountains of books, charts, files, and other. magical artifacts and talismans with which they planned hopefully to seek favor or at least to ward off executive displeasure.

The formal IC name for these occasions was PFD or Presentations for Decision. The obvious implication was that something resembling a decision was supposed to occur. That, of course, was misleading.

The structure of these presentations was highly ritualistic. Content was not necessarily of any importance. In fact, content -- and particularly logic -- often became a detriment to their successful conclusion. What was important was that a plan appearing to call for a top management decision was presented; that the seriousness of the plan be made manifest through the presentation of incredible detail; that the plan provide ample opportunity for irrelevant discussion and questions; and that no immediate penalty be attached to postponement of executive action.

The thing that most decidedly was expected to occur

was the creation of professional opportunity: opportunity to demonstrate one's own Olympian genius and wit; opportunity to make others look like certifiable cretins of low moral character; and opportunity for top management to look as if progress were being made. To the degree that these important objectives were achieved, a PFD meeting would be judged a success.

On this particular day, the Victims' Seats were occupied by Randall Dingle, vice president of the Goodtimes Division, and Les Gross, vice president of Corporate Information, along with the usual assortment of assistants. The Information Office group included Cookie and Lloyd Nightingale, an aging cynic of exotic tastes, particularly in connection with teen-age boys of good family.

Dingle, a tall, beefy booster with long, silky, styled hair and paunchy eyes, stood at the table at the opposite end from Wiggy and spoke first. Dingle was a particularly formidable figure in the corporate hierarchy because of the huge profits generated by his division. Accordingly, the Executive Office staff, as always attuned to protecting their leader, could hardly wait to find some way to maim Dingle. He, on the other hand, clearly smelled the current strong acrid aroma of debacle in the Tower and would seek every chance to advertise himself as a potential savior.

"Excitement, gentlemen," he began. "Excitement is what we have here today." And he pushed two buttons in front of him. One turned down the lights to funeral-parlor dim; the other turned on the slide projector. One word in Day-Glo red appeared on the screen. It said: EXCITEMENT.

"And I don't think I have to tell you, gentlemen," Dingle continued, "what excitement equals in the Goodtimes Division's markets." But he told them anyway. "It equals profits; more and bigger profits," he said and pushed the slide advance button. A new word in Day-Glo green appeared on the screen. It said: PROFITS.

"First I want to talk about House of Buns. As you know, we now have twelve thousand seven hundred House of

Buns restaurants in the United States, Europe, Aruba, Australia, and Japan. We have ten under construction in Kuwait. Sales for the last three years have been excellent, but recently the curve has flattened somewhat. Why?" In Day-Glo orange, the screen also said: WHY? "Well, just think about it. Our menu is too damn limited. Buns, coffee, tea. It's just not enough. Our market research shows that our customers are ready for something more. And that's what we plan to give them. Within the next two months, we plan to introduce a new product. (Day-Glo purple: NEW.) We have developed for the breakfast traffic the Fruitbun™. This is our standard Bun™ with one of twenty-five different fruit-type fillings custom designed for every customer."

Dingle paused to let the full grandeur of it all sink in.

"The fillings will be prepared in our central kitchens and packaged in large squeeze tubes. Each tube will be equipped with a portion-control applicator. When the customer orders his Fruitbun, the delicious filling of his choice can be quickly injected into the bun as he watches. Since there are. no natural ingredients in the fillings, they cannot spoil and require none of the preservatives to which many consumers object. We guarantee shelf life for six years. Furthermore, it is nonfattening." (Day-Glo green: NONFATTENING.)

Dingle held up what looked like a tube of bathtub tile calk. "Anyone for a little mango? No? Well, perhaps later." He tossed the tube to an assistant, rubbed his hands, and turned off the slides.

"Now for something very special. In the Goodtimes Division, we have been looking for ways to diversify our franchise offerings and thereby achieve new cost efficiencies and once more increase our profit contributions. For the last year we have looked at a number of possibilities. There was a pretty well-thought-out plan for a franchised divorce service called Split. It was a complete package: a home-counseling guide, legal work, a compensatory no-fault trip to the Virgin Island of your choice for both parties and post-divorce dating service. I am sure it would have been a winner, but because of unreasonable opposition from the American Bar Association and the Vatican, we ran into some licensing problems. Then we set up a small pilot company called Garagesale™ America. The basic idea -- truly a great one -- was to manufacture and distribute to franchise holders a full line of products with high nostalgia value: chipped dishes, scratchy phonograph records, ratty suits and dresses, 1939 World's Fair souvenirs, polychrome Jack and Jackie Kennedy plates. You name it. On the basis of early test-market results, we felt certain that we had another winner. But then we had a lot of trouble with some of the pinko consumer groups and decided the hell with it."

Dingle shook his head in dismay over the antibusiness attitudes that seemed continually to frustrate him.

"Again we went back to the drawing board and frankly I'm glad that we did. We have something new that is better than any of our earlier ideas. I know all of you are familiar with the tremendous success of the franchised health and slimming salons. These are fine for meeting the needs of the standard major segments of the market. But our market research shows that to date this service industry is not meeting the needs of this great nation's more than five million male gays in the all-important eighteen to forty-nine buying category. Gentlemen, I don't have to tell you what this said to us. It said opportunity.

"Nor do we have to start from scratch. We have found the very building block that we need to develop a new multinational chain. We have located in San Francisco a highly successful so-called minority health center called Mr. Y Salons, Inc. This is a relatively small public company that trades on the American Exchange and I have good reason to believe that we could acquire it at a reasonable premium. Moreover, I have assurances that we would be able to retain present management, including Mr. Y himself."

Dingle described how the Mr. Y Salons could be established in the forty top U.S. markets rapidly and at reasonable cost, particularly if IC were to acquire and refurbish buildings currently used by the YMCA. "Obviously," he said, "this would have the added value of using facilities already familiar to our potential customers."

Two Goodtimes executives began moving about the room, handing out thick booklets and plates of Fruitbuns. Lloyd Nightingale disdainfully declined.

"All of the detailed numbers are in the material we are now passing around," Dingle said. "But let me just show you some highlights."

For the next fifteen minutes he put on the screen a series of charts and graphs with a bewildering array of numbers. These were punctuated with words such as "obviously... you see...of course...and I hardly need to explain to you" However, the last slide was understood by everyone. It said (Day-Glo blue):

COST OF FILLING:	$ .01
FRUITBUN MARKUP:	$ .20

"Any questions?" Dingle asked, and the executive staff moved into action.

"How would we acquire?" someone asked.

"Oh, I'm sure that a friendly tender offer would be our best bet. No pun intended, of course.

"Do you see any possible advertising and promotion tie-ins between the Fruitbun and Mr. Y programs?"

"We've looked at that and, although initially it would seem that there is something there, we think that such an approach has too many downside elements."

"How much nutritional value will our Bun[c] fillings have?" Tommy asked.

"Absolutely none."

"Isn't that a pretty big negative?"

"Oh, only to a small degree. After all, with so much going for them, we can't expect everything. If customers really want nutritional value, we can always add some vitamins later."

Are there any other possibilities?" This from a Harvard MBA seeking to recapture the initiative. "It doesn't seem to me that you've thought this whole thing through."

"Well, this is only Phase One. For example, in France, where we are known as Maison des Brioches, we already have in test an injection of pastis. The problem is it makes the buns soggy."

"According to the latest Risklevich Survey, there is a declining buying power in the fifteen-to-nineteen-year-old market segment, particularly among high school dropouts, marijuana smokers, and early nesters. How much do you see this impacting on your market projections for the next two years, assuming that the inflation rate continues in the six point five to eight percent range?"

"We have looked very closely at the Risklevich numbers and find some basic flaws, particularly in the Sunbelt. However, even assuming reasonable relevance, we see only limited impact."

"Are you asking for trouble from the Women's Lib groups if you restrict the Mr. Y Salons to males?"

"As you appreciate, a basic sexist orientation is the essential ingredient in the Mr. Y marketing concept. However, should we detect sufficient demand from women's groups for our new service line, we have on the boards plans for a Ms. Sam ©."

"What kind of costs do we incur in getting into full production for Fruitbun filler? As usual, your numbers don't break that out separately."

"Very little cost. Fruitbun filler is in the great tradition of our company's growth — a direct derivative of polymer research. We have the know-how."

"Have you considered adding a kielbasa line to House of Buns?"

"No."

"Would we have to make Mr. Y an officer of the company?" This from Wiggy. "I am sure you appreciate that we could have some problems there with some members of the Board."

"No need at all. I think when you meet Mr. Y you'll find him a very delightful entrepreneur ready to do whatever is best for the company. I think he will make a first-rate ICer."

Tommy winced.

"Assuming we go with both of these plans, when might we see an increase in cash flow?" This from Or Boon.

"Within the next twelve months."

Boon laughed dryly and Wiggy ended the question period.

"Randy," he said, "I assume that no firm decision is needed from this group for you to continue to proceed on a pilot basis and report back?"

"Never has been," Dingle said cheerfully.

"Good," Wiggy said. "We thank you."

No date was set for the report.

Les Gross was the second man in the barrel.

He appeared under special auspices: the request of Tommy Lightmeade. Accordingly, the staff had the unusual opportunity for good fun in nicking the executive vice president by chewing at Les's generous form. This could be great sport, but it certainly was not for the amateur. And today Tommy sought to make clear great risks were involved.

Tommy himself opened the proceedings from his chair, which he edged as close to Wiggy as possible. "Les and his able people," he said to the room in general, "have been working on a very special program much needed at this time." As he said it, he nodded and smiled at Victims' Row where Lloyd and Cookie sat at the ready with various notebooks, boxes, and displays. Les stood in front of the room with his hands in his pockets and grinned back inanely. "Our company needs a great rebirth of spirit. And I think you will find that Les and his people have come up with some truly great ideas. Tell us about them, Les. We all want to hear."

"Thanks, Tommy," Les began. "I really appreciate your support because I think we have come up with just the ticket to turn around a lot of the bad-mouthing we've been hearing in recent weeks and get this company moving forward with the old IC spirit. We all know here how Wiggy and our top management are working around the clock to solve some of our problems. And we, who are out there on the front line with these crazy sharpshooters from the press, know how depressing it is to open the papers every day and read all this rotten stuff these guys make up. So what we think is needed right now is a new company-wide program that will get everyone marching in the right direction and show the world what IC is really made of. And here it is."

On cue, Cookie and Lloyd jumped up and unfurled a fourteen-foot orange and black banner which they tacked to the wall. It said: **OPERATION INTEGRITY.**

"I love it," Tommy said and winked at Wiggy. "I love it."

"Our plan," Les continued, "is to kick off the program with all-employee rallies in twenty major cities around the world. Wiggy, of course, will be principal speaker here in New York. I think we can get Shea Stadium. And we'll carry his message of leadership and inspiration by closed-circuit TV and satellite to all of the other meetings. Then we'll ask each employee to come forward voluntarily and sign a special IC Integrity Roll of Honor, pledging to work harder than ever to meet the high standards that IC sets for all of its products and services. Each employee who signs will be given a wallet-sized integrity card and a button that says: **BELIEVE IT!** We'll fly in the Boston Pops and we'll release balloons and doves at the finale."

As Les talked, Cookie and Lloyd passed out sample "Believe It!" buttons and integrity cards.

"That's just the opener," he said. "During the next month, every department will honor the ten employees who have made the biggest contribution to IC integrity. Each winner will receive one of a number of IC products and a special certificate encased in a block of orange-tinted Lucite. These will be suitable for display on their desks or in their homes."

There was more, but Wiggy slipped from the room and returned looking somewhat revived only in time for Les's conclusion.

"Finally, we will have three IC World Winners. Hopefully one will be a woman and one a black. We'll bring them to New York, all expenses paid, and announce them on a one-hour prime time TV special -- something with wide family appeal and true significance. I've already discussed this with the folks over at the agency and they think if we move now we can grab 'The Mickey Rooney Years.'"

Les then paused for questions before discussing operational details. But before anyone could begin, Tommy provided some immediate air cover.

"That's one hell of a program, Les. You and your guys are to be congratulated. I don't know how Wiggy and the rest of you feel, but I think we should not waste any time and announce this at the Management Meeting next week. I'd like to include it in my opening talk."

"Yes, I would agree in principle," Wiggy said. "But there may be some points that need clarifying. Does anyone have any questions or suggestions?"

"Sure," Tommy said, menacingly. "Let's hear what you other fellows think."

There was general shuffling of paper and a long silence.

"Well, how much?" Or Boon asked finally.

"Not bad, Or," Les said. "We don't have all the numbers yet, but we can buy the TV special with the ad budget we saved when we killed the Sunlamppe program and if we use some of our slower sellers for prizes we can get them for almost nothing."

"What about the press?" one of the braver staff men asked. "I think it's great, of course, but I could see how it might be twisted against us."

"No way," Les said. "They'll eat it up. Believe it!"

Everyone except Or Boon laughed this time, but everyone knew what a rotten sense of humor he had.

11

According to accepted MBA gospel, every good manager has at least three contingency plans in his desk at any one time. If Plan A fails, Plan B is ready to be unlimbered. If Plan B goes down the chute, Plan C can be rapidly deployed. Each is of increasing complexity and, needless to say, increasing cost. Each invariably involves higher personal risk; each, greater chance of total disaster. For these reasons, a Plan D at the highest levels often has something to do with Swiss banks and Costa Rica.

Plan A is usually beautiful in its simplicity. Such was the Plan A that Ward Winchester Read began to implement Thursday evening at the Sherry-Netherland Hotel in New York. His first step was to call on an aged international financier named Solomon Rosenberg.

SR, as Rosenberg was called with great respect in bank boardrooms, executive suites, and the U.S. Treasury Department, was an elegant, silvery gentleman in his mid-eighties who seldom appeared to do much of anything. Occasionally he bought a Dürer or a Vermeer; occasionally he went trout fishing in England; occasionally he attended a business meeting, but always briefly. Most of the time any business that he conducted was by phone from his apartment at the Sherry-Netherland, his home at Cap d'Antibes, or his country place near Shannon. Most of whatever he did was accomplished through others, who did not mention his name unless severely pressed.

Ward had met SR through a number of business contacts, but primarily through SR's position as one of the most influential members of IC's Board of Directors. He was also a major shareholder two ways: in various Street names and through several large trusts of which he was the principal executor. The combination was formidable. It amounted to almost 10 percent of IC's outstanding 250 million shares of common stock. As Or Boon once said: "If

SR needed a light for his cigar, Wiggy would immolate himself if necessary."

Ward hoped to enlist SR's support in what would be a clean, straightforward corporate coup d'etat directed by the Board. If SR did not appreciate the full seriousness of IC's financial plight, which was unlikely, he could possibly be shocked into action. However, even if he did know, he might not be aware of the Arab deal and that alone just might happily pink some long sublimated tribal loathing. Or, if that failed, a threat of exposure might bring him into Ward's camp.

SR's personal financial interest was enormous. IC stock had stabilized throughout the day. Despite continued selling by institutions in the morning, bargain hunters started a small rally that kept the stock from falling below 40. And, by the end of the afternoon, the stock closed at 43, down only one from Wednesday.

But 43 was still slightly more than half of what the stock had been selling for three months earlier. Since SR controlled more than 25 million shares of IC common stock, he had already lost nearly a billion dollars on paper. Ward could not believe SR would be eager to see much more disappear.

The door to SR's apartment was opened by his long-time butler, Bottle, a former British secret service agent of large proportions and deep suspicions. Although Bottle was in his sixties now, he appeared to Ward to be frighteningly fit and obviously carrying a service automatic of significant caliber underneath his tailcoat. Only a month ago Bottle had earned a mention in the French press when he had discouraged a photographer from taking SR's picture in front of the Crillon Hotel by crushing with one hand the man's Nikon. Ward also recalled an old story about Bottle in the Kenya uprisings: something unpleasant involving prisoners and a screwdriver.

"Mr. Read?" Bottle said, smiling.

"Yes. Mr. Rosenberg is expecting me."

"Quite. This way please, sir."

Bottle, although somehow watching him constantly, led Ward past three small Renoirs and a Degas (all purchased at auction from the collection of the late Hermann Goering) and into a two-story-high living room. SR was seated on a small silk-covered settee. Before him on a low, marble-topped table lay a portfolio of prints that he studied intently.

"Ward," he said, not looking up or rising, "you know Japanese art. Do you think this is a true Harunobu or have I been cheated again?"

He turned a beautifully colored woodblock print for Ward's inspection. It depicted a pretty girl student idly lying on a mat and sorting her writing brushes. Her playful instructor was seeking to stuff into her an amazing quantity of himself. Both smiled ethereally.

"I'm not really an expert," Ward said, dryly. "But I recognize the technique."

SR laughed. "Of course, of course. But here are some views even a man of your wide travel may find unusual." He pulled out another large print showing three Japanese ladies simultaneously engaging in wild athletic feats involving various parts of a famous nineteenth-century Japanese kabuki actor.

"Definitely a Utamaro," SR said. "And the ladies, I understand, were all shockingly identifiable at the Imperial Court. Would you like to see more of my collection?"

"Might we do it another time? I have something of tremendous urgency to discuss with you."

"So you said on the phone," SR said, putting the woodcuts back into the portfolio with resignation. "I offer to show you the greatest collection of Japanese shunga in the world and you choose the lesser course. Well, so be it. That, sadly enough, is our world today. No style. No pace." The old man shook his head, sat back, and closed his eyes. "Proceed," he snapped. "Five minutes."

"I think IC has about two to three weeks before it completely collapses," Ward said, dropping his cards one by one. "I have a plan to save it."

"Ah," SR said, but did not open his eyes. "So, I

63

understand, does the present management."

"It won't work. Wiggy will not be successful. You may not be aware that his deal is with the Arabs."

"Without concurring that such a deal is even contemplated, why wouldn't it be successful?"

"Because, if necessary, I will prevent it by blowing the whistle."

"And you would propose?"

"An immediate move by the Board to replace the present incompetent management with a new team headed by me. That would renew financial community confidence and enable a renegotiation of all short-term paper for a minimum extension of six months. That is all I would need to cut the losses, reestablish top-level control, and begin the turnaround."

The old man sat for more than a minute without responding. His eyes remained closed. Finally, he said one word: "Beautiful."

"You agree?" Ward asked. He was annoyed to realize he was actually sweating. He was excited. He was on the goal line.

"No," SR said. He opened his eyes and smiled. "Ward, you worry too much. You need diversion. Pace. Take the counsel of an old man. Leave this alone. Your IC options, which must concern you, will be fine. You will be better off thinking of other things. Try tying trout flies. I did it for years. I assure you there are few things more satisfying than tying a triple King Snapper. Then, when your manual skills weaken, you can move into something more vicarious, like Japanese shunga. Look, before you go, let me show you something few in this country have ever seen."

SR picked up a tube from a side table and began unrolling a thirty-foot scroll. Across it, a shipwrecked sailor and a group of truly uninhibited Japanese girls disported themselves with such imaginative frenzy that at the end of the scroll the sailor lay dead and covered with a sheet.

"Definitely Kiyonaga," SR said. "No later than eighteen

thirty. As you see, it is sometimes best not to be too original or too active."

"But then you miss all the fun," Ward said, and Bottle, summoned by an invisible hand, showed him out.

Moments after Ward left the room SR made two phone calls. The first call was to Greenwich, Connecticut.

"Wiggy?"

"Yesh?"

"Whatever you're planning to do, I suggest you do it rapidly." The second call was to a banker in Zurich.

"I think it would be prudent to begin selling IC for our account in the morning."

In neither case did SR feel it necessary to identify himself or mention Ward's visit.

As for Ward himself, he, of course, went directly back to his office to activate Plan B.

[12]

It was a glorious Friday in Washington.

Spring sunshine glistened brightly on the surface of the Potomac, completely obscuring the thousand tons an hour of important sewage roiling eastward to the sea; it glistened brightly on the white marble temples housing tho armies of the quick and the dead along the great river's banks, both groups currently providing equal service to a grateful people; and it glistened brightly on the aluminum shields of five thousand special police as they mixed it up with five thousand peace-loving Chicanos and Puerto Ricans on the Mall.

At the palatial headquarters of that greatest and purest of American enterprises, the Department of Health, Education, and Welfare, the assistant secretary for Suburban Blight announced the good news that employment at the department was up another 32 percent.

At the Watergate Apartments, the weather was so fine that Congressman Oskar Pazunski, Democrat from the great state of North Dakota, and his special assistant, Wanda Blaze, lunched on the balcony of her apartment. The congressman had rented the apartment for Wanda only the month before to enable them to work long hours without interruption.

At the Capitol, Senator Jefferson Jennings Bryan stood on the great inaugural steps blinking into the sunlight and an array of cameras. J-J's right arm embraced a chubby paraplegic Eskimo who waved with a tiny hand growing from his shoulder; J-J's left arm embraced a black girl with a face awash with unmistakable idiocy. "We know from experience that American industry misses a good bet when it passes over the handicapped," J-J shouted menacingly at the TV microphones and two passing K of C auxiliary matrons. "American industry better get with it."

And in the Oval Offico at thc very center of powei sal

the Commander in Chief of the Free World, President Gaston Edsel, catching the briefest post luncheon nap before his next appointment.

Gaston Edsel was one of the more colorful of the late emperors of the West. He had spent the first twenty years of his professional career as a fork-lift truck operator and failed union organizer in a K-Mart warehouse near Bayonne, New Jersey. Then, because of what some newsmen referred to as an amusing fluke, he was nominated for Congress. According to his detractors, someone shouted during a deadlocked meeting that they had to agree on someone even if he were an Edsel; so they did.

After ten years of totally undistinguished service in the House, he again demonstrated the historic American insistence that no special qualifications are needed for public office. In a moment of deep disarray and despair at the National Democratic Convention in Atlanta, exhausted delegates nominated a dark-horse aristocrat named Oliver Roosevelt Kernaghan for President. The party power brokers then insisted that a blue-collar nonentity of limited intelligence would be essential to balance the ticket. Gaston was the obvious choice.

Oliver Roosevelt Kernaghan or ORK, as he came to be known, was a natural winner. He had everything: Groton and Harvard; a decorated war hero and a stint as a gentlemanly peacenik; a good swimmer; a born-again mother and a Catholic father; a law degree but no practice; and no marring record of gainful employment. The Republicans, who had expected an easy win with Julie Nixon Eisenhower, were overwhelmed. ORK and Gaston were elected by the largest majorities in the twentieth century. The popular mandate for implementation of their honest program -- *Everyone Gets His* -- was clear.

Unfortunately, ORK was in trouble within his first year in office. After the election, with time on their hands, six crack investigative reporting teams, led by TV commentator Harvey Catoni, began to burrow into ORK's past. The result was a series of sensational exposures that eventually formed the basis of a dozen copyrighted articles, eighteen books, three full-length TV documentaries, and two movies. ORK was reported to be the totally synthetic product of the distinguished candidate-packaging firm of Straight Arrow Associates of Houston and Pasadena.

The real ORK was said to be an unknown summer stock actor who in the winter supported himself by doing impersonations of the late Presidents Kennedy and Roosevelt in obscure bars in Greenwich Village. He allegedly had been born in Worcester, Massachusetts, the son of a Unitarian mother and a high Anglican stockbroker of Northern Irish ancestry; had actually attended Groton but was expelled from Harvard in his freshman year for engaging in heterosexual activity in his dormitory and losing a swimming meet; served in Vietnam in the Peace Corps engaging primarily in the distribution of free birth control information to what remained of the native population; on return to Boston he joined an amateur theatrical group in Hyannisport and the rest became history. There appeared to be no foundation whatsoever to ORK's claim to a law degree, but, of course, it certainly was true that he had never practiced.

As the charges unfolded, ORK took the high road: he denied everything. He refused to discuss it. He declared war on Liechtenstein. He announced he was ill. He announced his mother was ill. He declared war on crime, poverty, indecent exposure and Montenegro.

Two years and two weeks to the day that ORK was sworn into office he went on national TV and announced his resignation. Some of the more extreme critics in the news media said he demonstrated small-mindedness when he said: "Well, you won't have ORK to beat over the head anymore." But even his worst critics agreed that he rose to greatness when he said: "As you might expect, I have received a number of handsome offers from the media to tell my side of the story. As a man of modest means with a growing family, I find these offers difficult to refuse. As I know all of you, my fellow Americans, can appreciate, one has to think of Number One."

Nor were his final words totally unmoving. Few can forget when ORK said: "Now we have a new President. It is up to Gaston Edsel to carry on the struggle for our great program. God save us all."

By this particular Friday in Washington, Gaston had been carrying on the great struggle for four months and the usual honeymoon with the news media and the public was ending. Along with the standard array of riots, peculations and foreign policy fiascoes, the national economy appeared to be taking a nasty turn. A major factor in that turn -- some presidential advisors said the causal factor -- was the situation at IC.

Gaston found these developments most regrettable.

"Hey, I didn't ask for the job," he would shout at his old friend Boom Boom Kelly, as they downed a late beer in the White House living quarters. "Now all I get is lousy comments."

"You're right," Boom Boom would say. "Pay no attention to the bastards."

"Piss on 'em," Gaston would say, pulling the ring on another cold one. "I'm doing the best I can."

"Right, but you gotta watch 'em. Lot of guys out there would like to be in your shoes. First class dough, big house, a car, a plane. Listen, pal, jobs like this don't come along every Tuesday."

"Sure as hell beats running them old fork-lift trucks," Gaston would say and slap Boom Boom on the shoulder and let fly with a long burp.

But that was late-at-night conversation when the beer was cold and the company was pally. Downstairs in the Oval Office, as he awakened from his short nap, Gaston felt a major clutch of terror in his stomach. He had felt like this briefly when he first went to Congress, but after only a few weeks he knew he was safe. No one really expected him to do anything there; all he had to do was take care of

70

some minor requests from his constituents in Bayonne and make a few unhinged statements periodically about how he favored taking all the money in the country and giving it to all the world's conniving losers and unjailed cut-purses of whom he was so clearly representative. But in the Oval Office the mysterious nightmare of the world's problems pressed on him; and enemies, or at least microphones, lurked in every file cabinet. The clutch in the stomach did not go away.

Gaston twisted in his desk chair where he had dozed and began absently probing a tooth with his thumbnail. He continued to do so for a full minute as his appointments secretary ushered into his office the Secretary of the Treasury, a short, saturnine politician named Warren Rasberry; a clutch of financial aides stamped from the Brooks Brothers' cookie cutter; and IC executive vice president Tommy Lightmeade, appearing somewhat strained but ebullient as ever. The purpose of the meeting was to discuss IC's financial woes. One might have guessed that the group was selling retirement condominiums of more than the usual dubious quality.

Secretary Rasberry, Tommy, and the aides arranged themselves in various upholstered chairs and couches near the fireplace. Only then did Gaston cease exploring his dental problem and join them. He sat in the presidential rocking chair, which he had had redecorated with souvenir pillows from Atlantic City.

"Mr. President," Secretary Rasberry began, and Gaston flinched visibly. No matter how much he worked at it, when someone used this mode of address in a rhetorical fashion he had an uncontrollable urge to look around the room for someone important.

"Mr. President," Rasberry said again for effect. "As you know, we meet here today to discuss the serious national problem involving one of our country's leading corporations, International Coagulants."

"Sure," Gaston said. "You can bet I'm just about as concerned as you are." And he nodded at Tommy in a manner that he hoped was reassuring.

"Yes. Of course," Rasberry said. "Well, to go on. As I am sure you are aware, IC is a principal defense supplier to the Pentagon of such vital products as the essential substrate to our most advanced nuclear weapons as well as a variety of other products, from the secret humane chemical warfare agent code named Perpetual Sleep© to a variety of medicinal social supplies and the basic chemical ingredients of all military field rations. Moreover, IC employs in the continental United States alone more than two hundred and fifty thousand people including ninety-six thousand five hundred blacks, Chicanos, Indians, Puerto Ricans, cripples, ex-convicts, mental deficients, and numerous disadvantaged residents of your home state of New Jersey, if that is not too much of a tautology. Accordingly, it must be obvious to you as it is to us at Treasury that IC is a national resource of major importance to the security and economic well-being of this great nation."

Gaston, whose eyelids had begun to feel heavy, sat up in his chair at the words "this great nation" and nodded sympathetically.

"Unfortunately," Rasberry pressed on, "as Mr. Lightmeade will tell you, IC has suffered for a variety of understandable reasons a few financial reverses. These are serious. In fact, I would go so far as to say very serious. In fact, if IC does not receive some small degree of temporary support from this government, we may have what my associates at Treasury and I feel would be a sticky situation."

"How sticky?" Gaston asked suspiciously, having already become familiar with Rasberry's penchant for euphemism.

"Bankruptcy, Mr. President," Tommy interjected, delighted to indulge his love of drama. "We could disappear."

Gaston rocked back and forth and returned to the problem of the troublesome bit of food in his teeth.

"Well, so what?" he said, finally, and everyone began to talk at the same time.

"Mr. President!" Rasberry exclaimed, talking over the others. "Collapse of IC could bring on a major recession. Look at what is happening in the stock market even as we meet. Also, IC is an essential partner in our private sector arsenal system. And anyway, if we don't do something, they may have to turn to the Arabs for help, a move that would be very unpopular in New York and Miami, among other places."

"Mr. President," Tommy said, "our problem is simple: the banks for some reason no longer have confidence in us. You know what bankers are like: a slow payment here; a defalcation there; and the next thing you know, they get itchy about credit. All that is needed is for us to find a way to reestablish confidence in this great American institution that has contributed so much to our country in this century through two world wars, two police actions, a dozen minor military supports, and, of course, the periods of normalcy in between. Happily, Secretary Rasberry and I have worked out a very simple plan. All that we need to reestablish confidence is for the government to guarantee some long-term loans."

"Precisely," Rasberry said and winked reassuringly at everyone. "It won't cost the federal government a dime. Just a guarantee for the banks to put their minds at ease."

"How do we do that?" Gaston asked.

"Well, sir," one of the aides said, "that's the one iffy area. Your statutory authority under the terms of the act limits you to a somewhat lesser number. I think it's about twenty-five thousand dollars. Therefore, we do have to go to Congress."

"Oh, shit," Gaston said, finally recognizing something about which he had some experience. "Those boys will eat us for breakfast."

"No, sir," Rasberry said. "We have a solution. We'll tack the guarantee instrument to the Rivers and Harbors Appropriations Bill next week. And if that doesn't work, we can tack it to the new Congressional Staff Expansion Appropriations Bill. They'll hardly notice."

"It's an act of patriotism, Mr. President," Tommy said. "It's pure statesmanshp."

"O.K., but listen you guys," Gaston said. "Gimme a clue: just how big is this damn guarantee?"

"About two billion dollars," an aide said quietly.

The leader of the free world stopped rocking and stood up to his full five feet three inches.

"That's one fucking lot of patriotism," he said. "I'm going to have a beer."

*   *

It took less than two hours for Senator Jefferson Jennings Bryan to learn what was afoot.

The good senior senator from Louisiana had just completed a meeting with six of his favorite oil millionaires in the new Late-Middle-Mussolini-Period offices of the Joint Congressional Committee on National Oversight when he received a phone call from one of his more able spies in the Administration.

"They are planning to send the bill up as quickly as possible because of the new downturn in the market," the muffled voice said from a coin phone. "If you want, we could delay it."

"No, no," J-J said, barely able to control his ecstasy. "Nothing should stand in the way of such an important piece of legislation. But just one thing. Make sure it's rerouted to my committee."

"They want it to go to the Commerce Committee for the Harbors and Rivers Bill."

"Of course. But your people are dumb. They're civil servants. They make mistakes. They send us a copy."

"I'll go pass out the dumb pills now."

"Your country is truly in your debt, sir."

A beautiful, dark-haired girl walked up to Ward, pinned a carnation to his jacket lapel, and kissed him. A large plastic button attached to her blouse said: LOVE EVERYONE LTD. A second plastic button displayed the smiling face of Mr. Moo, the celebrated Cambodian mystic, lute player, and banker.

"Help make the world safe for love," the girl said. "Give us a hundred dollars and become a benefactor of love."

"I think I'd rather be a beneficiary," Ward said.

They stood in front of the Bayou Airlines ticket counter at Kennedy Airport in New York. It was 10:00 A.M., Friday. Ward had just ten minutes left to catch the plane to Atlanta and he was having great difficulty moving through the noisy, chaotic crowd of passengers, friends, and airline personnel, all of whom were set upon by a swarm of supplicants for various causes.

Two bearded men in black shiny suits and hats carried a huge sign that said: MAKE GAZA THE 51ST STATE. A dozen bald young men in saffron robes beat tambourines and danced in a circle with their eyes closed. Rival barkers behind stacks of magazines shouted at the crowd and each other: "Stop irradiating our unborn" and "You'll freeze in the dark." An American Indian in full war bonnet and a World War II flight jacket carried a sign that said: THE CHEROKEES HAVE HAD ENOUGH.

"Love is what the world needs," the girl said loudly to Ward as she followed him to the gates. "We're helping make love a household word in forty-two countries, including Uganda. If you don't want to be a Benefactor, you can be a Sponsor of Love for fifty dollars. It's all tax deductible because we qualify as a church."

"What do I get for ten?" Ward asked, dodging around the saffron-robed dancers.

"You get to be a Friend of Love," the girl shouted back

over the noise of the tambourines and chanting. "And you still get the magazine. Can I sign you up?"

"Not today," Ward said.

"For only five dollars you get to be a Follower of Love, but the magazine is extra." She reached out to grab his arm but missed. A sudden surge in the crowd separated them and a new group of black men and women with Afro haircuts and white robes rushed down the gate ramp with signs that said only: IT'S COMING! As Ward reached the baggage inspection station, he heard the girl shout after him: "Hey, give me back my flower, you cheap bastard."

Only five passengers were in the line in front of the inspection station, but it seemed to Ward that the processing was interminable. A plump, dark matron in an ill-fitting Ralph Lauren skirt and jacket had a huge velour suitcase that would not fit into the machine. She had to rummage through her Gucci purse to find the suitcase keys so that the suitcase could be inspected manually. It was filled with toilet tissue, Tampax, and cans of Campbell's chicken soup with 00 noodles. "It's for my daughter from Barnard," she explained. "She's working in a commune in Alabama." A bearded, suspicious-looking man was turned back from the inspection station because his attaché case was full of throwing knives which, he tried to explain, were part of his TV act. Another man, who said he was an Atlanta museum curator, tried to get through with a bass viol case that the inspection machine x-ray screen made clear housed a crossbow. He was allowed to pass when searchers failed to find any crossbow darts. Finally, with only four minutes before take-off, Ward reached the x-ray machine and handed his attaché case to the uniformed and booted attendant, a surly, spavined woman with a harelip.

She hurled the case onto the conveyor belt and he walked through the adjacent detection doorway. But his attaché case was not waiting for him on the conveyor belt emerging from the x-ray machine. In fact, the conveyor belt was not moving.

"What happened?" Ward said sharply to the first attendant's counterpart, a two-hundred-pound harridan in a rumpled, lemon yellow guard's uniform, complete with lanyard and whistle. "Where's my case?"

"Don't get excited, dearie," she said. "The goddamn machine broke again. It does it all the time."

"Well, inspect my case and give it to me. I'm trying to catch a plane."

"So's the whole world. I can't get your case, dearie. It's in the machine. Banjo has to go in and clear the belt. Don't worry. He's quick as a garbage rat. Here he comes now."

A three-foot midget in lemon yellow, armed with a screwdriver, jumped up on the conveyor belt and crawled into the machine. Only moments later the conveyor motor started, the belt began to move, and a picture came on the viewing screen showing a small skeleton with its arms hugging an attaché case. Then Banjo himself emerged feet-first through the rubber flaps at the machine's exit, followed by the case. Ward grabbed it and ran toward his plane's gate.

"No hurry," the girl at the check-in desk drawled. "We're running a teensy late."

"Goddamn, how late?" Ward asked, breathing hard and handing her his ticket.

"Just a teensy. Something about the cargo door coming open when the plane landed. But, oh my, Mr. Read, your ticket is for first class. We just don't have a thing left in first class today so I'll have to put you-all in our special businessman's section, compliments of Bayou, of course."

"Does that cost more than first?"

"No, not exactly, but it's always reserved for just businessmen like I guess you-all are, and we give you a free copy of the *New Orleans Times-Picayune* and serve a special snack that you order in advance. Now, would you like to be in the smoking or nonsmoking section of the special businessman's section?"

"Smoking,"

"Oh, I am sorry, Mr. Read, but we just don't have anything left in smoking. Will nonsmoking be all right this time?"

"Just grand."

"Good. Now, Mr. Read, about the special snack. Would you-all like the fat-free, low-salt, kosher, low-cholesterol, soul, or regular?"

"What's the regular?"

"Well today it's breast of turkey on white bread. We call it the Wasp but the fellows back in the Bayou PR department get kind of mad if they hear us."

"I'll have a Wasp," Ward said.

"Now, your complimentary beverage selection, Mr. Read. Would you like hard liquor or a bottle of fine Arkansas wine or would you like a soft drink like maybe some Rainbow fruit punch or low-cal Gatorade? If you'd rather have a soft drink, we give you two little bottles of the hard stuff of your choice in a cute little gift package that slips right into your attaché case. We all call it the Bayou Boozy Bag."

"I'll have black coffee," Ward said.

"Well, then, I guess you're all set. Here's your seat ticket and I guess we'll be going in just a little while. It's been a real pleasure."

"Thank you," Ward said and left to look for a phone. He wanted to let some people know that the start of Plan B was just a teensy delayed.

*   *

Less than one day's march away -- a manner of speaking not entirely inappropriate under the circumstances -- something close to pandemonium was developing at the New York Stock Exchange.

It began earlier that day in Europe. In Zurich, in Geneva, in Frankfurt, in Amsterdam, large blocks of IC stock were dropped into the market by SR's agents. At first blocks of 100,000 and 200,000 shares moved across the

European tapes; then several 500,000 share blocks; then the numbers rose to 2 million.

By 10:00 A.M. in New York, when the New York Stock Exchange opened, more than 1.2 million shares of IC, mostly from SR's personal accounts, had been traded and the panic was on. The Dow index opened down 3, then plunged swiftly downward 9, then down 15. First blue chips, then secondary issues fell with the selling trend; margin accounts began to be called; the market began to feed on itself.

By 11:30 A.M., when Ward finally boarded his delayed plane to Atlanta, the Dow was down 23 points and IC had dropped from 43 to 31. Losses in IC stock alone were more than $3 billion and the market had entered what appeared to be a free fall. Without touching the trusts, SR agents had unloaded his entire personal portfolio of more than 10 million shares and were now selling IC stock short in cities throughout the United States.

The floor of the New York Stock Exchange was ankle-deep in paper. Investors were clawing at the sealed windows in high buildings. Or Boon went for a walk to get away from his phones while Wiggy took a salutary alcoholic nap in his office. Les Gross issued a statement saying that "IC knows of no reason for unusually high interest in its stock at this time." SR told Bottle that he would have a little Scotch salmon fumé for lunch with a 1970 Montrachet. And TV crews began to gather in Wall Street and at brokerage offices in midtown Manhattan to bear witness to the debacle.

Finally, shortly before Ward's plane landed at 1:30 P.M., the Board of Governors of the Exchange met in solemn session and ordered all trading in IC stock halted.

But by then the disaster was almost spent. IC stock stood at 20, down 23 points. The Dow was at 650, down 40. IC losses totaled nearly $6 billion. The national economy tottered. However, at the Sherry-Netherland, SR was sufficiently undismayed to have a second glass of wine. He had not only successfully emptied his IC portfolio, but he had sold short an additional 12 million shares.

SR was now positioned for whatever developed. If Wiggy cut his deal with the Arabs, SR agents were ready to cover his shorts and more and ride the stock back up. If Ward blew the whistle, as he had threatened, and killed the Arab deal, SR agents would simply cover his shorts when IC hit the subbasement.

He sighed happily and opened a new portfolio to a Hiroshige. Mount Fuji loomed beautifully in pinks and grays over a quiet stretch of water where two young ladies and a samurai warrior of truly astounding proportions cavorted gaily in a boat.

Hours before Ward landed in Atlanta, R. C. Y. de Salida, formerly of the CIA, prepared for their meeting.

Carefully, carefully, he dismantled and put back together the telephone, lamps, radio, TV set, and small refrigerator in his hotel room at the Atlanta Hyatt Regency.

Carefully, carefully, he looked behind the pictures, inserted long thin needles in the pillows, and explored the toilet.

Carefully, carefully, he used his minimicro tie-clip recorder to listen to his neighbor on the right tell his boss by phone about his plans to sell at premium prices twenty gross of king-size sheets to an Atlanta department store; a couple on the left argue about the man's stupidity in picking up a dinner check the night before when they ate with their deadbeat friends. Three times the woman used the old Vietnamese code word "shitforbrains."

Carefully, carefully, he employed his special zoom-lens fountain-pen camera to photograph the street in front of the hotel. He paid particular attention to a green Mercedes 250SL- XA_{45}-T that circled the block three times before parking. As everyone knew, the XA_{45}-T was a special model reputedly custom-made during the 1960s for Baby Doc of Haiti.

Technique! Good technique! How many were dead who had not followed it? Control would have been proud of him. De Salida had not been with the Company now for a decade, but he remembered his lessons well. Technique! Your life depended on it. The lives of others. The life of your country.

R. C. Y. de Salida, known as Ricky, had been born Charlie Potter in New Bedford, Massachusetts, of an old whaling family; graduated from Princeton University; drafted for army service in the Korean War but assigned to code work at a Mississippi chemical warfare depot; and finally recruited by the Company at a drunken alumni reunion in the mid - fifties.

A romantic mind made him one of the most enthusiastic recruits in the Company's history. He loved the training; he reveled in intrigue; he could not get enough of the whole black grab bag of wild electronic wizardry, devious weapons, and triple codes. Most of all, he had a passion for disguise. In fact, it was in pursuit of disguise that early on he developed as a master disguise for himself the scenario that he was the Baron Ricardo Castilles Yberra de Salida, a name that he composed one day at the airport in Managua after he missed a courier plane. Poor old Charlie Potter of New Bedford had disappeared from a train somewhere between Princeton and Newark. Apparently he had been done away with in a delightfully disgusting fashion by a gang of queer black muggers.

Unfortunately for Ricky's career with the Company, his favorite and most successful disguise was to dress up as a somewhat undernourished but quite lovely-looking young college girl. Much to his credit, he used a variation of this disguise to smuggle Polish designs for a nuclear zeppelin out of Cracow in 1959. And, in the early 1960s, he used a similar disguise with even more notable results in a complex caper involving a top official in the Moroccan Secret Police. But, after this triumph, Ricky was found to be using this disguise whenever he went on leave in London and New York. With deep regret, the company had to let him go following the appearance in the *London Telegraph* of a picture of Ricky and a certain peer of the realm strolling together at Derby Day. The caption said in part: "A Palace spokesman denied any special relationship between the Duke and Miss Gridley, socialite daughter of an American fast-food restaurants millionaire."

Since his retirement from the Company, Ricky had employed his many talents in private foreign service. He was particularly active in helping the governments of emerging nations in Africa acquire military equipment in defense of their freedom. He also was active in helping the governments of various Latin American countries maintain order. And, in the same countries, he also was known to have been helpful to various patriotic groups on a strictly COD basis.

In the last few years he had made himself useful as a link between American businessmen and foreign government and business leaders. Usually his work involved the making of key contacts and helping American companies manifest their appreciation for contracts in a meaningful manner. This work often involved nothing more arduous than making sizable deposits of cash in Swiss banks.

However, in other cases, Ricky would perform the difficult role of middleman-- particularly when the principals were overly modest and disdained undue publicity.

It was in this latter, delicate role that Ricky had come to Atlanta to meet secretly with Ward. His principal was Joseph Xypaxtyxl, a Mexican oil billionaire and full-blooded Zapotec Indian known in Houston circles as Joe the X. He was dedicated to two great passions: making money and Indian causes. He was able to indulge both of these passions through his personal ownership of a once worthless Mexican province that lies on top of proven oil reserves about the size of Lake Michigan.

Ricky looked at his watch. It was 10:45 A.M. Ward should be in the air somewhere over New Jersey. Ricky checked his cigarette lighter blowgun and dropped it into his jacket pocket. The phone rang and he jumped for it.

"Arthur Detroit speaking," he said smoothly.

82

"Mr. Detroit," Ward said, feeling immediately like a damn fool but playing along. "This is Philip Carcassone. There has been some delay in my flight and my arrival may be delayed several hours."

"No problem, Mr. Carcassone. However, I suggest that in view of the delay it would be best if we canceled our meeting here today. Instead, I suggest you attend to the charitable work that you have in Atlanta and we can get together another time."

"Excellent," Ward said, almost beginning to enjoy the game. "I'll be in touch, Mr. Detroit."

Technique! Good technique! Ricky immediately moved into his alternate plan. When schedules change, you never could tell what might be going on. Anyone can delay a flight while positioning a counterstrike. Best to play it safe. Change your own plans. Switch meeting sites on them. Switch identities. Keep them off balance. Control would be proud.

By prearranged code, Ricky had canceled his meeting with Ward at the Hyatt Regency. They would meet instead at the Admirals Club at the Atlanta airport.

But not as Mr. Detroit and Mr. Carcassone. Now Mr. Carcassone would meet at the Admirals Club with the Reverend Billy Sam.

Technique! Good technique! In an instant Ricky stripped off his necktie. From his attaché case, he took a clerical collar and bib, a set of large porcelain front teeth, and a full wig of long, silvery white hair. He inserted the teeth in his mouth along with two cotton dental rolls that puffed his cheeks; put on the collar and bib; adjusted the wig on top of his straw blond hair; and called the hotel desk.

"This is Arthur Detroit in room five forty-six," he said loudly so that any microphones that he might have missed could clearly pick up the message. "When the Reverend Billy Sam arrives, please tell him to come right up."

He spent the next five minutes wiping his fingerprints from the phone, doorknobs, and faucets, took one last picture with his fountain pen of the Mercedes 250SL -- XA_{45} --T, and walked casually to the elevator and left the hotel through the garage.

*   *

"My name is Philip Carcassone," Ward heard himself saying to the blonde receptionist at the Admirals Club. She had a lovely shape and vague eyes revealing an IQ just under 20.

"I'm looking for the Reverend Billy Sam," Ward added.

"Oh my, yes, Mr. Carcassone. The Reverend Billy has been waiting for you and the others from the National Gospel Committee. You-all will find him right over there in Meeting Room B. Shall I send the waiter in so you can order some refreshments? You must be right worn after your long trip from Phoenix."

"I definitely think we'll need refreshments," Ward said and walked through the crowded lounge to Meeting Room B. When he entered, he found Ricky in his Reverend Billy outfit making one final sweep of the walls with a radiation beam detector.

"This little old place is clean," Ricky said reassuringly and winked. "I've checked everything. Did you spot anyone following you from the plane?"

"Christ, no," Ward said. "Why would someone follow me? No one has any idea that I even left New York."

Ricky smiled condescendingly. "Don't kid yourself," he said. "Play it smart. Begin with the idea that they know. Then work the problem from there."

There was a knock on the door and he jumped to the wall by the door. Signaling silence to Ward, he called in a soft corn-mush accent: "God bless us all, who's there?"

"A-men. I'm the waiter," a voice said on the other side of the door. Ricky signaled to Ward to open the door while he remained in a position from which he could strike to kill whoever entered. Ward opened the door and a small, very black waiter about seventy-five years old ambled into the room.

"Can I get anyone a drink?" he asked, looking first at Ward and then looking around until he found the Reverend Billy emerging from behind the door.

"I'll have a double Scotch," Ward said. "What will you have, Reverend?"

"I think a little Tab with a lot of ice would just hit the very right spot," the Reverend Billy said. "And the Lord save you."

"A-men," the waiter said. "Would you gentlemen like some nuts? We also gots pretzels."

"Just the refreshments," the Reverend Billy intoned. "God save us all."

"A-men," the waiter said and ambled out.

"O.K.," Ward said. "Let's talk."

Ricky put up his hand and deliberately opened the door halfway to allow for the waiter's return.

"We are meeting here today to discuss how corporate America can contribute to the great rising of spirit that is taking place in this great nation," he said in his Reverend Billy voice. "You, sir, Mr. Carcassone, are one of the first to appreciate the great work of our National Gospel Committee. You, sir, will be delighted to learn that the spirit of the National Gospel Committee can infuse the great corporate enterprises that you represent and help prepare the American people for the great day when we will all join hands in fellowship in that great Fast-Food Restaurant in the Sky."

"A-men," the waiter said, coming back into the room with the drinks. "Save us all, brother."

"I'll take the check," Ward said.

"Lord be with you," the Reverend Billy said. Ward handed the waiter a five-dollar bill and the Reverend Billy ushered him to the door and locked it.

"Now?" Ward said.

"Now," Ricky said. "But let's keep it to a half hour. How have you been, dear boy? I haven't seen you since you were in the Middle East."

85

"I would hardly say that things are looking up."

"Of course. But that's why we are here, right? To make things look up. First, how bad is this situation at IC?"

"Very lousy. There is need for a major transfusion of new money immediately. On the other hand, with the right management, the company is a tremendous institution and can be highly profitable."

Ricky smiled. "I assume, dear boy, that by the right management you are speaking of yourself and your associates."

"If you'll pardon the expression, Reverend: Is the Pope a Catholic? What IC needs at the top is management muscle."

"Now that does sound like fun. What's the timing?"

"Right away. I think a stock deal may be cut privately with Arab interests in the next few days. The Board, at least so far, is a captive of management. What we need is a white knight to come in and pick up all the marbles immediately."

Ricky laughed, took a drink of his Tab, and made a face. "I can't imagine anyone describing Joe the X as a white knight. He looks more like Tonto by Pierre Cardin out of Chase Manhattan. One of the problems is finding the dear man. You won't believe it but now he's somewhere up in the Dakotas talking to the Cheyenne Indians. He's very big in that area: he likes helping Indians. For some crazy reason he thinks the Indians in North America have had a bum deal. Only last month he was so upset over living conditions among the Navajos out in Arizona that he sent every family a flush toilet. The only problem is that where these Navajos live there isn't any running water."

"What are they doing with them?"

"Using them, of course. No one wants to make Joe the X feel unappreciated."

"Assuming you can find him, what do you see as the next step?"

"He'll ask two questions: How much money and how much control?"

"IC needs at least five billion dollars. For five billion dollars, he can move it to Acapulco."

"How would we explain the involvement of a great Mexican financier like Joe the X?"

"It would be a triumph of free enterprise and the individual entrepreneur. A philanthropist and champion of the downtrodden Red Man such as Joe the X is another plus."

"And you can help make it happen?"

"As long as I'm part of the program."

Ricky stood up, opened the meeting room door slightly, and, in his mushiest Reverend Billy voice, said: "Lord bless us all, Mr. Carcassone, I do think that the National Committee will be interested in hearing about your proposition. You, sir, will certainly be hearing from us right soon.

"A-men," Ward said. "You didn't finish your Tab."

Ward left immediately to catch the next plane back to New York. It was not until he was somewhere over the wreckage-choked sands of Cape Hatteras that he opened a copy of the *Atlanta Constitution* and read the front page. A five column headline screamed:

MARKET DISASTER HITS WALL STREET
IC DROP PACES DOW INDEX PLUNGE

It was only then he began to fear that all might be overcome by events and took some satisfaction that his Plan C was already being prepared.

Ricky had stayed behind at the Admirals Club to wipe prints from the glasses, door knobs, and other furnishings and in general secure the room. Then he stripped off his Reverend Billy collar, bib, and wig; removed the big teeth and cotton from his mouth as well as an elongated putty nose and some bushy eyebrows that belonged to Arthur Detroit; put on his Charvet crested necktie; extended his fold-up, gold-headed walking stick; and strode elegantly from the Admirals Club as once again the Baron R. C. Y. de Salida.

Master of disguise! Technique! Control would have been proud.

[14]

World in Brief— Two
(Friday P.M. EST)

MORE THAN 60 PERCENT of America's HUTS (known to the elect of the Tube as Households Using Television) are standing by. Emerging in a star-spangled roll of color on their TV screens are those familiar electrifying words, "Your Evening News." Drums. Horns. Clarinets. And there they are: Anchorman Martin Dasher! Anchorwoman Betsy Poke!

"Hi ho there, Betsy. It's a wonderful spring night here in New York."

"Hi ho to you, Martin. It is indeedy. And tonight, Martin, we have for the first time the long-suppressed Matthew Brady photographs of Walt Whitman relaxing with some of his more ardent admirers at a first-aid station just after the Battle of Chancellorsville. We can't show them all, of course, during family viewing time. But we'll have with us the man who found the pictures in the vice squad file of police headquarters in Camden, New Jersey."

"Yes, Betsy, and our roving correspondent, Paolo St. John, is going to give us by satellite an on-the-scene interview with a family of Red Chinese shoppers at the Peninsula Hotel in Hong Kong. And, of course, we'll have Jim Jump with the weather. And Sid Crunch with the big game from Houston. And plenty more."

"But first you have the headline stories for us, right, Martin?"

"Right, Betsy. The news this evening is not too good!"

Despite his words, Martin bravely maintained a broad grin on his sun-tanned face, and the more discerning viewers noticed that he even winked.

"Just off the Westchester County shore in southern New York two Italian oil tankers collided this afternoon in Long Island Sound. The *Luigi Visconti* rammed into the stern of the *Luigi Condottiere II* at four P.M. in bright sunlight. Both sank immediately with all hands. Fortunately the water was shallow at the point where the ships sank and did not cover their decks. Therefore, many members of the crew were able to fight their way to safety and walk to shore. Network Oil Spill Correspondent Joe Garden talked to some of the survivors only a few minutes ago at the bar of the Larchmont Yacht Club."

Fade to Joe Garden and two oil-covered sailors, each holding a bottle of grappa from which they take an occasional pull.

"I guess the big question is, how did your ships get so far off course?" Joe asks with a friendly chuckle.

"Hey, whatsa mat? You wanna the oil. You gotta the oil."

"There is the problem that some see in the method of delivery," Joe Garden persisted amicably. "And some are asking whether the captains of the ships took timely notice of the Larchmont Yacht Club squadron out for its spring trials."

"Hey, bigga deal."

Fade back to Martin Dasher and a picture of the U.S. Capitol.

"Members of the House Armed Services Committee expressed alarm today over a top-secret report on the loan of twenty-four Soviet Mig nuclear bombers to French radical nationalists in Quebec. The report, apparently leaked by Pentagon spoil-sports to the *New York Times* and *Rolling Stone,* states that the Russian jets will be delivered to the Quebecois group known as Souvenez Montcalm Committee sometime next month. Questioned about the report, SMC leader René Bonchance said the Migs will be used strictly for defensive purposes against the language chauvinists of Ottawa. But, in Washington, congressmen noted that the Migs were capable of nuclear

90

strikes as far south as Birmingham, Alabama. Asked for comment, Bonchance said:

'Pourquoi voulez-vous bombardier Birmingham?'"

Close-up headshot of Marvin Dasher shaking his head in mock disbelief, followed by a big reassuring smile.

"New trouble on Wall Street today, folks! For that report, we take you direct to the floor of the New York Stock Exchange and Chief Network Economic Disaster Correspondent Joe Garden."

Fade to Joe Garden on the littered floor of the darkened Exchange.

"Only a few hours ago this room witnessed one of the great crashes in American history. More than sixty million shares were traded as money disappeared like snow in a microwave oven. Biggest loser of the day was International Coagulants, which dropped twenty-three points before trading was stopped in IC stock. Mr. J. Wigglesworth Pratt, president of IC, came to Wall Street to meet with Exchange governors and we talked to him briefly."

Fade to crowd outside a huge, mahogany door which opens to reveal Wiggy refreshing himself from a paper cup.

"Mr. Pratt," Garden says, "what is the problem at IC?"

"No problem, Joe. No problem. This is merely a bit of market hysteria and what they call on the Street a market correction. I assure you IC is as sound as America."

"But, sir, why the sudden selling?"

"We really don't know, Joe," Wiggy says and smiles his most convincing smile into the cameras. "We think IC is solid as a rock and we have been buying all day."

Fade back to Martin Dasher.

"Two additional comments on the big drop in the market from Washington," Martin says oracularly. "President Edsel's chief economic advisor, Nobel Prize winner Sigismund Occam, called the drop in the market a fully expected occurrence in line with the National Econometric Model. And Senator J-J Bryan said he was considering a full investigation."

Fade to Betsy Poke, who leers winsomely through a

great quantity of long hair.

"Finally, in other developments in the news," Betsy says, "we had two somewhat unusual funerals today.

"In Santa Monica, Reconstituted Orange Juice Heiress Cindy Amsterdam was buried today in her Rolls Royce Grande Corniche. As specified in her will, Cindy, who died Wednesday, allegedly from an overdose of ginseng root, was sitting in the driver's seat of her white Rolls as it was lowered into the ground at private ceremonies conducted by the noted evangelist Dr. Moo.

"Meantime, in Bug Tussle, Texas, Oilman Jimmy Hedge was buried on the site of his first oil strike alongside the remains of his Irish setter, O'Brien. The burial took place in a pet cemetery known as the Kennel of Heavenly Repose, despite local protests that the cemetery was not licensed to accept human remains. Hedge's attorneys pleaded before a federal judge that to block Hedge's burial beside O'Brien would raise the specter of segregation against every dog owner in America. The judge, who can count dog lovers, agreed.

"And now, before we go to Jim Jump and the weather, a few words from the folks at Wildflower Lubricants and the continuing fight against serum cholesterol."

15

Archibald Kennedy sat nervously in his room at the Hotel Pierre in New York and picked at an early supper of eggs Benedict and Pouilly-Fuissé. On the basis of his inside information, Archibald had decided that he must abandon the relative safety of his post as IC Vice President for Southern Europe and the African Littoral and protect his interests at the IC Management Meeting. He had just arrived from Milano and, despite Alitalia's loving first-class care, he felt exhausted, and that increased his state of growing panic. It was now 5:00 P.M. -- 10:00 P.M. his time— and he had to wait until morning to catch a plane to West Virginia. But he was uncertain as to whom he could safely talk; therefore he hid in his room.

His informants had told him that he was about to witness a corporate disaster. Even if Wiggy could move successfully in time, there would be vast disruptions at IC. If Wiggy failed, the disruptions could be cataclysmic. Accordingly, Archibald did know where to turn; where safety might lie. Under such circumstances experience had taught him to hedge against the vicissitudes of corporate politics: his objective had to be the purchase of as much insurance as possible.

Archibald's problem was that he was not even certain where to make the purchases. If not Wiggy, then who? As he sipped his Pouilly-Fuissé, he slowly turned over the problem. A veritable college yearbook of corporate officers passed in review. Each had a little italic nickname under his picture. And each was seen in Archibald's mind as he had last seen them: Dr. Sydney Plumb, vice president of research, and his horrible wife, Laura May, sitting in the lobby of the Grand Hotel in Rome while Laura May said she had never seen so many Catholic churches in her whole life. Nickname: "Kansas." George Queen, vice president of the New Materials Group, wondering aloud in

Archibald's office if Wiggy could ever be replaced. Nickname: "Dumbo." Harold Quincy Harold, vice president -- international relations and Tommy Lightmeade's brother-in-law, telling Archibald that there would be no need to bother Wiggy about the special commission payments to an alleged third cousin of the former Shah of Iran. Nickname: "Lancelot."

None of these and a dozen or so others seemed to Archibald to be of any particular use to him at this dread hour. Then he thought of two more: The first, of course, was Randall Dingle, vice president of the Goodtimes Division. If anyone were prepared to push Wiggy down an elevator shaft the moment he felt such an act would be applauded, it was friendly Randall. The second name that came to mind was a long shot but Archibald decided it might be the best possibility of all. He knew Ward Winchester Read was currently doing a life sentence in IC's New York purgatory and stood a long way from the throne. But Archibald felt that if anyone could pick up a sword in a time of open confusion and cleave his way to the top of the Tower it probably was Ward.

Archibald made two phone calls. One was more satisfactory than the other.

"Randall," he said into the phone in his clubbiest tone, "how the hell are you? Archibald Kennedy here. I'm on my way to the Greenbrier and frankly, Randall, on the basis of what I'm hearing, there are a couple of things that I thought you should know. Might find them a bit helpful and all that."

"What kind of things, Arch?" Randall said cheerily, and Archibald winced. He hated being called Arch. He hated having his ploys called even more.

"Nothing I can really talk about on the phone, Randall," he said. "I thought maybe you and I might share a little Scotch in private tomorrow at the Greenbrier. Very, very confidentially, of course."

"Fine, Arch. But let's play it by ear. You know what a circus that place will be. I'll keep an eye out for you when I can break free. And thanks for the call, old friend."

"Wonderful, Randall. I'll be looking for you. Just great talking to you."

Archibald shook his head sadly as he contemplated the evanescence of gratitude. Surely it was but one more proof of the baseness of human nature when one considered the number of fantastic two and three-star dinners financed by IC that he had given for Randall Dingle from Venice to London; the hours that he and his much-suffering wife had been bored beyond endurance over cocktails while Dingle's mousy wife worried out loud about what her beautiful, brilliant children were doing at that very moment; the days spent getting those same dear children out of a Spanish jail where they had been sent forever for smuggling pot.

Feeling both driven and disheartened, he obtained Ward's home number from Information and dialed it. The phone rang a long time; then Ward answered. He seemed out of breath and expectant.

"Ward, old friend, Archibald Kennedy here. How the hell are you?"

"Archibald!" Ward said, readjusting his tone. "Good to hear from you. I just got back from a trip and had to race for the phone."

"I'm on my way to the Greenbrier and I thought we might have a drink here at the Pierre. I have some new funny stories that you might find amusing."

"Archibald, don't you know I am practically embalmed? My sense of humor is very thin."

"That'll be the day," Archibald said and then tried a long shot. "I hear you might become a lot more active than some suspect. After all, who else can pull the irons out of the old fire the way you can?"

Ward only paused for a moment, but for a political listener like Archibald the pause was enough.

"Crap," Ward said and laughed. "But I would like to see you. Unfortunately I can't tonight. And I won't be going to the Greenbrier, which shows how far out of things I really am. However, I'd be curious to know just what I might find amusing other than maybe a tip about a new job."

"Ward, you are the most disarming guy. I can't really talk anymore right now myself. But as you may recall, one of my many chores has been to do some banking legwork and there are a couple of Swiss numbers that I thought would you might find entertaining."

"The man at the Greenbrier who really loves to hear Swiss numbers is Jocko Burr. You remember Jocko? Tell him I suggested that you look him up."

"I'll do it."

"Good. Jocko can tell me when he sees me. Then we all can have a good laugh."

*　　*

As Harvey Catoni liked to tell it, there were for him only three kinds of news stories in the world.

"First," he said to his agent, an outsized lesbian named Helen Palm, "there are the big ones you have to cover. Shit, you know, like presidential assassinations, world wars, really major disasters like maybe a Concorde crashing into the middle of London and killing the Queen. You've gotta be a bum in this business if you're not on the scene for that kind of stuff. But the trouble is that it's hard to make a buck out of it because everyone is running around trying to do the same thing.

"Second are the big stories that I find or, better yet, make and then get some kind of arm lock on them. That's when you and I, Baby, can really make out. Before anyone knows what is going on, we have the syndicated, copyrighted series of articles, the TV series sold, the paperbacks on press, and the movie rights in the bag.

"Third are the big, windy zeros: the always momentous socioeconomic changes of our times, tax reform, the world's inexhaustible supply of little men, growth in the GNP, and, oh God, all the rest of that whither whither crap which I gladly yield to all those double-domed, thumb-sucking geniuses who can't even figure out how to pay

96

their American Express bills next month."

Harvey paused, took a sip of coffee, and looked around the restaurant where they were sitting to see if anyone he knew of any importance had entered since he last looked. Harvey Catoni and Helen Palm themselves made a highly noticeable couple. He was a slight, homely, sad-looking man with thinning black, curly hair. He usually wore expensive unpressed suits and flowery Countess Mara ties. Helen Palm was a towering linebacker with a round, pretty face. She favored silk suits and enough gold jewelry to make onlookers suspect she had located a sunken Spanish galleon.

"I love your speech, Sweetie," she said. "I love it every time you give it. But why bore us tonight?"

"Because, you big, cuddly bag of concrete blocks, I want to remind you what it is that attracts us so much to each other and get you going on something that could be our biggest hit to date."

"Harvey, Sweetie, if I were interested in boys, your dripping-wet eighty-five pounds of Italian nothing would hardly make you Number One on my list. But, believe me, Sweetie, I *know* what you can do for me and my creditors and *you* know what I can do for you. Now tell me all."

Harvey waited deliberately while the waiter put a plate with the dinner check in front of him. He studied it carefully through his large glasses which as usual were halfway down his aquiline nose; with equal care he added with his pen an unusually modest tip and signed the check; then in silence he waited until the waiter who had been eagerly standing by took the check away and commented on Harvey's level of generosity by emptying the ashtray and spilling ashes in Harvey's coffee.

"I'm on to one of the biggest business blow-ups of the century," Harvey said finally, in a low steady voice. "Everyone is involved: the President, the Arabs, Wall Street, the whole goddamn national economy; it's a cast of thousands. And, at least right now, I have an inside track."

Helen Palm looked at Harvey Catoni in open

admiration. You really had to hand it to the rotten little weasel. He really knew where to locate the mother lode.

"How absolutely yummy," she said. "Details?"

"Not here. I'll give you everything you need at breakfast at my place tomorrow morning at eight. Then you'll have forty-eight hours, maybe a little more, to peddle our usual package. O.K.?"

"Sweetie, I'm already at work. I'll see you for breakfast at your apartment. You're such a romantic little devil."

*   *

Mayhew Stark, editor of the *Specialists' Insider* and stock tipster extraordinary, had been having a splendid week.

Beginning without a share of IC stock, he had been happily selling IC short for more than two days. Then on Friday morning he found himself short one hundred thousand shares when SR agents put IC on the express elevator going down. Before trading was halted, Mayhew had covered all of his shorts and he and presumably many of his readers were considerably richer.

That evening, as he sat in the front row at one of Christie's more select auctions, he put away from his mind the dangerous thought that had he stayed in the game he might have doubled his winnings next Monday. Mayhew was not greedy. He was happy to limit his risk. There were other things to do in the world. For example, contemplation of the Tang warrior on the block in front of him.

"I have one hundred twenty-five thousand," the auctioneer said in his most cultivated tone. "Do I see one thirty?"

Mayhew, who was sitting with one elegantly tailored leg crossed over the other and his hands folded in his lap, raised his program slightly and smiled. The simple pleasures were always best after all. Sometimes a man just had to forget about business and have a little fun.

16

The Grand Ballroom of the Greenbrier was most certainly designed by an architect who had in mind swirling young belles in white and ribbons and dashing young officers in gray. Great crystal chandeliers, gilt paint, frescoed ceilings, and boxes from which to observe the loveliest and the bravest all posed a challenge to be met by IC's eager meeting engineers, for an entirely different tone was required. By Saturday afternoon, when the first advance forces arrived for rehearsals, the goal had been achieved.

The Grand Ballroom had been converted from a piece of Old Vienna by way of Richmond to a cross between the Stadium at Nuremberg and the Court of Versailles. Chairs marched rank on rank from the front of the huge room to the rear, every twenty or so separated by a slight break and a standard emblazoned with such names as GOOD TIMES DIVISION, GROCERY and GOURMET FOODS DIVISION, OUTER SPACE DIVISION, NEW LIFESTYLES DIVISION, and PEACE PRODUCTS DIVISION. Hanging from boxes were festoons of orange bunting and huge portraits of IC's directors and principal officers, including, among the more prominently displayed, a frowning Or Boon, a warmly smiling Tommy Lightmeade, and a statesmanlike SR.

The ballroom stage had been expanded from a small area suitable for a string orchestra to a huge platform designed to accommodate a raised dais. There IC's leaders could sit in an appropriately imperial manner and speak from an elevated rostrum that looked like the prow of a ship. Behind the dais was a giant screen for projecting slides and movies or both simultaneously. And to the front of the dais was a stage large enough to accommodate a full chorus line. The side areas of the stage were covered with orange bunting, heroic pictures of Heinrich Volksblatt, Wingate Cotton and Wiggy, plus two gigantic IC monograms painted in Day-Glo orange. An orchestra section was placed at the opposite end of the ballroom in the balcony for the Boston Pops, which had been hired for the meeting's opening session on Monday. And everywhere in the balcony banks of lights had been installed to create excitement and other special effects.

Two broad aisles, each carpeted by a thick, orange runner made of Purwul™, an IC product developed from reconstituted paper drink cartons, separated the room into three equal sections. Aisles were also created in the front and rear, making it possible to circumnavigate the entire room for the product demonstrations planned by some of the divisions. There were also more than fifty microphones scattered throughout the room for full participation. However, as a precaution, Tommy Lightmeade arranged to have it possible to cut off some or all of the microphones if necessary.

"I think we should run through Wiggy's slides now; then go into the Peace Division stuff," Cookie Tollhouse said from the rostrum in an electronic voice that boomed through the sound equipment.

"We don't have them yet," an unidentified voice boomed back. "All that shit is coming down with Gross on the second flight."

"O.K., then. Let's do the Peace Division. Just a quick walkthrough because the talent won't be here until tomorrow."

Cookie half walked, half jogged down from the rostrum and sat in the front row of the nearly empty ballroom between Lloyd Nightingale and Sally Laurence. Both Cookie and Sally wore IC-orange slacks, white button-down shirts, and sneakers. Lloyd wore a pair of Chip purple slacks dotted with embroidered trout flies, a rough linen shirt open to the navel, gold chains, and white Gucci loafers.

Successful production as vast and complex as the IC Annual Management Meeting called for an infrastructure staffing of equal vastness and complexity. Inertia and incompetence were built in everywhere by the usual

100

organizational and political realities of the corporate bureaucracy. Therefore, in order to make certain that a meeting took place at all, it was vital to have a structure within the structure. Such a structure was the small group seated in the front row.

Les Gross was in nominal charge of the program under the overall command of Tommy Lightmeade. But Lloyd, as Les's deputy, was specifically in charge of all administrative detail and was unquestionably the person to whom to go if you really wanted to get something done. Cookie, as chief speechwriter, had more to say than anyone about the program's content. And Sally, as Tommy's executive secretary and special assistant, was there to make sure that whatever Tommy wanted to see happen happened. Each, in turn, had a half dozen assistants of varying capability in the usual range: outstanding to rotten. As a group they had to deal with the total panoply of the Executive Office corporate staff and all of the barons and their staffs from each of IC's dozens of divisions gathering from throughout the world. The job, of course, was impossible.

First to be contended with this afternoon was Joe Burnside, the ramrod manager of communications of the Peace Products Division. He worked directly for Harmon "Buzz" Malone, the division's vice president and general manager and a one-time Navy carrier pilot. Joe always sought to anticipate his leader's wishes and to emulate him in every way. For example, Joe was never seen without his outsized, light-sensitive, pilot eyeglasses, shirts with epaulets, or half boots. Neither, of course, was Buzz. Only once did Joe overstep in this area. Buzz often carried a silver-tipped swagger stick that he used as a pointer at meetings. The first time Buzz saw Joe with a swagger stick of his own, he offered Joe several scatological suggestions on where the stick should be stored and implied that Joe's career might be about to suffer a sudden malaise. "Sometimes I don't understand the man," Joe said later. "My stick didn't even have a silver tip."

"Joe, I think it would be easier if you stood in for Buzz at the rostrum while we walk through this," Cookie said, giving Joe his ego fix for the afternoon. "Just talk through the entertainment part".

"I pray the talent won't be the Rockettes again this year," Lloyd said. "I hate to see all those old ladies huffing and puffing."

"It's the cheerleaders for the Dallas Cowboys," Cookie said.

"Chauvinist pigs," Lloyd said. "Sally, if I were you, I'd protest to Tommy. Really, all those half-dressed women wiggling and jiggling. I thought this was supposed to be a serious meeting."

"Undoubtedly," said Joe, who had now reached the rostrum, "you would prefer the soccer team from some good boys' school."

"Delicious," Lloyd said. "Simply delicious."

"Come on," Cookie shouted. "Start the slides and music. Joe, please walk us through."

Drums rolled; trumpets blared ruffles and flourishes; and a huge American flag a appeared on the screen behind the rostrum. The flag faded into the words:

IC PRODUCTS FOR PEACE

This, in turn, faded into the division's slogan:

KEEP 'EM SCARED

The sound system began to roar, "The Eyes of Texas Are Upon You."

"At this point," Joe said, "the cheerleaders will rush down the aisles and come up on the stage waving pompons and IC banners. Then they go into their group numbers as the band plays 'Deep in the Heart of Texas,' 'Dixie,' and 'The Battle Hymn of the Republic.' That sets us up for Buzz to walk up to the rostrum and begin the main presentation. O.K.? Everyone with me?"

102

"Couldn't be clearer," Lloyd said. "I love it."

"As you know," Joe went on, "the presentation falls into two major parts. First, some comments on our major product lines...the H-bomb warheads, the chemical stuff like Peaceful Sleep . . . and the old favorites from our napalm line that we've upgraded like Well Done II."

As Joe talked, slides began to appear rapidly on the right and left screens: pictures of exploding missiles, clouds of gas engulfing attacking tanks, entire city blocks covered with flaming goo. These were followed by a lot of numbers showing kill rates and cost per thousand.

"First we show a lot of shoot-'em-up just to give everyone the flavor," Joe said. "But the guts are in these numbers, of course. This is all pretty much as you and your guys wrote it, Cookie, but Buzz wanted to get in a lot more shoot-'em-up than you had in your draft."

"Looks just fine," Cookie said. "Can't have too much."

"Now," Joe said, "we get to the second section, which everyone has been waiting to hear. The division has been doing beautifully but the world peace market gets more competitive every year. Not just new stuff, either; the market in used peace products is booming. Here we show the series of satellite photos from the captured Soviet satellite Uk XXXV."

Pictures appearing rapidly on the screens showed happy Nigerian troops opening crates of guns with Polish markings; happy Honduran troops opening crates of guns with Nigerian markings; happy Polish troops opening crates of guns with Honduran markings. Then came pictures showing Israeli airmen painting out the U.S. markings on a new jet bomber; Indians painting out the Israeli markings on a somewhat used jet bomber; and finally Bolivians painting out the Indian markings on a shot-up jet bomber. These were followed by the usual series of slides filled with indecipherable but impressive-looking numbers and curves.

"And now our biggie," Joe said. "Our marketers have sensed a growing need to pay more attention to the peace needs of the smaller nations. Something nonnuke oriented; no Cadillacs; just the plain-Jane hardware designed to keep the peace. So here it is."

Both screens lit up with the same phrase:

THE IC SPECIAL MINI-PEACE KIT

"The rest of the slides outline the various special kits," Joe said. "Essentially, there is our basic five-million-dollar package for equipping small units. Then it goes up by multiples of ten. The big sales plus, of course, is IC reliability. You're buying from someone you know; not just from someone who picked up a lot of junk on an old battlefield. And here's the final slide."

The screen showed a picture of a crane hoisting an enormous box from a freighter to a dock. On the side of the box stenciled letters spelled out the slogan, KEEP 'EM SCARED.

"Joe," Sally said. "When Mr. Malone finishes, he should plan to introduce Mr. Lightmeade for a brief comment."

"That's not in our script," Joe said.

"Yes it is," Sally said. "Mr. Lightmeade put it there this morning when I talked to him from the airport."

"I have just one question, Joe," Lloyd said. "Do you really think it's a good idea to open this presentation with 'Dixie'? You know we have some spoilsport black managers who might take umbrage."

"Lloyd," Joe said with strained patience, "you ought to know by now that 'Dixie' is Buzz's favorite song."

"We love the whole thing," Cookie said.

"Particularly the Cowgirls," Sally said. "Don't change a line."

*   *

The IC lead corporate jet — the Haltblut I — greased onto the runway at the Greenbrier Valley Airport precisely at five o'clock Saturday afternoon. The stretch Boeing 727 carried Wiggy, Tommy Lightmeade, and Or Boon, along with a half dozen staff aides, including Les Gross and Jocko Burr.

For most of the two-hour trip from New York to White Sulphur Springs, Wiggy, Tommy, and Or closeted themselves in the CEO section of the aircraft, occasionally summoning one of their assistants. Tommy, as usual, was expansive and optimistic; Or was depressed; Wiggy drank a lot and said little. However, by the time the Haltblut I landed, they had decided on a strategy for their meeting with Major Mamoud and Marvin Ikworth.

"I say we have them in our pocket," Tommy said for about the fifth time. "The Arabs have been trying to get into the pants of a major U.S. multinational for years. They won't be able to resist."

Wiggy twirled the ice in his glass. "Seeing that it's the Arabs, I wish you would find another form of expression."

"I still say we have it backwards," Or said sourly. "I think you will find that it is we who are in the pocket of the Arabs. Maybe before the market yesterday we had some leverage. Now we have to take what they'll give."

"No, sir, by God," Tommy said. "We haven't even played our big cards. I have the solemn word of Gaston Edsel and Warren Rasberry that we have their full support. I tell you it's a blank check. We can bring to bear on this bunch of camel drivers the full power of the United States of America."

"As wielded by Gaston Edsel," Or said, and got up to fix himself another glass of Perrier with a squeeze of lime.

"While you're up, I'll have another short one," Wiggy said.

"Or, you just have to take a more positive approach," Tommy said. "If we are going to win, we have to play like winners. I'm not blind to our problems, but we have to keep our eyes on the horizon and not at our feet. We play our cards as if they were all trumps and keep the deuces and threes in our pocket. And don't worry about Edsel. He may not be a Lincoln but he isn't a Tucker either."

"Tommy's right," Wiggy said, turning to Or. "We have to play from strength regardless of the facts. And, after all, we're pretty good at that. At least, that's what everyone has always said."

Or smiled for the first time in a week.

"No argument, gentlemen," he said. "As you will see when we get Jocko in here in a few minutes, my department has not been idle. I just feel it is important that we don't kid ourselves. The collapse of our stock yesterday did not go unnoticed by the sheiks. And I have to believe that it has even come to the attention of the President and his good friend Boom Boom. I submit that we may have to fall back and open the way for the Arabs to gain absolute control. That may have to be Plan B."

"Never," shouted Tommy. "Never, never, never!"

"Unless, of course, we have to," Wiggy said.

Or summoned Jocko, who laid before them a series of newly minted numerical exhibits and graphs. Jocko's appearance had continued to deteriorate and he looked increasingly like a customer of an inept funeral home. When he saw the bottles of liquor on the CEO bar, he literally licked his lips and panted quietly.

"These are our latest numbers," Or began. "They are designed to show us in our very best light and I think you will appreciate that Jocko has performed another miracle. Lazarus continues to walk."

"Haltingly," Jocko essayed, and immediately regretted his unfortunate tendency to whimsy when all three men glared at him.

"What we suggest," Or said, "is that, armed with these displays, we push for the sale of only convertible stock to the Arab consortium. That would give them a holding of about twenty percent of IC common if they convert. We may also have to give them a couple of seats on the Board. But we would still be able to outvote them as long as they don't convert. And two things should make conversion unlikely. One is our offering price of a hundred dollars a share for the convertibles when our common is

106

down to twenty. Two is Arab queasiness about a bad reaction from Washington. Anyway, that's Plan A."

"We can sell it," Tommy said. "Those monkeys will love it."

"But you, Or, think that they may not," Wiggy said.

"Unfortunately, I suspect that Major Mamoud and Mr. Ikworth did not join forces because of any mutual inability to add. That's why we must be ready with Plan B. If necessary, we may have to give them the store."

"Never," Tommy roared. "Jocko, you better plan to be with us to help explain your masterpiece," Or said. Wiggy said nothing and drained his glass.

*   *

Cookie Tollhouse was hardly overjoyed when he found out that Sally Laurence was at the Greenbrier.

He had arrived Friday morning on the Haltblut IV, an aging turboprop, along with the meeting setup crew. By noon he had had the great good pleasure of meeting Tina Vitello, the Italian movie star, at the indoor Greenbrier pool.

Cookie was not aware that so far Tina had starred in only two movies, both a special blend of Milanese kiddie porn and art photography designed for easy showing worldwide without the need of subtitles or voice translation. Nor was he aware that Tina was at the Greenbrier through the good offices of the Count di Conti, IC's roving vice president for Italian government relations. The count, an elegant gentleman in his late fifties with a small beard and a monocle, had invited Tina to the IC meeting to keep him from being bored and to give her the opportunity to meet important Americans who could further her acting career.

However, despite these gaps in his knowledge, Cookie was very much aware of Tina herself as she stood beside the pool with warm spring sunlight streaming on her through the pool's glass enclosure. She was a perfectly formed, doll-like woman in her early twenties who could have passed for fifteen. She had long, black, straight hair;

a tawny porcelain face; large blue eyes; and a bathing suit composed of a broad red hair ribbon and two red cocktail coasters.

Even as Cookie took note of Tina, she took note of him. The count was lunching and plotting in their suite with IC counter-parts from other parts of the world. All had arrived early, of course, to gain an extra day or two of respite from their busy schedules and to learn what intelligence they could in advance of the meeting. "Cara Tina, go play in the sun," the count had said. Therefore, as Cookie's creative mind concocted scenes of early afternoon seduction, similar thoughts occurred to Tina. Within five minutes they had met accidentally and were chatting and laughing; within twenty minutes they had taken a swim and decided to have a cocktail in Cookie's sitting-room suite since a bar had conveniently been set up there for IC planning meetings; within forty minutes Tina was entertaining Cookie with some remarkable feats that she had learned in her starring movie roles. And so the afternoon sped.

"Cookie bambino, Sainted Mother of God, it is four o'clock," she said suddenly. "The count will be anxious. It is time for his sauna and massage."

With exquisite grace, she put on her beach robe; grabbed a handful of peanuts and a handful of Fritos; and started for the door.

"Caro Cookie, no lunch is bad," she said. "Ciao." And she was gone.

Cookie saw her again at dinner. She was with the count. He was distraught. He saw her again at midmorning Saturday in the lobby. Again she was with the count. Pain! But then, as the count talked to a bellhop and bought newspapers, Tina made little swimming motions at Cookie and rolled her eyes. Ecstasy!

He was at the pool at 11:30. At 11:45, Lloyd Nightingale appeared and announced that he and Sally Laurence had just arrived, somewhat shaken, on Haltblut V, a refurbished DC-3. At 11:50, Sally appeared. At noon,

Tina walked up to the table where Cookie sat with Lloyd and Sally, smiled warmly, and said:

"Buon giorno, Cookie." Then she walked to a nearby beach chair, stagily removed her robe, and dived dazzlingly into the pool.

"Who is your cute little friend?" Sally asked.

"She is the protégée of the Count di Conti," Cookie said, as casually as possible.

"I didn't know that you knew him."

"No doubt a vicarious friendship," Lloyd said unhelpfully.

*   *

Kings and presidents, maharajas and generals, dukes and premiers had occupied the Presidential Suite at the Greenbrier for more than a century. Some great, some dishonest, some merely totally incompetent, but all unquestionably familiar with the feelings of suppressed stark terror that now prevailed in the half-sober brain of the latest occupant of the suite: J. Wigglesworth Pratt.

"As chairman and chief executive officer of one of the world's largest multinational corporations, I am in a position to have far better information about the world economy than most," Wiggy told the small group gathered in large, comfortable chairs around a huge glass coffee table in the suite's two-story living room. Beginning at Wiggy's right sat Tommy Lightmeade, Major Ibn Mamoud, Marvin Ikworth, and Or Boon. Jocko Burr hovered outside the magic circle, fixing drinks and waiting to be summoned. The time was nine o'clock on Saturday night. The major and Ikworth had arrived only a half hour earlier aboard their Yankee Properties Learjet. From outside the heavily draped high windows of the suite came the muted sound of an orchestra playing "San Francisco," followed by "Arrivederci, Roma."

"Our corporation has positioned itself to achieve major benefits from what I see as a forthcoming world boom,"

Wiggy continued. "What today look like major setbacks in some areas, tomorrow will be regarded as minor blips on the curve. Your principals, through Yankee Properties, have the kind of opportunity that may never come again."

"Please, please, Mr. Wigglesworth," the major said, raising a beautifully manicured hand that bore three large rings, "we do not speak of principals. This is a Yankee Properties investment and, of course, Mr. Ikworth is our president and chief executive officer. I merely am a…leading shareholder"

"Of course, of course, excuse me," Wiggy said and smiled his most sympathetic and pleasantly conspiratorial smile.

"We fully understand that all legal agreements will be made with Yankee Properties," Or Boon interjected. "Any questions on the resources of Yankee Properties would be deferred to Mr. Ikworth or you. I presume you are prepared to provide satisfactory answers in view of the sums involved."

"Absolutely," the major said, and Ikworth nodded. "We are extremely successful entrepreneurs. We have the strong support of certain major European banks. We are, in sum, a bloody good example of the free enterprise system at work."

As the major said "bloody good," he sat back and self-consciously smoothed his impeccably trimmed Sandhurst mustache. Then he looked over his shoulder on the conclusion of his statement and said to Jocko, "I'll have a whiskey now. No ice."

"Then let's get down to it," Tommy Lightmeade said. "We have what we feel is a splendid and most generous package, the kind of opportunity, as Wiggy has pointed out, that is most rare and may never come again. Or, why don't you give our good friends from Yankee Properties the details?" Tommy smiled and made a sweeping gesture toward the two little dark men in black pin-stripe suits. "As you will see, we are prepared to welcome you as major partners."

110

Or leaned forward from his huge boat of a chair and spread before the group the exhibits previously prepared by Jocko. Then he used them, along with substantiation that he invited from Jocko, to present a picture of the current financial position of IC that would have made the Rock of Gibraltar look spongy by comparison.

Billions in debts had miraculously disappeared or become assets. Huge losses turned into bookkeeping footnotes of the most inconsequential nature and in the smallest of print. Great new ventures not expected to realize a dime in profits for a decade or more became absolute certainties upon which large new borrowings would soon be possible. Great new tax benefits materialized out of the ether in dozens of countries in which IC had not conducted business in years. Minor physical assets such as burned-out warehouses in Chile became enormously valuable. Gold, oil, bauxite, and other unproven mineral reserves were discovered beneath Alaskan tundra, Honduran swamps, and slum property in Watts, the upper Bronx, and downtown Singapore even as Or talked.

"It is only lack of confidence in an uncertain market that is troubling us today," he said finally. "Cash flow is our problem. If we can cure this temporary minor matter, all else is possible."

"We have the management team, the resources, and the know-how to do the job," Tommy interjected. "We can double this great corporation in a decade — maybe less. And you can be a part of that dazzling opportunity. You and your associates.

"How much?" the major interrupted and looked at Wiggy, who had been concentrating on drinking throughout Or's presentation. "How much to join this great management team and participate in this great opportunity?"

"We are prepared," Or said in his coolest bookkeeper voice, "to offer you fifty million shares of IC convertible stock at one hundred dollars a share."

"Son of a bitch," Ikworth said, "that's five billion dollars."

"That should be no problem for an enterprise like Yankee Properties," Wiggy said.

"Not a problem," the major said. "But not a good deal either."

"Now just a minute," Tommy said. "IC today is one of..."

"Please, Mr. Lightmeade," the major said. "Our research indicates that IC today has not quite the high gloss that you would suggest. But that is not the point. The fact is that you need five billion dollars and, for whatever reason, that kind of money is unobtainable to you except from a company such as Yankee Properties with its excellent resources. In fact, we are ready to spend much more but not, as my friend Mr. Ikworth might say, for a lousy fifty million shares of convertible. Bluntly, gentlemen, we are interested in a deal only if we gain absolute control."

"Impossible!" Tommy said. "No way, sir! I can assure you that the great International Coagulants Corporation is not on the block. We are not here to barter away a great American institution."

"But let's talk about it anyway," Wiggy said quietly and waggled his empty glass at Jocko.

*   *

At eleven o'clock that night Cookie Tollhouse and Sally Laurence had been arguing in the sitting room/bedroom of his suite for about two hours.

The immediate cause was the burning question of whether Cookie did or did not have more than a nodding acquaintance with the lovely companion of the Count di Conti. But by now the way this question was resolved was almost irrelevant since the answer had already been settled in Sally's highly competent head.

The underlying cause was whether there was still any kind of a mutually satisfactory relationship between Cookie and Sally. To this more important question, Cookie kept saying yes if only Sally would be sensible; Sally increasingly felt the answer was no.

"Your problem," Cookie shouted as he fixed himself a seventh vodka on the rocks, "your problem, goddamn it, is that you just want too damn much of too damn much. That's what your problem is, goddam it!"

"And your problem," Sally shouted at Cookie from the end of the couch where she sat almost in a fetal crouch, "your problem is that you're an emotional eunuch, a sexist womanizer, and you're drunk."

"Don't start telling me how much to drink. I guess, goddamn it, I know how much I can drink, goddamn it. And don't start giving me all that Women's Lib crap."

Cookie hurled himself into a chair and spilled his drink. Sally laughed, and the phone rang.

"Sally, this is Tommy Lightmeade," Tommy said. "I've been looking all over for you. I need your help."

"Should I come over?"

"No need. But get packed. I want you to go back to New York on a company plane tonight, get the sealed Project Z files out of the safe in my office, and bring them back here tomorrow. You're the only person besides myself who has the combination and I can't leave. I've ordered a plane to get ready. Can you go?"

"Sure," she said, looking across the room at Cookie, who had fallen asleep in his chair. "I don't have anything else to do here tonight. I'm happy to help."

An hour later the copilot ushered her aboard the Haltblut II, Tommy's personal Learjet secretly refurbished to include an electric organ. As she adjusted her safety belt she realized that she was not the only passenger aboard. Jocko Burr was sitting two seats forward, clutching an envelope handed to him by Archibald Kennedy, and staring blankly into a glass of gin.

Then the engine came on and the jet started to roll.

17

Cookie sat in the Colonnades Dining Room and pushed scrambled eggs around his plate. They were disgusting. The day was disgusting. Life was disgusting. He had a terrible headache.

An army of black waiters moved silently about the elegant white and gold room, serving eggs and kippers and smoked salmon; bowing and smiling and emptying empty ashtrays and wiping chins; making the more than a hundred late Sunday morning breakfast guests scattered throughout the room feel as if nothing had really happened since 1890. Or maybe 1790. It was delightful. It was wonderful. "Mo sweet rolls, suh? Watch yo fingers. Dey is hot." It beat the hell out of a world of Tab and Big Macs with a hefty helping of surliness on the side.

But Cookie's depression was such that the ambiance which the Greenbrier called in its promotional literature "life as it should be" only served to make him feel worse. He had awakened on the couch in his room. He was wearing a familiar costume — the one he had been wearing the previous day. His mouth was arid.

His taste no longer functioned. A note pinned to his shirt said, "Drop dead." It was signed: "Sally." When he had finally focused his eyes on his wristwatch, he learned that the time was 10:30. At noon, he had a program planning meeting for which he had not prepared.

Cookie's lust for life was not enhanced a half hour later when he entered the Colonnades as Tina, dressed in riding clothes, walked out, leaning on Buzz Malone. Malone, also in riding clothes, carried a riding crop instead of the usual swagger stick. Cookie wondered if Tina went in for whips too.

Behind Buzz and Tina more than a dozen more of his executive team from the Peace Products Division swarmed, wearing a rainbow of sports clothes. They, along with more than two hundred others, had been arriving steadily since the previous evening. It was like a convocation at Rome. The Cardinals of the True Corporate Church were clearly identifiable by the clusters of Archbishops and Bishops who surrounded each of them. Meantime, on their flanks, the Monsignors and clouds of high-paid spear carriers hustled this way and that, fetching and hauling and shouting to onlookers to make way for the great men passing by.

"Miss Vitello and I are going riding," Buzz said to two vice presidents walking near him. I'll meet you at noon for the presentation review."

"Buzz and I will meet you later at noon for the review," each of the two vice presidents said to others near them. "Make sure you have everything."

"Get that damn material cleaned up for a noon meeting with Buzz," the others said to others. "This is no kidding. Buzz doesn't want any damn slips-ups."

And those others along with still others went to look for the material, saying things like: "Buzz is really putting on the old heat"; 'The balloon goes up at noon"; and "Buzz says, 'Kick ass. Let's go.'"

As Cookie gave up on the eggs and tried to get down some dry toast, he realized that someone was talking to him. Vernon Schlitz, vice president of marketing for the Corporate Planning Division and IC's highest ranking black executive, stood at Cookie's table. It occurred to Cookie that Vernon looked exactly like Tyrone Power when he played a handsome Hindu doctor in an old movie about heavy rain in India under the Raj.

"May I join you?" Vernon asked, and did. "I find I need some personal advice."

Cookie tried to reassemble his mind. He had worked with Vernon a number of times and they had developed a certain amount of camaraderie. But when an IC officer started asking for personal advice, all of the warning and tilt signals went on in Cookie's head even in its present deranged condition.

"Sure, Vernon," he said. "Happy to help."

Vernon looked around to make certain that he would not be overheard and leaned forward confidentially toward Cookie.

"I just got a funny phone call from Square Root," he said. "He won't be coming down to the meeting and wants me to give his corporate planning presentation for him tomorrow afternoon. He says he's involved in a special project."

"Must be one hell of a special project. But, hey, that's a break for you. Guys kill for an opportunity to speak at these meetings."

"Usually. But I'm not so sure about this situation. Have you read the presentation?"

"I wrote it."

"I thought so. It's pretty wild stuff, isn't it?"

"I'm not in charge of content. My job is to make it sound good."

"Sure, but you have to admit this is no ordinary presentation. It has all the proposed plans for acquiring Penn Central Railroad and the Postal Service and maybe Ozark and Frontier Airlines. The presentation says we're going to show what big-league management and technology and know-how in private enterprise can do. You know, this is really Tommy Lightmeade's big idea. I've never gone along with the scenario. Do you think I'm being set up?"

Cookie sipped cold coffee to give himself time to think. Vernon was truly a first-class corporate dream: son of a successful basketball star; graduate of Colgate and Harvard; brilliant business careerist; smart; cultured; beautiful manners; good looking; and black. The only thing he lacked was a minor disablement attributed to combat. It was a combination that would put him at the top of every manager's private hit list.

"You've got to be kidding," Cookie said. "Why would anyone set you up?"

"Well, maybe Square Root feels he would prefer not to

be associated with the plan. Maybe he figures that if it bombs, they can blame it on some dumb disadvantaged black. Maybe he thinks this is a good chance to dump me."

"Dump you! You! For Christ's sake, you're one of IC's star performers. Other than the top brass, you're the only guy whose picture always makes the Annual Report."

Vernon tapped his well-manicured fingers on the table.

"You may be right," he said. "I guess this place makes me a little paranoid with all these escapees from Class C movies running around saying things like 'Does you want some mo coffee?'"

"Forget it," Cookie said. "I have it on good authority that every waiter in this hotel owns a condominium in Florida and learned to talk the way they do in a special course at Cornell Hotel School called Servility one ten."

Vernon laughed for the first time.

"You're probably right," he said again and got up. "But do me a favor. The presentation rehearsal is scheduled for the Jefferson Davis Suite. See if you can get it moved."

*   *

Tommy Lightmeade arrived at the President Millard Fillmore Room promptly at noon. Cookie, Lloyd Nightingale, and Les Gross were waiting for him.

"Where is Sally?" Tommy asked, as casually as possible, but he almost choked on the phlegm in his throat.

"Can't find her," Les said. "No one has seen her since last night."

It was the fourth disturbing discovery for Tommy in an hour. First Or Boon informed him that Jocko Burr seemed to have mysteriously disappeared. Then he had learned that Square Root Randolph had phoned to explain that he would have to stay in New York for unexplained medical reasons. And, only a half hour ago, he could have sworn he saw that rotten bastard columnist Harvey Catoni checking in at the reception desk.

Usually Tommy, by nature, would ignore all such

information, no matter how obvious the pattern became or how negative. Had he been a German staff officer in World War II, he would have been first at the Führerbunker with the glad tidings of high Russian losses at Stalingrad. Had he been a Spanish grandee at the court of Philip II, his report on the Armada would have begun with the wonders of circumnavigating the British Isles. But even Tommy had begun to feel twinges of unease and found his mind wandering as Les Gross excitedly outlined details of the Management Meeting program as it currently stood.

"You have the whole first morning," Les said. "You open the meeting and give everyone the charge for Day One. Then you introduce Wiggy for his State of the Company Address. Then we move right into your follow-on remarks and the unveiling of Operation Integrity. Then you give everyone another shot of Old Lightmeade Inspiration and they break up into teams to decide how to implement Operation Integrity in their divisions."

"Good. That sounds plenty exciting," Tommy said without visible excitement. "What's next?"

"Lunch," Lloyd said.

"After lunch," Les continued, "we get everyone back in the ballroom for Buzz Malone and the Peace Products Division. You follow Buzz with some comments and then we break for the golfathon. That's Day One. Except for dinner when you or Wiggy give everyone the charge for Day Two."

"I'll do it," Tommy said. "Wiggy doesn't like to talk at dinner."

"O.K.," Les said, elaborately making a note. "Now here's Day Two. Randall Dingle does the big story on the Good Times Division. As per your good suggestion, you follow up with a few comments. Then we break up into the workshops. We have one on Advanced Marketing, one on Advanced Planning, one on Advanced Accounting, and one on Advanced Career Development."

"Then we advance to lunch," Lloyd interjected.

"Right," Les said. "Then we have Or Boon's wrap-up on

the big financial picture. You make a few closing comments of course. Then we have the tennisathon."

"The formal dinner that night is in the Crystal Dining Room," Cookie said. "We have three speakers: you, Johnny Carson, and our good friend, the cousin of the Shah of Iran."

"Day Three," Les said. "Just a morning session to allow everyone to get back. You open with The Charge. Then we all look at the future with Doc Plumb. This is our big newsmaking day. The research boys are planning to trot out their latest and best and we'll be broadcasting some of the presentation to a special news conference in New York."

"Have we checked out that presentation yet?" Tommy asked suspiciously.

"Not really," Cookie said. "Plumb told us he may unveil his new major diet pill. It's called Shed©. It enables you to live on a banana and a glass of gin a day for two months and lose up to fifty pounds. But he's still waiting for some final test results. If Shed is a no-go, he says he has a backup secret program that he can use but he won't tell us what it is."

"You damn well find out," Tommy said. "Tell him he doesn't go on until I approve what he plans to talk about. The last time he pulled a secret out of his hat it turned out to be that damn death ray sun lamp. One other thing. ."

But he was interrupted by a bellboy with an envelope. The message inside said:

"Haltblut II still at La Guardia. Where girl with your file? Arabs restless." The initials on the message were O.B.

"All right," Tommy said to the group. "It sounds as if it's going to be just great. Press on. I'll talk to you later."

And he hurried from the room to make some phone calls.

*　　*

"Wiggy-pie, I do really think that you are mad to go on with this thing. You and I could be sitting at the club in

Aruba right now instead of being just trapped here in this godforsaken place. Wiggy-pie, are you listening to me at all?"

The soliloquy in the best Foxcroft tones came as it so often did from Lydia Winthrop Pratt. The intended auditor was the chief executive officer of International Coagulants. They sat alone in the two-story sitting room of the Presidential Suite.

As a rule, wives were banned from the annual IC Management Meeting. But there were special cases. Lydia always attended. So at various times did the wives of Tommy Lightmeade, Or Boon, and a half dozen other top IC executives, on the theory that they acted as corporate hostesses and would introduce a social note into the otherwise Machiavellian atmosphere of the dinners and receptions. In practice this was a dubious theory. With one or two exceptions the wives devoted their time at the meetings to playing bridge, complaining about the service, gossiping among themselves, and advising their husbands of the questionable deeds of their business associates.

Lydia, as the wife of the CEO, made the requisite number of appearances. Otherwise she rode, stayed in her suite, and read books. At fifty-seven she was still trim and retained her scrubbed, attractive, finishing-school-girl looks. She always wore only two basic costumes: tweed suits or simple, black, designer dresses and pearls. Corporate wives who were her contemporaries were totally intimidated by always feeling that she consciously put them down. That was untrue. She did it subconsciously. No effort was required. Younger corporate wives often were devoted to her particularly because of her offhand, simple way of dressing. They did not recognize that her pearls were oriental and were insured for $100,000. Nor did most of them understand Foxcroft.

Lydia's pearls not only were real but, even better, she had inherited them from her great-grandmother Winthrop, a monstrous old tyrant whom everyone called Tatti. Among Tatti's other charms had been a small New York farm that became the site of the Hotel Pierre. Tatti's pearls were particularly treasured by Lydia since that was all she had inherited. Everything else had disappeared with her father in 1931 when the Justice Department started to ask a lot of unpleasant questions about some bank overdrafts.

"I truly am worried about you, you know," Lydia went on. "You haven't been sleeping well and you are drinking a lot. And all over this stupid company. I know you have to do it all by yourself. Certainly you can't rely on that absolute ass, Tommy. I don't know why you've kept him around. And his wife! God! Betty Lightmeade is one of the most impossible people I know. All she does is eat and talk about her idiot grandchildren. You should see their pictures. I swear they all have hydrocephalic heads and funny pink little eyes.

"And you certainly can't trust Or Boon. It gives me chills just to look at his bald head. Have you ever noticed that when he smiles his teeth are actually pointed? Thank God his wife isn't here. Everytime I see Eleanor Boon she wants me to subscribe to some new insane cause. Last year she spent the entire meeting trying to raise money for the descendants of Japanese who died at Hiroshima. She went around asking everyone, 'What do you say when you look into the eyes of someone whose parents were at Ground Zero?' She was just furious when I said, 'How about Remember Pearl Harbor?' The woman has no sense of humor.

"Wiggy, if you must keep on with this thing you must get some help. Whatever happened to that delightful fellow, Ward Read? Now he was really clever. And the two of you got along so well. I heard that his wife has remarried some former Nazi flyer. She always had a lot of spunk. He must be quite something for her to leave Ward. Anyway, you do have to get some more competent people to help you. It does seem some days that all the idiots have floated to the top of this company.

"That's what really puzzles me, Wiggy-pie. Why do you care what happens? And don't tell me all that gibberish about your responsibilities to the shareholders. I always remember my father at Southampton in the summer laughing and telling the story ad nauseam about the man looking out into the harbor and asking 'Where are the customers' yachts?' I guess nothing changes. All of you would still put up with anything just to have the coolies carry you around in the sedan chairs a little longer.

"But I do think you should watch how much of that whiskey you're drinking, old boy. You know that's your fourth since lunch. I don't care how good a head you have, four stiffies since lunch is a lot. If you want to relax before your meeting with that perfectly dreadful Mr. Ikworth and that funny little Arab with the mail-order Oxford accent you should try taking a nap or practice your putting or take a steam bath or something. I suppose both of them will be at the reception tonight. Oh, fear not, I shall be perfectly charming.

"There's the phone. I'll get it. Hello. Yes, this is Lydia Pratt. Why, yes, of course. What a surprise! Of course, I remember you, Ward. It's good to hear from you. What a coincidence. I was just talking about you. Just a minute. I'll call him. He's right here. Wiggy, darling. It's for you."

*   *

Wiggy gave them the bad news in the James Buchanan Room.

Tommy Lightmeade and Or Boon met there to prepare in secret for a five o'clock meeting with the major and Marvin Ikworth. The purpose of that meeting was the signing of papers that would pass 50 million shares of IC convertible stock to Yankee Enterprises in exchange for $5 billion. They would also give Marvin and the major a piece of paper indicating Board approval of a tender offer by Yankee Enterprises for 125 million of IC common at $30 a share. Wiggy had already devoted most of the day to obtaining that approval by conducting a dial-a-board meeting with his tame outside directors. By early afternoon he had enough telegrams with proxy votes to provide the required assurances and sell the convertibles.

"But we have to have the goddamn certificates," Or Boon said, pacing the small meeting room beneath the glazed, foggy eyes in the portrait of one of America's more ineffectual Presidents. "Are you sure that girl is still in New York?"

"She has to be," Tommy said. "We've checked the pilot of the Haltblut II. He arrived back here without her after he received word from Square Root Randolph that arrangements were changed and Sally would not be returning. Square Root apparently told the same thing to the limousine driver at the IC Tower".

"Square Root? What the hell has he to do with this? What was he doing at the office? He's supposed to be here, isn't he? This is absolutely insane. But we damn well better get those certificates that you sent her for or we are in deep trouble on this deal. I just don't understand, but somehow you screwed this thing up."

"I understand," Wiggy said in a doomsday voice from the door, shut it quietly, and slumped into a chair. "I understand and you will too."

Both Or and Tommy stared at him in horror. Wiggy looked bloodless and suddenly about 105. Even more frightening, he had become cold sober. No one had seen him that sober in ten years.

"I have just received a telephone call from our old friend Ward Read," Wiggy said. "He seems to have been calling from my office. He says he has occupied the Tower in the name of IC shareholders and he is making certain demands. We have only a few hours to meet them or he threatens to give the press materials on IC's true financial condition and call in the Justice Department.

"Outrage!" Tommy shouted. "We'll put the bastard in jail. We'll crucify him."

"How do you know he isn't faking?" Or asked very quietly in his take-him-out-and-shoot-him voice.

"I know," Wiggy said. "He was definitely in my office.

124

He read to me some personal correspondence that was in my desk. He also has our Miss Laurence under what he calls house arrest and has Tommy's Project Z File with the convertible certificates."

"Trespassing!" Tommy shouted. "We can put him away for trespassing and theft of company property. I'll call the police. He's bluffing us. What can he say to the press or anyone else? I never liked that opera warrior bastard. I told you he had a crazy streak."

"Tommy, for God's sake, shut up," Wiggy said. "Listen to me. He's sitting there in my office with all the cards. Jocko Burr is with him. So is that ingrate Square Root Randolph. I'm sure there are others. They're rummaging through the files now. Tomorrow it will be *Forbes* and the AP doing the rummaging. How would you like to spend the rest of your life in Costa Rica?"

"Well, what do we do then? Just cave in? Crawl?"

"We may have to. He wants our written resignations by tomorrow. He wants the Board to name him CEO. And he wants the Arab deal dropped unless it can be renegotiated back to a maximum of ten percent of the company. Or, what choice do we have?"

Or had a set, funny look on his face. He merely stared silently out the window, as if he had left the room.

"We can still win," he said finally. "We have to bluff him out. Tell him we'll meet with him tomorrow afternoon to work out his deal. Stall him. Meantime, we'll get our Arab friends so far into the swamps they won't be able to get out."

"Now you're talking," Wiggy said. "I knew we could think of a clean way to do it."

"Yeah," Tommy said. "But later we have to get that bastard. Christ, he's violating private property. Breaking into our offices. Reading your mail. It's un-American. What was the letter he read to you?"

"Nothing important," Wiggy said. "It was a note from the Count di Conti asking me if I would be interested in a little personal investment in some Italian movie."

Two brief meetings.

First, in the Greenbrier suite named for Martin Van Buren, statesman and wheeler-dealer.

"Here is the letter of Board concurrence," said Wiggy. "I think that you will find it quite in order."

"Oh, good show," said the major.

"And the certificates?" said Marvin Ikworth.

"Only a slight delay," said Tommy. "A little logistics mix-up. We will have them tomorrow afternoon."

"Regrettable," said the major. "You realize, of course, no deposits can be made without the certificates in hand."

"Of course, of course," said Or. "No hurry. Our deal is solid as a rock."

"I do hope so," said the major. "Our chief shareholder at Yankee Enterprises is so unpleasant when he feels cheated."

"Not to worry," said Wiggy. "What have you got to lose?"

"My hands."

Second meeting, compliments of A. Bell, inventor, via cable from West Virginia to New York.

"Tomorrow afternoon, then," said Wiggy to Ward in tones of celestial reasonableness. "It will be too obvious if we don't open the meeting here. As soon as that's taken care of, we'll fly to New York to meet with you.

"All right," said Ward. "We'll make no moves until then. But be ready to cut the deal or we'll go public immediately."

"Ward, Ward, you can trust me. You know we both want the right thing for the Company. That's paramount."

"Of course."

*   *

They were drinking at the Old White, the Greenbrier's exclusive private club that admits Greenbrier guests to temporary membership for a dollar and a half. Membership is essential. Otherwise the thirsty guests would be unable to drink in West Virginia where the benevolent legislature protects its hungry hill folk from the evils of alcohol.

…Kim Dingle, the vaguely pudgy and overdressed wife of Randy Dingle, stood near the bar spreading sociability as a good corporate wife should.

"I just can't understand these young managers' wives anymore," she said. "These girls who don't want to move are just wrecking their husbands' careers. They are absolutely wrecking them. Randy and I have moved twenty-five times in the last twenty-two years and I never have had any trouble making new friends. All I do is I just join the Newcomers Club wherever I go until we move again. Oh, I used to feel a teensy shy, you know, because I was one of the younger members. But now wherever I go I'm the oldest."

"Have you ever lived near our plant in Reading, Mrs. Dingle?" The question from a red-faced sales manager named Douggy drew a few uneasy laughs. Douggy, whose career had plateaued ten years ago, was known for his bold wit.

"No" Kim Dingle said, unperturbed. "But we lived in Fort Wayne for two years and I get more Christmas cards from the gang we met there than from anyplace else. Of course, that always was a big Christmas-card-sending town."

…Across the semidark room Lydia Pratt sipped with glacial slowness a vodka and Perrier and acted as if everything that Major Mamoud and Marvin Ikworth said to her was worth inscribing in marble.

"Isn't that simply marvelous," she said for the tenth time. "Tell me, Major, how many palaces does His Highness actually have?"

"I don't think that even he is certain," the major said. "His family, you know, keeps moving out of them and sells them to their friends."

"And is it true that some of them have neon signs in front?"

127

"His Highness is very found of neon. Ever since he visited Los Angeles. He also has installed hot tubs and water beds in the women's quarters. He is a great student of the West."

"How perfectly wonderful," Lydia said. "He must be such an amusing man."

She took another invisible sip from her glass and turned her very very cool, very very polite smile on Marvin Ikworth.

"Now do tell me, why didn't you bring your wife? I hear she is lovely. And this hotel is such fun."

"She is always so busy at home," Mr. Ikworth blurted, somewhat taken off guard by a description of Mrs. Ikworth that he failed to recognize.

"Oh, I knew it," Lydia said. "You look like a family man. There must be a lot of little Ikworths at home."

"No, no, just the boy, but not at home. He's a pediatrician in Cleveland."

"How nice. So useful."

"And you, Mrs. Pratt," Mr. Ikworth said. "You have children?"

"Indeed. Both are in the restaurant business. My daughter waits on tables in a restaurant on Cape Cod and my son, Wiggy the second, is a bartender at a Club Med on Guadaloupe. Do you know the Club Med, Mr. Ikworth?"

…Beneath a many-faceted crystal chandelier hanging halfway down from the low ceiling, Buzz Malone, Randy Dingle, and Doc Plumb stood around a small tray of cooling cheese puffs and carefully fenced with each other. Buzz sought first blood.

"What are you going to wow us with this year, Randy?" Buzz asked pleasantly. "I hear you have a hell of a new secret weapon."

"You're our top secret weapon runner," Randy said with equal good fellowship in his voice. "But we do have a few new goodies that should keep the shareholders from becoming restless."

"Franchised fairies," Buzz said, pressing on. "That's

128

what I heard from someone. But he was probably kidding."

"All will be revealed in good time," Randy parried. "We have a winner."

"Well, at least they can't give you cancer."

"Listen, old pal, we're not turning tail on the sun lamp business yet. Doc's boys still think they can work the bugs out of Totalpower. Right, Doc?"

Doc shrugged.

"Maybe yes, maybe no," he said, his eyes glinting behind his silver-metal-framed glasses. "But I think we have something anyway. Some of the latest reports from the Lab show that with only a few modifications we may have a ray that pierces six inches of armor. Funny how some of these things work out for the best."

...Tina Vitello, wearing a white silk jersey dress open coyly to her navel, smiled and shook hands with Or Boon. The count, who had introduced them, discreetly went to look for another drink with Archibald Kennedy.

"I have heard so much about you," Tina said in a half whisper. "Buzzy says you are a great financial wizard who can turn mothballs into gold. Is that true, Signor Dottore Boon?"

"Mr. Malone tends to exaggerate," Or said stiffly, his eyes roaming the room as he prepared for escape.

"Maybe only silver from the mothballs," Tina said and, laughing lightly, she moved closer to him. "Tell me Signor Boon, do you like the films of Italia?"

"Do I like the what?" Or said, feeling exceedingly uncomfortable and feeling irritated with himself that he did. His state of mind was not improved by the fact that Eleanor Boon had absented herself from the Greenbrier to attend a workshop on rehabilitating rapist muggers through handicrafts.

"The films of Italia," Tina repeated. "I have one with me that I would like to show you. You might want to invest in it with some of the silver from the mothballs."

..."I have heard absolutely nothing more from New York," Wiggy told Tommy Lightmeade as they came together through eye signals near the bandstand. A trio was playing a medley from *Camelot.*

"We've got that bastard," Tommy said. "By tomorrow it will be all over. We announce the Arab deal: everyone agrees; and by the time we get back to New York tomorrow afternoon there will be nothing to discuss but which jail Read prefers."

"Don't underestimate him. He's damn smart."

"Wiggy, that's where you're so wrong. He's dumb. What's so smart about taking over an empty office on a Sunday? He just got a little lucky about the stock certificates. But now we have him trapped right in our building. I've already got our private security people all over the place. Tomorrow morning, when the regular office force starts pouring into the Tower, I wouldn't be surprised if Read and his cronies try to sneak out. And, Wiggy, let me tell you, if they do, our guys will be right on top of them."

Wiggy took a long, consoling swallow from his glass.

"Poor Ward," he said.

…Outside, on the Old White Club terrace, Cookie and Lloyd Nightingale found an unexpected small, thin guest stretched out in a reclining chair.

"Hi there, fellows," Harvey Catoni said, cheerily. "Thanks for breaking away from the party."

"I got your page," Cookie said. "What's so important?"

"Oh, you fellows know that better than I do." Harvey said. "Now don't start giving me a lot of shit. I'm here because I want to give you a chance to give me your side of the story. I want to be fair. I want to give the whole picture. You know me."

"You bet your ass we do," Lloyd Nightingale said. "We don't know what you're talking about, Sweetie."

"O.K.," Harvey sighed. "This is what I get for trying to be a straight-shooter. It doesn't make any difference anyway. I've already talked to Wiggy Pratt."

"The hell you have."

"No, no really. I walked into the Men's Room and there

130

he was. Well, maybe I didn't talk to him too much but we sort of stood side by side. That means I'll be able to say I got together with him tonight but that IC had no comment. You know, that reminds me of a guy I used to know who was one of General Eisenhower's security guys. When Eisenhower was President he was staying here at the Greenbrier one time in one of the bungalows. One night late he and some of his buddies were playing bridge and drinking a lot and they stepped out on the porch to relieve themselves. My friend was on duty and he had sneaked into the bushes below the porch just to rest but then he started to doze. All of a sudden he heard the presidential party and before he could move he was getting all wet. For years after that my friend went around saying 'Do I know Dwight David Eisenhower? Hell, we couldn't get any closer without being arrested.'"

18

When the Haltblut II landed at the Marine Air Terminal at LaGuardia Airport at 1:30 A.M., a waiting IC limousine took Sally to her apartment in Manhattan. She made arrangements to be picked up immediately after breakfast and went to bed, comforted by the thought that Cookie, in the spongy alcoholic state in which she had left him, was in no condition for nocturnal adventures exploring modern Italian culture.

Jocko Burr, who had recognized Sally's presence on the plane with a brief nod and had immediately disappeared again into his own gloomy thoughts, took a taxi to Ward Read's apartment and awakened him. Ward was not happy.

"Jocko, what the hell is going on?" he asked, irritably snapping on lights in his living room and randomly kicking sections of the early edition of the Sunday New York Times. The main headline on the Real Estate section read:

WIDOW BUYS RANCH WITH FOOD STAMPS

"You're supposed to be watching things at the Greenbrier," Ward said. "You're supposed to be organizing things down there. Jesus, you look as if you've been exhumed. Take a tip from Wiggy. Learn to relax."

"We have to move now or there will be nothing to watch," Jocko said. "If we're going to do anything, it has to be now or you can start sending me the magazines and candy at Allendale. For Christ's sake, where's your gin?"

Then Jocko, as Ward kept his glass full and chain-smoked, described the proposed Arab deal. Yankee Properties would buy 50 million shares of IC convertible at $100 a share. That would give IC a transfusion of $5 billion in cash within the next few weeks. At the same time, Yankee Properties, with IC's endorsement, would tender publicly for an additional 125 million shares at $30 a share. The first ads would appear Monday. The Board would recommend acceptance. Wiggy would remain as CEO, but Yankee Properties would get four seats on the Board. Along with the five management seats, that would give Yankee Properties absolute control.

"Maniacs," Ward said. "The dumb bastards are giving away the company. Book value is sixty dollars a share. They're selling it for thirty-five dollars. Wigglesworth ought to be turned over to a mob."

"That's what he's afraid of," Jocko said. "They're all dead if they don't take the deal. I keep telling you: It's a disaster zone. They won't have enough cash to meet the payroll in two weeks or less. And no financial man outside of the funny farm would lend them a quarter unless maybe it were for a drink of Drano."

Ward, still in his pajamas and a blue silk bathrobe bearing on the pocket the arms of the old Army Tank Corps, began to pace the room, slapping his leg with a copy of *Financial World Magazine*. The cover was a picture of a badly wounded bull. A sword stuck in the bull's neck was labeled "IC."

"If we're going to make a counteroffer, our ads should be out in twenty-four hours," Jocko said. "We have to move faster than we planned. Even then, we'll have a lot of trouble. But that's our best shot."

Ward stood at the window and looked out at the spring haze glimmering over the green pastoral beauty of Central Park. Only yesterday the mayor had announced that muggings in the park had been cut back to less than ten a night. Ward turned and squared his back to the window. His voice took on a decided military tone.

"Plan C," he said. "We can go with a counter tender for backup. But now that's not enough. Plan C is the only way. We move now."

Jocko stared at him as if he were looking into an open grave.

"They'll put us away forever," he moaned.

"No, we'll put them away, goddamn it. We're going to do what has to be done. We're going to show them what free enterprise can really do."

"Well, if we're going to Plan C, I guess you'll want to know about this." Jocko took the envelope from Archibald Kennedy out of his pocket and removed a couple of sheets of memo paper covered with numbers. "Archibald gave me this tonight, apparently as a little insurance on his villa. These are the numbers for the IC Swiss bank accounts. If we call them this morning when they open at three o'clock our time, we can have the whole bundle transferred to new accounts that Wiggy can't touch but we can. I don't know how much is still in the accounts but I should think it would buy more than a few bowls of fondue. I know Or was counting on them."

"Jocko, you rotten rummy, you're huggable," Ward said.

*   *

No one slept.

By four o'clock Ward and Jocko had completed three major moves:

One -- the Swiss accounts were successfully transferred into two new numbered accounts at the Union Banque Suisse in Zurich. To the delight of Ward and Jocko, they found that the accounts totaled more than $200 million.

Next -- three companies of battle-hardened PKs -- IC's Peacekeeper security forces -- that were enroute from Bolivia back to their base at New Life City, Iowa, were ordered off planes at New Orleans and rerouted to New York.

Finally – a small cadre of current and former IC executives, later to be known as The Five, were located at their homes and given instructions.

The Five had been carefully selected by Ward during the last week on the basis of their talent, loyalty to him, and

-- most important -- deep personal hatred of Wiggy, Tommy Lightmeade, or Or Boon -- or all of the above. Each of The Five also continued to be increasingly distressed by their ownership of sizable blocks of depreciating IC stock or stock options.

At 0630 hours, Ward and Jocko approached the guard at the locked Fifty-sixth Street door of the IC Tower, showed identification cards, and were admitted to the building. Each carried a large suitcase.

"We are having a big meeting here today," Ward told the Puerto Rican guard.

"Others will be coming along. Also, some food for the meeting."

"O.K., you betcha, chief man," the guard said. "No problem. I, Manuel, am here."

Between 0700 and 0830 hours, The Five arrived one by one, each carrying an enormous suitcase; showed either current or strangely smudgy identification cards; and were admitted by Manuel.

At 0835, two delivery trucks from the Waldorf arrived and unloaded three dozen large boxes of gourmet treats and liquor. Manuel and the other three helpful building security guards -- Fernando, Paulo, and Julio -- helped unload the trucks and deliver the boxes to the Board Room.

At 0900, two chartered 747s with IC-orange markings touched down at Kennedy airport. More than six hundred disadvantaged black, Puerto Rican, and Chicano PKs disembarked, wearing freshly pressed, lime green uniforms with orange IC arm patches centered with a black Mickey Mouse. They were under the command of Colonel Trader John Pinkington, a six-foot five-inch white Rhodesian mercenary. They marched in formation from the planes and immediately boarded waiting orange buses while shouting in cadence their favorite marching ditty:

Grab 'em by the ears
Grab 'em by the balls

136

Grab 'em quick
Freedom calls!

As the motor convoy swung out of the airport complex and picked up speed on the almost empty highway, it included two light-blinking motorcycles at the front and rear and fifteen buses, each flying from its roof two white flags with orange stars. All PKs wore combat helmets with Plexiglas riot visors, goggles, and combat boots with knives. All wore sidearms; carried automatic weapons; and were equipped with three-foot fighting batons, gas masks, riot shields, and a variety of gas and smoke grenades. All smiled a lot.

For nearly thirty minutes the convoy sped unnoticed through the ratty urban encrustation known to its fans as Queens; past the overgrown Mafia-crowded cemeteries, the miles of fast-food parlors, gas stations, and used car lots; past the tacky reminders of two long-deceased World Fairs; and finally plunged onto the Triborough Bridge. There -- confronting the unconscious wall of Manhattan's towers -- the motorcyclists turned on sirens for the first time. Toll gate bars flew up as the convoy approached at full speed and the toll gate guards stood outside their booths saluting smartly as the convoy roared past into the sleeping city and down the East River Drive.

At 0945 the convoy arrived at the IC Tower and Ward returned Trader John's salute at the Fifty-sixth Street door. By 1015 hours all PKs and their equipment had been moved into building; the buses and motorcyclists dismissed; and Manuel, Fernando, Paulo, and Julio were locked in a computer storeroom in the subbasement. Lime uniformed guards were placed on all doors. A platoon with warning flares, tracer bullets, and automatic weapons but nothing big was stationed at the helicopter pad on the roof. A heavily armed reserve unit occupied the main lobby. At 1030 hours Trader John reported to Ward, who by then had a command post established in Wiggy's office, that IC World Headquarters was secured.

"Well, I guess this calls for a little old drink," Jocko said to no one in particular. He was working the bottles behind the elegant semicircular bar in Wiggy's office.

Everyone else was sitting around a large oval table. It had been installed in the midzone of the endlessly long room bounded at one end by sliding mahogany doors and in the mists of the other end by Wiggy's huge glass and steel desk. Papers, telephones running from jacks, coffee cups, and plates with Waldorf Danish pastry were scattered on the table and had started to spill over the various side tables among the German and English porcelains.

Ward sprawled in a chair in front of a small TV set and three phones. He was wearing chino trousers, a blue shirt with epaulets, and an ascot. He also wore a sidearm.

Besides the Leader, the others at the table dressed in a variety of costumes were:

Randolph "Square Root" Randolph (suit and tie including vest), IC's disaffected manager of corporate planning. Every good idea conceived by Square Root for the last ten years had been stolen by Wiggy or Tommy Lightmeade. All disasters had been directly attributed to his allegedly fallacious plans.

Buddy Jones (Levi's and Frye boots), a computer genius whom Or Boon personally had fired a year earlier for refusing to play funny games with the company's data retrieval system. He could make a pile of electronic junk work by breathing on it.

Hobart York (designer tweeds), a former IC public relations executive and free-lance writer shoved out of IC for treating Les Gross with the professional contempt he so richly deserved. York had since written two major books — the brilliant, tedious *Decline of the West Revisited*, total sales 375 copies; and the best-selling novel *Wanda*, the story of a witty call girl who, as the fun-loving mistress of Jack Kennedy, Nikita Khrushchev, and Fidel Castro, ended her career as the missing second gun at Dallas.

Sid Bloom and Paddy Laval (polyvinyl double knits),

138

two faceless detail experts and corporate killers who had followed Ward from corporate adventure to corporate adventure for fifteen years. Sid's specialty: bugging phones. Paddy's: stealing files.

"Everyone has their assignments," Ward said. "Square Root is pulling together a statement from his records on how the corporation's long-range plans have been constantly screwed up. Buddy and Jocko are doing a fast update on the company's true financial position; and be sure you get into that central computer memory and get all the gory numbers. Hobart is preparing the draft for the statement to the press. And Sid and Paddy are working with the lawyers."

"What's our timing?" Hobart asked. "When do we push the button?"

"To be determined. I'm going to fire the first shot over Wiggy's bow at three o'clock. Then we'll see."

"What about the Mexican connection?" Jocko asked.

"That's out of our hands. They're running around the reservations looking for Joe the X. I'm keeping them advised. But we can't wait for them."

"How about those Mickey Mouse guards?" Sid Bloom asked. "I think your friendly hoods messed them up a little when they encouraged them to go to the basement. We don't need any problems like that."

"Trader John is taking care of it. He's filling them full of booze and sandwiches. By the time we let them out later tonight, they won't know what world they're in. Anything else? O.K., go to work. I've got some calls."

Before anyone could move, Trader John came in and performed an elaborate British salute that included stamping his feet four times.

"Yes?" Ward said, delighted, and returned the salute.

"We have a prisoner, sah?"

"For Christ's sake, who?"

"Young woman, sah. Says her name is Sally Laurence. Says she's secretary to a Mr. Lightmeade. Bit indignant, sah. Some of the troopers had to restrain her."

139

"Oh shit, oh dear," Jocko said.

"Show her in," Ward said.

Two black troopers in lime green uniforms propelled Sally Laurence into the room. She looked somewhat tousled. And she obviously was in a state of advanced pique.

"What the hell is all this?" she screamed as she entered. "What the hell are you people doing here? When Tommy Lightmeade hears about this, you'll all be in jail. Tell these thugs to let me alone. Tell this Hollywood actor the show's canceled."

Ward kept putting up his hand to interrupt her. It was useless. Only when he hit his fist on the table and told her as suavely as possible to shut her goddamn mouth for a minute did he get to talk.

"This building has been occupied by a committee of IC shareholders," he said. "How did you get in?"

"You're kidding. Manuel the guard let me in. I've been here for two hours pulling some papers together for Mr. Lightmeade. He's waiting for them. When I tried to leave, these big limedrops stopped me in the lobby. I don't know where you escaped from or what you're smoking, but I have to go now."

"I'm sorry," Ward said. "But we can't let that happen. Now that you're here, you'll have to stay. At least for a while."

"I want to call the Greenbrier. I have a right to make a phone call."

"Miss Laurence," Ward said. "This is not Manhattan South. You will have to be our guest for a while. Trader John will escort you to the small Executive Apartment on the next floor. He will also remove the phones, of course."

"Hey, what are those papers she's talking about?" Paddy Laval asked with sudden inspiration.

"They're confidential," Sally snapped.

"Good," Ward said. "Paddy, get the papers. Trader John, please escort Miss Laurence to the small Executive Apartment. It's the one without the dome."

Trader John hustled her from the room. Sally offered a parting admonition. "Lightmeade will have your ass," she screamed.

"Spunky," Hobart York said.

"Let me tell you, she's right," Jocko said. "Wiggy is going to be damn mad when he sees this mess in his office."

19

"Good morning!" Tommy shouted into the microphone in his sunniest voice. "I hereby declare the world Management Meeting of International Coagulants open for business."

The time was exactly 8:30 Monday morning. For the last hour the three hundred top managers of International Coagulants had consumed large quantities of orange juice, Danish pastry, and coffee in the Greenbrier's sun-drenched Spring Room; pulled themselves together from the alcoholic bath of the previous evening; and wandered into the adjoining orange-spangled Grand Ballroom. Inside a rump group from the Boston Pops played special wake-up music especially selected by Tommy for the occasion. The repertoire included "Roll Out the Barrel," "Anchors Aweigh," and "Waltzing Matilda."

One by one each of the true princes of the IC church found his marked section of the hall and, as he sat down, his retinue rapidly filled the chairs around him. Some read newspapers; others started meetings; a few made telephone calls from the orange phones set up in each section. The noise level rose until it almost overpowered "East Side, West Side" and "Chicago."

"Nice decorations," Archibald Kennedy said dryly to the Count di Conti.

"I always find it a special experience," the count said.

At precisely 8:33, Wiggy, Tommy, and Or, followed by Les Gross, walked out on the stage and sat down in front of the king-sized IC portraits. The four men appeared dwarfed by the heroic faces behind them. Tommy, standing at the prowlike podium, grinned broadly, and gaveled the room into silence.

"Good morning!" he shouted again. "And welcome! Welcome! Welcome! In the spirit of international ecumenicism and for other reasons that we will be talking

143

about a little later, the Invocation will be given today by the Ayatollah Hassan ai-Saladin Buggertouti of the Little Mosque Around the Corner in Los Angeles."

Tommy stepped back and a black-robed and turbaned man with a huge drooping mustache walked from the wings to the podium.

"Yiyiyiyiyiyiyiyiyiyi . . . ahahahahahahahahahahah," he undulated and three hundred managers bowed their heads.

"I remember him," Randy Dingle whispered to his second-in-command. "He used to sell BMWs in Beverly Hills."

"That's not all he sold," second-in-command whispered back.

"Yiyiyiyiyiyiyiyiyiyi . . . ahahahahahahahahahahah," the Ayatollah concluded and swept from the stage.

"Many thanks for that great moving prayer," Tommy said, recapturing the podium. "And now, to set the tone for our work during the next three days, I will turn this microphone over to a man we all know so well, the corporate statesman who is leading our great corporation toward the twenty-first century, our chairman and chief executive officer, Wiggy Pratt."

Wiggy stood before them in a beautiful blue suit and red regimental striped tie, looking every inch the corporate statesman described. Two baby spots glinted light from his full head of carefully clipped white hair. His mind was unusually clear, his eyes bright, his face ruddy. Except for a little shooter or two of vodka in his orange juice, he had not had a drink since the night before. As the applause of the managers swept over him, he almost did not want a drink. He became euphoric. He was a great corporate statesman after all. Listen to that applause. They really loved him. By God, he was their leader. Finally, he held up his hands for silence and began to read for the first time the introductory remarks that Cookie had handed him ten minutes earlier.

"This is the largest annual Management Meeting in the

144

history of International Coagulants," Wiggy said. "It is symbolic of the bright future ahead. And as I stand here and look at you, the management of this great worldwide corporation, I feel truly proud. I have to say: What an array of talent! What a company!"

New applause swept the room as the managers clapped for themselves and Wiggy grinned. There followed about five minutes more of this sort of thing. Then Wiggy moved into his traditional "Message for Tomorrow," an annual compilation of whatever wisdom had been churned out by the resident wizards in Corporate Strategic Planning and spoon-fed to Wiggy's speechwriters. Wiggy pointedly assumed an oracular tone as he read on:

"A future unfolds before us like the open prairies -- the prairies that once unfolded before the endless wagon trains moving westward to the shimmering Pacific beyond the mountains. I want to talk a little about that future. And about some of the new directions for our wagon trains. The excellent people who run our econometric models have been working overtime for the last few months. And they have come up with some trend lines and some analyses that should be part of our thinking during the next three days. I understand that you will be getting all the details tomorrow in a fine report from Vernon Schlitz. Vernon will be standing in for Square Root Randolph who has come down with an avoidable emergency. I don't want to take any of the megatonnage away from Vernon. But I do want to give you just a brush over the mountain tops this morning. In brief, we see three major trends that will influence every market in this country.

"The first of these major trends involves work. The country is rapidly approaching the point where very few Americans will do any.

"Let me cite just two outstanding examples of foreign countries that our planners see as obvious role models: Switzerland and Saudi Arabia. In Switzerland all physical effort is put forth by itinerant Italians, Portuguese, and Spaniards. The Swiss, in turn, spend their time counting money, running hotels, and whiling away the days circulating official documents. It took the Swiss several centuries to achieve this nirvana. The Saudis have done it in a decade. This was made possible, I am proud to say, through a magnificent gesture by the United States. As you know, in the spirit of international friendship, we are paying the Saudis more than thirty times what it costs us to extract oil from the wells that originally we dug. In Saudi Arabia all physical effort is put forth by itinerant Africans, Indians, and, of course, expatriated Americans not bright enough to stay home.

"Our planners feel that the process will be complete in this country by the end of the century. The luckiest, naturally, will continue to be the mentally, morally, and physically disadvantaged. They will be totally supported by the government and do nothing at all except for breeding and a little fun pillaging.

"Next will be the increasing numbers of Americans employed by the government. They, of course, will do nothing either beyond appearing at their posts. And, finally, will come those employed by the large bureaucracies of the private sector. They too will do nothing but will be kept busy working on strategic corporate plans and processing reports to the government. The entire American industrial plant will have to be run by no more than six workaholic engineers from MIT and two deranged wet backs from Juarez.

"The second major trend will be the total conversion of the public to preferring substitutes to originals. For example, few Americans have tasted a real hot dog for a generation. Hot dogs made of unmentionable chicken parts, oatmeal, and nuclear waste are considered to be what hot dogs are supposed to taste like. Give a child a hot dog made of pure meat and he throws up. The lesson for any marketing man worth his salt is clear. We must stop trying to force the products of the past on the unsuspecting consumer.

"The third major trend involves a thrifty and mature improvement over the cost and trauma of face-to-face experience. More and more Americans are willing to stay at home and experience day-to-day life on television. Accordingly, there no longer is any need for the expense and risks of having events actually take place. Either they can be filmed in Los Angeles studios or, still better, they can be developed from old films of past events. Presidential elections, football games, wars, space exploration, and parades can all be efficiently produced as prime-time TV programs and broadcast to millions of Americans who never leave their homes.

"Here then is an important look at tomorrow -- a world of leisure. . . crowded with consumers who can be satisfied only with simulated products. . . and who are no longer distracted by direct participation in riots, ballgames, and wars. The marketing opportunities and challenges to IC are obvious and I can see by the agenda for the next three days that you are already moving in the right direction.

"Who can help but be reassured when he sees discussions planned on such new products as Bricklook™ and our big pharmaceutical breakthrough, Nokid™; our new Trompe L'Oeil Division with its Great Quikart™ line; and our ingenious plan to train thousands of disadvantaged ghetto boys and girls as medical doctors through special TV crash courses. With this kind of thinking I am confident that you will be able to keep IC out front and on the cutting edge.

"I have one other important announcement to make about our company's future. But first, Tommy will tell you about an exciting new program that he has planned to help all of us."

Tommy began by swiftly providing the managers with his unmistakably personal view of how IC was perceived in the world. IC was a leader among the great corporations of the West. But because of its size and its success, because of its great contributions, because of its importance to the Free Enterprise System, because of the very critical role that it played in Defense of the West, IC was indeed Target

Number One on the hit list of the Soviet Conspiracy and its numerous handmaidens. The handmaidens included anyone who ever opposed IC for whatever reason or said any negative thing on any subject about IC. For example, labor unions, consumerist groups, many security analysts (most of late), a broad variety of politicians, nearly all former employees (why would anyone good ever leave?), dissatisfied customers, irritated plant community neighbors, competitors, and all of their wives and children just in case. These enemy forces were now taking advantage of the recent superficial problems affecting IC. Moreover, a sensationalist press of questionable loyalty was agitating the situation.

"We need to be bold," Tommy said. "We need to engender among our people and among our friends a new spirit that will broadcast our true lovable nature and maintain our plucky spirit in the challenging days ahead. To build this spirit, we will launch a new company program worldwide within the next two weeks. All of you will play a vital part. All of you, I am certain, remember ten years ago when, in the depths of one of the nation's deepest recessions, we successfully conducted **OPERATION SELL**. And I am sure you recall the great success of four years ago when we combated antiwar rioters throughout the world with **OPERATION PEACE IN OUR TIME**. Now we have something even bigger. Les Gross is here to tell you about it. We call it **OPERATION INTEGRITY**."

The projection screen came alive with orange and black letters spelling out

OPERATION INTEGRITY

and

TAKE THE IC PLEDGE.

The Boston Pops musicians began to play "There's a New Day Coming." And twenty miniskirted models ran up

148

and down the aisles passing out "Believe It!" buttons. Tommy waved and stepped from the podium to be eplaced by an inanely smiling Les Gross.

"Thank you, Tommy, thank you," he said. "All of you can *Be-lieve It* that this is going to be big. Let me give you a few of the highlights. The rest will be in your kits at the door when you leave this morning and in your mail next week."

For the next ten minutes Les described to a totally bored management a program which had grown considerably since it was first presented in the CEO Conference Room in New York.

"We definitely have Shea Stadium for the New York kick-off," Les bubbled. "There will be an elephant parade down Fifth Avenue with floats illustrating great moments of integrity in history: The hanging of Nathan Hale! Washington in the snow! Babe Ruth steps down! The Crucifixion!"

"Wiggy drying out," Archibald Kennedy whispered to the Count di Conti.

"I'm trying to get Billy Graham as a guest speaker," Les continued. "He will join with Wiggy in calling on all IC employees to sign the Integrity Honor Roll. Then, while all the world watches on TV, thousands of IC employees will come forward to take the Integrity Pledge."

Thirty slides later Les moved toward his surprise conclusion. Not even Tommy knew about it. Les could hardly contain himself.

"The grand winner — the IC employee chosen for having the greatest integrity — will be flown to Peking and Moscow to deliver a special plea to the Chinese and Russians for world peace. He -- or *she*, or *she* -- will carry IC time capsules containing the Integrity Roll of Honor and a special letter from our two Presidents, Wiggy and Gaston Edsel. And the socko highlight of the trip will be the burial of the time capsules in the Kremlin wall and the Great Wall of China.

Wiggy returned to the podium. He looked nervous and

he spent more than a minute arranging papers. He sipped from a plastic orange mug. He arranged papers again.

"I told you before that I had an important announcement about our future," he said at last. "I do. Yes, I do. In order for this company to achieve its great objectives, we have a critical need for new investment dollars. A great many investment dollars. Yes, a great many. Happily, we have found an ideal partner to provide them. Yankee Enterprises, one of the fastest-growing companies in America, has agreed to link arms with us. Your board has agreed to sell a significant number of shares of preferred stock to Yankee Enterprises. Your board also will look with favor on a tender offer that is being announced in this morning's newspapers."

Wiggy stopped and cleared his throat. The room, which had been pervaded with a low hum throughout Les's presentation, was absolutely silent. Wiggy noticed Major Mamoud and Marvin Ikworth standing near the rear. The major held up two fingers in a V sign. Wiggy's eyes lost focus.

"I want to assure everyone in this room that there are no plans to change the management of this company in any way," he said with no conviction whatsoever in his voice. "We will continue as before but reinvigorated with new resources. I look to the future with great optimism."

Three managers in the front row clapped. Then stopped when no one joined in.

"I believe it," Les shouted.

No one else said a word.

Wiggy, Tommy, and Or left immediately for the Haltblut I to fly to New York. The managers adjourned early to the Old White and to phone their brokers.

"The Market is wild," Or told Wiggy and Tommy in the limousine on the way to the airport. "IC is up five in the first half hour of trading, but now something funny is happening. All trading in IC has been temporarily stopped by the Exchange."

"That S.O.B. Read must be trying something cute,"

Tommy said with extreme unpleasantness in an exhibition of what for him was unusual prescience. "We have to get to him fast."

Wiggy nodded remotely and clutched his plastic mug.

20

As IC's top management gathered to sip orange juice at the Greenbrier on Monday morning, an unusual event occurred in New York.

Normally, every weekday, more than five thousand people began arriving at the IC Tower at approximately 7:00 A.M. It was almost a natural phenomenon. First a few individual units, then clusters, then streams of living matter carrying attaché cases or little brown paper bags flowed from the streets and subways into the Tower and up its dozens of elevator shafts into all parts of the IC organism. Lights came on. Xerox duplicators and IBM word-processing machines began to hum. Scruffily bearded computerniks in white coats attended the banks of blinky lights at the giant central mainframe computer complex. And IC world headquarters once again was doing whatever it did. But on this particular Monday morning the phenomenon did not follow its usual pattern. Someone had locked the Tower doors and posted handwritten signs on them. The signs said:

**THE IC TOWER IS CLOSED
TODAY FOR RENOVATION.
GO HOME. THANK YOU.**

The IC Shareholders
United Committee (ICSUC)

Hundreds of people, delighted by the news, turned around and happily went back to the suburbs to clean lawnmowers, play golf, or think seriously about beginning a number of projects that had been pending for the last ten to twenty years. Hundreds more crowded neighboring restaurants to eat huge plastic breakfasts. But the majority were so stunned to find that they had no office to go to that they milled aimlessly about the locked doors, talking knowingly about the renovation, concocting and spreading rumors, and looking longingly up at the dark windows in the Tower's Early American pine façade.

As usual, all direct sunlight was reduced to a gloomy half light by smog. But the weather was quite warm for early spring, a condition that encouraged standing around on sidewalks despite the morning gloom. Accordingly, the growing crowd of IC employees attracted additional thousands of passers-by who apparently were in no hurry to reach their offices and had a passionate desire to find out what was happening. Within two hours more than ten thousand people completely surrounded the Tower, blocked the sidewalks, and spilled out into the streets.

The local fraternity of sidewalk madmen who worked the area for ten blocks around hustled to join the crowd. Juicy the Button Man, a huge mountain in a World War I overcoat covered with old political campaign buttons, took up a position near the main door. One button on his left lapel said: "If I Were 21, I'd Vote for Willkie." One on his right said: "All the Way with LBJ." And a very large one on his tie said: "Nixon's the One." Not far away, Seymour the Gay, wearing a silk caftan and a flowered hat, passed out massage parlor brochures which he carried in a large Gucci shopping bag. He also wore a button. It said, "Kiss Me Quick." And Knocko the Drummer, who usually helped change traffic lights by doing a roll with his drumsticks on the asphalt in front of the Hilton Hotel, performed helpfully in the middle of the street in front of the IC Tower until the crowds became too large even for his mystic powers.

Vendors selling hot chestnuts, obscenely large, and very stale pretzels, a dozen varieties of bagels including chocolate, and hot, watery coffee hawked their goodies. Two aging winos promoting a new disco passed out inflated purple balloons that said: **DISCO DREAMS.** A small instrumental group comprised of two lutes, a lyre, and a hornpipe began to play fifteenth-century French court music. A lady dwarf with a light mustache sang in Olde

154

French.

But, beneath the veneer of normality, even the less astute in the crowd felt that matters were out of joint. Certainly the few lime green guards inside the locked doors did not generate feelings of good fellowship. A number of times, when employees had knocked on the doors merely to ask a few diffident questions, the guards had grinned unpleasantly and made rather hostile gestures with their fingers.

Many also noted the unusual display of flags over the Tower main entrance. The U.S. flag hung, as always, in the center and the orange IC flag hung on the right. But from the companion pole on the left hung a huge battered battle flag that some recognized as the World War II divisional banner of the U.S. Third Army.

Finally someone reported seeing a small man in a rumpled suit hand a guard what looked like a bloody mary, emerge from a side door, buy copies of the *New York Times* and the *Wall Street Journal* at a kiosk, and go back into the building. The guard holding the bloody mary also appeared to be holding an M-16 automatic weapon.

The feelings of disquiet were greatly strengthened when reports spread through the crowd that the late city edition of the *New York Times* carried an ad announcing a tender offer for International Coagulants from some obscure company. Many scoffed and said the report obviously was garbled. Then actual copies of the ad began to be passed hand to hand. Its thrust was fairly clear. The headline said:

YANKEE PROPERTIES OFFERS
$30 A SHARE FOR IC COMMON

The noise level in the Street rose appreciably. All traffic on the Avenue of the Americas was now blocked by the crowd, which instinctively felt that something unusual was about to happen. At 9:05 it did.

Warren Ohms, a hot-headed workaholic in Peace

155

Products Planning, began wildly pounding his attaché case against the Tower's main glass door and shouting that he wanted to go to work. He was immediately joined by several other men who also began pounding the door with their attaché cases. In a flash reaction, the many became inspired by the few. The crowd began to pick up the cry "We-want-to-work!" Large cracks began to appear in the thick glass. The cry "We-want-to-work!" became a roar. The crowd surged forward against the doors.

Suddenly the lime green guards opened the main door inward, grabbed Warren, and again shut the door. The crowd surged forward shouting but then fell back in horror immediately. Warren, his face crimson and his eyes popping from his head, was ejected through a nearby revolving door. At first they thought he was dead. Then they discovered his only affliction was a temporary inability to talk because his tie had been cut off and stuffed in his mouth. But the moment had passed. The crowd took up the chant again but stayed away from the door.

Police arrived at 9:30. Two squad cars with sirens on and blinking lights edged slowly through the crowd and parked on the sidewalk in front of the Tower. Four policemen then made their way on foot to the main entrance and the largest of the three knocked on the shattered glass door with his baton. The conversational exchange, as later reported with some discreet family newspaper deletions, was as follows:

"Open up," the lead cop shouted at the lime green men inside. "Police."

"You kidding," the lime green guard nearest the inside of the glass door shouted back. "Hey," he called over his shoulder, "these cats are the police." The half dozen other guards laughed, showing how well they enjoyed a good joke.

"Open this goddamn door," the lead cop shouted and hit hard with his baton. "Now."

"Easy," the cop next to him said nervously. "Look at those cannons in there."

"Hey, man, don't you mothers have no respect for private property?" the guard shouted. "You got a search warrant or something?"

"We can get one, wise ass."

"Well fine. When you do, come back. Meantime, we is IC's official PKs and we is in charge of guarding this fuckin' building. So buzz off."

During the next several hours more than two dozen policemen arrived, but no one challenged the locked doors. When Police Headquarters telephoned IC, Jocko quite reasonably told the captain who called that the Tower was closed for repair work; IC regretted any disruptions caused by the crowd; and any help the police could give in getting the crowd to disperse and go home would be appreciated. Accordingly, until they heard later -- much later -- from Wiggy, the police directed their efforts to urging the crowd to disperse and to trying to open up the Avenue of the Americas.

By 10:30, when the first TV cameras arrived, no one had gone home but one lane had been opened up for northbound traffic. By 11:30, the crowd had grown, but two lanes were open and the crowd was contained behind police barricades. Police then helpfully cordoned off the Tower entrances to prevent any further attempts by IC employees to rush the doors. By now TV cameras and mobile broadcasting units dotted the area in anticipation of the next act.

It started at noon with the arrival of a limousine carrying Wiggy, Tommy, and Or. The long, black automobile glided past the barricaded rows of people and stopped in front of the Tower.

When Wiggy stepped from the limousine, hundreds of the crowd began to applaud. Some shouted, "Open the building." Others shouted, "Save IC." Still others shouted, "Don't sell."

Juicy hurled old MacArthur buttons. Balloons were launched. Knocko did a drum roll on the curb. The musical group played "Hail to the Chief."

Wiggy was absolutely astounded. He, along with Tommy and Or, had driven directly from the airport and had little idea of the events of the morning in New York. However, Wiggy's instantaneous evaluation of the situation was that it could be used. He decided to play to the crowd. Amid the pandemonium, he waved and smiled and moved toward the door. The crowd parted for him and his party. Four policemen formed a wedge to help it part faster. Then, just before he reached the entrance, two newsmen and a TV cameraman burst through the crowd and blocked his progress.

"Mr. Pratt," the first newsman said breathlessly as someone poked a mike-boom into Wiggy's face, "what about this charge that you've been juggling IC's books and that you're arranging a sellout to the Arabs?"

Wiggy paled visibly. It was as if he were struck in the chest with an ax. Juggling books! No one should use such words. It was positively scatological. Before he could comment, Tommy broke in.

"Absolutely absurd," he said. "We can't imagine where you could ever hear such totally unfounded accusations."

As Tommy spoke, Wiggy for the first time saw over the newsman's shoulder two grinning lime green guards holding automatic weapons inside the main door. It was a second ax blow. He panicked.

"We have no further comment at this time," Wiggy snapped, cutting Tommy off. "Nothing more at this time. Nothing. We have to leave."

And he turned around, rapidly led Tommy and Or back to the limousine and drove away. As they turned the corner, Wiggy looked out the rear window half expecting to see Ward Read and the PKs pursuing in a half track.

Unfortunately for Wiggy, his intelligence service had been very poor all day. Or had learned by phone prior to taking off from White Sulphur Springs that the market in IC stock had opened late and that when it did the opening bid was 28 — up 5. Arbitragers obviously were moving in on the strength of the Yankee Properties offer and were

158

buying heavily.

Once in flight, because of atmospheric disturbances, the Haltblut I was unable to obtain further information on market developments. Meantime, the drama at the New York Stock Exchange began to take some unexpected turns.

In the first hour of trading, IC continued to climb and pull much of the Market with it. IC rapidly rose to 32, two points over the Yankee Properties tender offer. There was a brief period of profit taking, but the 32 level held. There was a pause; an almost audible huge intake of breath. Experienced traders could almost sense the phone calls from Major Mamoud from a lobby phone booth at the Greenbrier: first to a robed figure in Sharm overlooking a tanker-filled harbor; then to a banker's office on the thirty-fifth floor overlooking the Statue of Liberty. The pause was ended by Yankee Properties announcing an increase in the tender offer to 40. A wild half hour ensued, when suddenly trading was again halted with IC at 37. The Dow Jones broad tape reported that the halt in trading was ordered because of an important forthcoming announcement.

As the Haltblut I had landed at the Marine Air Terminal at La Guardia, the promised announcement began to appear on Broad Tape printers in offices throughout the world.

New York — A top executive of International Coagulants Corp. and leader of an activist shareholder group today accused IC management of "grossly misleading financial manipulation" and a "sellout to Arab interests."

Ward W. Read, an IC vice president and chairman of the selfstyled IC Shareholders Unified Committee (ICSUC), said, "IC management has instigated a takeover bid designed to cover up a financial disaster of mind-boggling proportions."

Read issued the statement after Yankee

Properties, Inc., a privately held U.S. corporation reputed to have heavy Arab support, initially tendered for IC stock at $30 a share. IC stock closed Friday at 23. Yankee Properties increased its tender offer to $40 after the stock rose to 32 in active early trading.

Ten minutes later the Broad Tape carried some interesting reaction.

Add IC Charges — Tender

An IC spokesman reached for comment at IC's annual Management Meeting at White Sulphur Springs, W.Va., said the accusations "were absolutely absurd, a web of fantasy, and inaccurate."

"We do not engage in name calling," he said. "But I believe that Mr. Read is wanted in Yemen for bribing public officials and pederasty."

J. Wigglesworth Pratt, IC chairman and chief executive officer, was unavailable for comment. He was variously reported to be enroute to New York, ill, and overseas.

*   *

As soon as the Haltblut I landed, they had sought to find out what was happening. While Wiggy and Or had waited impatiently, Tommy had stood on the shortest public phone line in the crowded terminal while a man at the phone shouted into it: "I don't care what the plumber says about having to go to his sister's funeral; it used to flush and now it doesn't. Tell him to fix it." When Tommy had finally obtained command of the phone, he called his prime investment banker in downtown Manhattan. The direct line was busy; the call was transferred to a receptionist; she transferred the call to the Auto Loans Department in an uptown branch; Auto Loans transferred the call back to the receptionist who said "First World

160

National, may I help you?" and automatically the call switched to Pensions; Pensions apologized, promised to transfer the call immediately to Investment Banking, and hung up. Tommy, out of change, asked Wiggy for a dime to try again. Wiggy, out of patience, insisted that they proceed to the Tower to settle with Ward Read without further delay. And so they did.

"You said he wasn't dangerous," Wiggy said through tight lips. "Now you know just how dangerous he can be: public charges, armed guards, building lockouts; it's all pure Ward Read, damn him. Do you know what probably would have happened if I'd gone into that building? I'll tell you. There probably would have been a nice little item in tomorrow's newspapers about how I unfortunately jumped out of a window. You'd be surprised how many people have conveniently fallen out of windows all over the world when Ward and some of his CIA friends were in town for the day."

"Oh for Christ's sake, Wiggy, stop being paranoid," Tommy said. "And I never said he isn't dangerous. I just said he's dumb. And we have to be smart."

"Smarter," Or interjected. "Much smarter."

They were sitting in what they had converted in the last thirty minutes into the new temporary World Headquarters of International Coagulants. Following their unseemly and sudden departure from the IC Tower, they had immediately done three things: They checked into the Waldorf Towers and occupied a large part of the twenty-second floor for an indefinite period; they ordered back to New York from the Greenbrier a half dozen managers; and they engaged private security guards from Omni S.A. of Lausanne, Switzerland, a most discreet worldwide supplier of a wide variety of security services, including F--14s, howitzers, and tanks with or without crews.

"We must be ready to meet the challenge," Tommy said, after talking to Lausanne. "M. Pont has assured me that he can meet our needs."

"Did you remind M. Pont that this is New York, not

Addis Ababa?" Wiggy said. "M. Pont sometimes gets confused."

"M. Pont is a man of exquisite discretion,' Tommy said. "I think Or will agree."

"Here is where we are," Or said, ignoring Tommy and referring to some notes on a yellow legal pad. "The stock was under heavy upward pressure from the arbitragers. They were being obscenely greedy once they understood that the Arabs were serious. Yankee had to up the ante to forty dollars a share. Then these damn charges were made by Ward. The stock fell back to twenty-seven as soon as trading was resumed. However, under renewed buying pressure, some of which I suspect came from our own straight-shooters, the stock ran up to thirty and has continued to trade in a narrow twenty-nine to thirty-one range. That's good. Yankee should have no problem sweeping in the necessary shares at forty. And, in the meantime, all we have to do is get back the convertible preferred for delivery."

"Under the less than happy situation at the Tower, how do you suggest that we do that?" Wiggy asked, pouring with a more than generous hand his first drink of the afternoon.

"As soon as you've reinforced yourself with that, I suggest you personally call Ward and use all of your charm to convince him that it is in his best interest to turn them over."

"And should good old Ward find me uncharming?"

"We will have to turn to M. Pont, I suppose. But I think if you say the right things he'll come around. It can truly be in his best interest to cooperate."

"What the hell are you suggesting?" Tommy asked, wary as always when the best interests of his associates were mentioned.

"Just that we make his plate full enough so that he'll go away."

"I hate giving that bastard a dime."

"Would you rather wrestle him in the elevator for the

162

certificates which you were dumb enough to leave behind and your cover girl secretary failed to pick up?"

"Of course. I suppose it's also my fault that we need the certificates because there is hardly a bank in the world that will give us a loan. Incidentally, I certainly hope that you aren't planning now to use our last remaining credits in an Italian movie investment."

"Wiggy," Or said, flushing only slightly but mentally jotting down Tommy's name on his private hit list, "call the man."

Wiggy, who had been busying himself reinforcing his reinforcement while Or and Tommy bickered, sat down at a large reproduction Louis XV desk. For a moment he felt that he might throw up as he dialed his own office number. But, by the time he heard Ward Read answer, Wiggy was back in the game.

"Hello, Ward," he said jovially. "We're in New York."

"So I hear. But for some reason you only got as far as the front door and decided not to come up. Don't you like us?"

"Oh, you know how it is, Ward. Guns always make me so damn nervous. I'm sure an old international hand like you feels that same way."

Ward laughed. "Wiggy, you have to be kidding. A couple of guards on the door shouldn't bother you. Those are our own PKs. One of your better ideas. Hell, I'm your old friend."

"Well, of course, so you are. That's why this whole thing is all so stupid. Just the other day Lydia was recalling what fun we all used to have and how we ought to get together for some laughs about the old days in Mexico and the Far East. Remember how you and I tried so hard to get that funny little guy, Teng Giap Songh, to retire to Palm Springs and you showed him all the real estate brochures on property near Nixon's place?"

"Sure. And then there was that long hilarious boat ride that you and I took. Remember that was just after Teng turned down Ricky de Salida's special sauce beurre blanc

163

on his fish but Teng's pet Siamese cat who didn't expired in twenty seconds at his feet."

"Yes, good times, Ward. Well, now look, you know what we're trying to do. We're trying to save this company. And we need your cooperation."

"Anything for IC, Wiggy. You know that. What can I do?"

"You can make two major contributions. One is to turn over the Project Z file with the preferred certificates to me. And the other is to take back that rather nasty statement you made and drop this whole crazy thing you've started. You know, just fuzz it all up and say you've been misquoted. Now, if you do all that, Ward, I can assure you up front an increase in your options of say one hundred thousand shares and I feel confident that, when this is over, management will want you in a very key position."

"How confident?"

"Well, as confident as anyone can ever be about these things. I give you my word."

"I see. Now, just for discussion among friends, what if I tell you folks to stick it?"

"Oh, that would be very unwise, Ward. As someone who has always had your best interests at heart and a very real sense of responsibility for your personal advancement at IC, I think that you would be making a poor career development judgment."

"O.K. then, Wiggy, I think I understand the picture. How much time can I have to think about it?"

"I'll hang on."

They both laughed, wallowing in the spirit of good fellowship and an old corporate joke.

"O.K., Wiggy," Ward finally said as the chuckles subsided. "Here is how I see it. I truly appreciate your offer and I most especially appreciate your concern for my career. IC always comes first with me. And, in the end, I guess I know whom I can really count on."

"You accept?"

"No, Wiggy. I think you should stick it."

Wiggy could hardly believe it. He had just offered to make Ward a potential billionaire; to push him for a top slot; to let bygones be bygones. What an incredible ingrate! Wiggy felt personally insulted. And, as the clear danger of the situation ricocheted through his mind, unthinking blind anger welled up inside of him and took control.

"All right, goddamn it, Ward," he shouted savagely into the phone to the horror of both Tommy and Or. "You've made your decision. Now here's mine. You're fired, goddamn it, effective immediately. You understand? You're out! Out! And that goes for that whole crowd who have been crazy enough to join you over there. And that includes that dumb secretary who works for Tommy."

"O.K., Wiggy," Ward said very quietly. "I'll tell the payroll people what you said as soon as I decide to let them back into the building."

It was not clear who hung up first.

21

Ward called a council of war in Wiggy's occupied office. Jocko Burr and Square Root Randolph had been sitting there enjoying Ward's phone conversation with Wiggy. The group now was joined by Hobart York, fresh from his triumph achieved in the release of Ward's statement; and Buddy Jones, who had been living for more than twenty-four hours in IC's World Data Processing Center five floors below the street.

Ward had changed his blue shirt with epaulets for a green one with matching ascot. He also had added a pair of light-sensitive pilot's glasses. Otherwise his costume remained unchanged, including his sidearm.

For the meeting he had set up both a flip chart and a white plastic briefing board on which he had drawn in red crayon a complex map of the Tower, showing strong points and secret routes of supply. As he talked he paced in front of the two boards. His auditors lounged in various postures at the large, makeshift conference table, drinking coffee, Dr. Pepper, and, in one case, bloody marys.

"Time, gentlemen, is our objective," Ward said. "With enough time, we can win one way or another. Briefly, I see three scenarios: A white knight such as Joe the X will buy control. The government will force a reorganization through us. Or we will be able to take control through our own proxy solicitation. Naturally, we could have some combination of all of the above. In that case, I suggest that the entire corporation runs the risk of dissolving into a massive pool of shit."

Ward tapped his flip chart where he had written two words:

PUBLIC DISCLOSURE

"This is our weapon," he said. "We must demonstrate

to the public the un-American manipulations of IC management. At the same time we must emerge as the champions of American free enterprise. The fact that this happens to be true for the most part is beside the point. To rally support to our side, words will not be enough. We need a public demonstration of Wiggy's evil intent -- a demonstration preferably on prime time. Hobart, what do you think?"

Hobart York, who had replaced his J. Press sport jacket with a roll-top ribbed sweater, was toying with one of Wiggy's Emission figurines.

"Absolutely on target," he said. "All three networks already have great film of Wiggy refusing to comment and fleeing the scene this afternoon. But we still look like the aggressors because, after all, we did seize the building. What we need is some way to clearly show the Arab connection."

"Like a picture of Wiggy and Major Mamoud drinking orange soda at the Riyadh Hilton," Jocko said, helpfully.

"Or a bunch of sheiks touring the nuclear warhead works," Square Root suggested.

"Both good," Hobart said, seriously. "Not easy to pull off."

"O.K., but you get the idea," Ward said. "Now, what about our legal action?"

Jocko put down his bloody mary and opened a file folder.

"Excellent progress," he said. "Sid Bloom and Paddy Laval have been on the phone all morning. Once they were able to convince the lawyers that we had the money in Switzerland to support our legal tastes in New York, everything has moved ahead as planned. We have filed or are filing injunctions in a dozen courts from here to Los Angeles to stop the Yankee Properties tender. We also have filed minority shareholder actions in Federal Court here and with the SEC in Washington, accusing Wiggy and his friends of criminal mismanagement, fraud, insider trading, embezzlement, violation of various security

168

statutes, and failure to meet the requirements of the Clean Air Act. We had only one hitch. Our lawyers felt that under the unusual circumstances they could perform better in our behalf if they received some advances in cash. We solved that by sneaking Paddy Laval out of the building through the subway entrance. He is picking up the cash from the Swiss New York branches this afternoon and making the deliveries."

"What security have you given him?" Ward asked.

"Paddy left here disguised as a plumber. The money will be given to him in large bills wrapped in wax paper in a workman's lunch box. Should he be stopped, no one would ever question a plumber making a major withdrawal from a Swiss bank account or having large amounts of cash in his possession."

Ward nodded approval and moved on to Buddy Jones and his work on IC's worldwide information processing system.

"We're just about finished," Buddy reported. "All the reports that you'll ever need on IC's financial fun and games have been retrieved and passed along to Jocko and Square Root for analysis. And as a by-product we have a lot of really great stuff involving a half dozen labor unions, at least seventeen pension funds, four South American republics, and someone named Benny 'The Pliers' Vanetti of Las Vegas."

"How about the codes?"

"All changed. The whole system is now accessible only to us: The central memories in New York, London, Sao Paolo, Melbourne, and COMSAT X plus all auxiliary memories answer only to the new codes that I have here. All anyone using the old codes will receive is one of six amusing quotations from the works of Gilbert and Sullivan. However, we did have a couple of glitches. Unfortunately, in making the changes we wiped out the entire memory file on all IC warranties. Also, I'm afraid that we ordered an extra five thousand pounds of Mother Smucker's marmalade for each House of Buns east of the Mississippi.

We accidentally tripped the Master Dun Key for the credit card system so that all **ICCARD** holders will be receiving our standard property seizure threat notices next week. And I think we may have released a phantom bug into the continuous process plutonium plant in Santa Monica. But, hell, Ward, you can't expect perfection on a rush job like this."

Ward gave Buddy a thumbs-up sign and finally turned to his most pressing problem. With a dramatic gesture, he turned the page on his flip chart and revealed the words:

ASSAULT ON THE TOWER.

"It could be imminent," he said. "Wiggy can't use the police. If they come in here with a search warrant, the preferred certificates could be seized as evidence. Also, Wiggy certainly wants to minimize publicity just as much as we want to maximize it. Therefore, he has to do the job himself."

"You really think Wiggy and Tommy are going to karate their way in here?" Jocko asked, delighted at the image he had conjured.

"Not exactly. But according to my intelligence they have been in touch with the Omni organization. I think that they are assuming we have only a few guards and that a swift, surgical attack will carry the building with a minimum of casualties, if any. We need to prepare immediately to repulse it. I would expect that they will hit us anytime after nightfall."

"Sonofabitch, wouldn't that be super," Hobart York said and clapped his hands together exultantly. "Right in prime time."

*   *

Sally Laurence had gone through a series of mental states since she had been locked in the smallest of the three apartments that IC maintained for late-working top

170

executives and visiting dignitaries.

Initially she was infuriated and devoted several hours to a maniacal hunt for means of escape. With an increasing sense of futility, she reviewed the same possibilities. The door was locked from the outside and through the peephole she could see a large lime green guard. No matter how many times she paced through the apartment's living room, bedroom, and kitchen, she could find no other door. All of the double glass windows were sealed. And even if she were to break one, outside there was an eighty-six-floor drop to the Street and no ledge in the sheer pine panel face of the Tower. Nor, except for the passengers of an occasional inbound Boeing 747, was there anyone at whom she might gesticulate from her prison.

At one point, she developed a plan to break a window and drop a note for help to the street. She would enclose the note in a weighted box of Hi Ho sugared oat puffs that she had found in the kitchen. She had even written the note. It said:

I am being held captive on the 86th floor of this building. Call the police. This is not a test marketing program.

But she discarded the plan, certain that unless the box maimed or killed someone it would be ignored. "Sheldon, don't touch that box," some mother would shout at her ten-year-old. "It's probably a bomb."

Her second phase involved a series of elaborate plots. When the guard brought her dinner, she would seduce him; steal his M -- 16 as he undressed; shoot him in the shower and blast her way out of the building. Or she would ignite the drapes and scream *"fire"* to the guard. In the excitement of the fire being put out, she would easily be able to slip into the elevator, descend to the lobby, and bluff her way out of the building by saying she was soliciting contributions for the PLO. Or she would ask the guard to deliver a sealed envelope to Ward Read. The note inside would say,

Let me out and I'll give you the microfilm copies of the agreements.

The specific agreements were cagily not identified. In fact, she had no knowledge of any.

All her plots fizzled. When the guard brought her dinner, she said "thank you" and ate it. There was no point in trying to steal his M --16 because she did not know how to operate it. Later, when the time came to ignite the drapes, she could find no matches. And the note to Ward which she shoved under the door was indeed picked up, but the response was disheartening. His reply, also under the door, said,

> *Thanks but the microfilm is*
> *already in our possession.*
> WWR

Her third phase was a combination of boredom and despair. She sat in the living room and watched network television as she waited for the eleven o'clock news, which surely would report her kidnapping or at least her disappearance. There was "Barge Billy," the story of a crotchety but lovable tugboat captain who met eccentric but basically good-hearted dock folk as he hauled garbage every day from Staten Island to dump it in the Gowanus Canal. Next came "Jemima and Company," the story of a poor but lovable black lady who printed her own food stamps to support her unemployed, fun-loving friends and relatives. There was "Big 0 Valley," the story of a disagreeable but basically kind-hearted rancher named Flint who helped a lot of colorful Mexican purse snatchers and cock fight handicappers hide from the mean, narrow-minded border guards while lecturing his new friends on the benefits of hard work and clean living. Finally, just before the news, Sally watched "Crotch," the story of a seamy but street-wise and good-guy detective who was able to expose through tricky questioning the diabolical plans for world conquest of a blue-blooded tycoon from

Las Vegas and his snooty wife from Vassar.

At eleven o'clock Sally watched the news. It offered only very thin gruel: the usual local muggings, inconsequential mayhem, and incidental incinerations of unsuccessful restaurants and vacant tenements. No mention of lime green armed forces capturing one of the largest buildings in the center of Manhattan. No mention of any mysterious disappearances of beautiful administrative assistants. No mention of whatever the hell it was that she knew was going on around her.

Only toward the end of the program did the subject of IC intrude. It was a thirty-second spot commercial. The scene *was* laid in the chrome and glass business mecca of downtown Düsseldorf inside a SchneckenmitschlagHaus, West Germany's franchised chain of House of Buns. A friendly druggist purporting to be Heinrich Volksblatt but looking suspiciously like Henry Fonda sat at a small table sharing a plate of pastry with a young, boyish-faced American journalist.

"Who vould haf suspected it?" I-leinrich said. "All doz vunderful products all doz years from my original research."

"And still they come, sir," the journalist gushed. "What do you think will be next?"

"Who can tell? Vonce inspired der scientist is unstoppable in der search of better things for all mankind, ja? It is der vay of der American, no?"

"The world owes you much, sir"

"Ach, I enjoy it. But, if you insist, der is one thing."

"Of course. Anything. Name it."

"More schlag on der schnecken," the old man said and passed the empty plate to a buxom, apple-cheeked waitress with thick blonde braids.

Upbeat music. A blazing orange IC emblem that quickly fades to make way for the words:

BETTER THINGS FOR ALL MANKIND

Back to Heinrich with a new mound of goodies for a folksy wink at the camera. Fadeout.

Sally went to bed and dreamed of lime green troops fighting floor by floor for the Tower against hordes of police who all looked like Cookie, Lloyd Nightingale, and Heinrich Volksblatt.

Nor did reality please her much better the following morning. Not that anything very bad happened. The problem was nothing happened.

A new guard brought her breakfast clearly catered by Chock Full O' Nuts. He said nothing. And again she was left alone.

It was at this point that the enormity of her situation began fully to impinge upon her and her mental outlook entered a new phase. She began by reassessing her position. Obviously she was in the middle of a major corporate struggle which, unlike so many she had witnessed through the politely cushioning media of double entendre letters and sneaky memoranda, had been escalated to a considerably more macho level. She found it difficult to assess her personal danger. Normally she would have brushed aside any worry. After all, what excessive unpleasantness conceivably could happen to an attractive and intelligent young woman from Cos Cob, Connecticut, in an office building held by armed mercenaries and a possibly deranged group of corporate executives? But now matters seemed to be getting out of hand.

Earlier her feelings centered on guilt for failing to deliver to Tommy Lightmeade the Project Z File. As his administrative assistant she could not help but recognize through daily exposure to his mental processes that he was basically a terrible horse's ass. On the other hand, she felt he had treated her reasonably well; she enjoyed her work at the summit of a large corporation; and, despite occasional flashes of doubt-inducing reality, she tried to take that work seriously. Accordingly, for twenty-four hours all of her thinking turned toward returning to the Greenbrier to tell Tommy what had happened.

174

But certainly by now she felt they must have missed her and sought to find her. If they had, they would know the building had been captured. Why didn't they call the police? Why didn't they come and get her? Surely by now Crotch, Flint, and Billy Barge would have arrived. Maybe they couldn't. Maybe they didn't care. This entire trend of thinking was highly unnerving. And her agitation was not lessened by her lack of a change of clothes.

She spent most of the morning pacing the apartment. It was an increasingly depressing day. Three times she slipped under the door notes addressed to Ward Read. The first merely demanded her release and threatened instant retribution by the FBI, CIA, and the Secret Service. The second threatened massive damage suits and suggested a parley. The third offered to provide unspecified corporate secrets including photographs. She would say anything if only someone would pay some attention to her. She was bored.

At last, shortly before one o'clock, she heard a knock on the door. It was the guard with lunch arranged on a rolling table. The table bore settings for two. Then Ward Read walked into the room.

"Since we've become such pen pals, I thought we might have lunch together," he said.

"When do I get out of here?"

"Have a little vichyssoise. I think you'll find the Waldorf does a fairly good job. May I offer you some Montrachet?"

He poured the wine while she glared at him. The guard retreated from the room and shut the door behind him. Ward tasted his soup, deliberately took a sip of wine, wiped his lips with a well-pressed linen napkin, and smiled at Sally.

"Don't be too upset," he said. "How would you like to work for me as a special assistant? I find that I need someone right away."

"Thanks. I already have a job."

"Not really. I was just talking to Wiggy Pratt. He wanted me to tell you that you're fired."

"I don't believe it. That's ridiculous."

"Don't feel bad. He fired me too."

"I don't believe you. What did I do? Did you tell him that you're holding me here as a prisoner?"

"Frankly, I don't think he cares. But don't be hard on him. He's really quite upset. He has a lot of problems today. Listen, if you don't believe me, you can try to call him. He has a room over in the Waldorf Towers. Your ex-boss and that great humanitarian Or Boon are over there with him."

"I do want to call him. What phone can I use? As you are aware, the one here has mechanical problems."

"Finish lunch first. I want to give you some background information so that you can properly consider my job offer."

For the next twenty minutes Ward briefed her on the financial situation at IC; the Arab deal and its possible consequences; and his plans to block it and force the ouster of IC top management. The longer he talked, the more Sally recognized on the basis of what she already knew that everything he said had the poignant ring of truth. Ward was in full flight. His cerulean blue eyes brightened as he described Wiggy's various gropings and duplicities. He continually chopped the air with his hand in a karate gesture as he made telling points about Or Boon's financial manipulations. Meantime, Sally found herself increasingly concentrating on him and his physiognomy: the dashing streak of gray at his left temple, the strength and agility of his mind, the forcefulness of his character. The longer he talked, the more attractive she found him. Her thoughts became more and more libidinous. After all, how many women find themselves as a luncheon guest in the pirate captain's cabin and discover that he's a handsomely graying movie star fighting for justice and the American Way and she has been on the wrong side all along? Billy Barge and Crotch would not have waited an instant.

"I think we have them if we can hold out," he said in conclusion and poured some more coffee. "But we need the time. Now, how about my job offer? Will you accept?"

176

"What happens if I refuse?"

"Nothing really. But I can't let you go for the duration. In either case, I have a present for you. I had Paddy Laval pick the lock of your apartment and bring over a suitcase full of clothes."

Sally laughed. "With that kind of gallantry," she said, "how can I refuse? Besides, if that bastard fired me, I guess I need a job. Do I get to learn how to run an M--16?"

22

Ward, accompanied by Sid Bloom, Trader John, and Sally Laurence, conducted a midafternoon tour of the Tower. Their purpose was to check the disposition of the PK forces in anticipation of an assault. Both Ward and Trader John carried swagger sticks. Sally carried a pad. Sid Bloom carried a bottle of Dr. Pepper.

The tour began six floors beneath the street. The four stood in an overlighted orange tile hallway embedded with large mosaics forming IC monograms. The hallway connected at one end with two huge double doors that led to the subway. The other end of the hallway connected with two high-speed escalators that led to and from the Tower lobby. Every weekday thousands of people pushed and jostled each other up and down this hallway, in and out these doors, up and down these escalators. Today the escalators ran silently without passengers. The doors were bolted. The hall was empty except for the unusual addition of six lime green PKs behind a barricade of cartons filled with computer paper rolls. Another unusual addition was the muzzle of a machine gun poking through the barricade in the direction of the locked doors.

"Blanks," Trader John explained as they walked past the guards and the machine gun. "Anyone comes through these doors, we give them a warning burst. Second time around, of course, we have plenty of stronger stuff if we need it."

They unlocked the doors and stepped into the subway station. Directly outside the doors sat a gypsy nursing an infant. A dead lily was attached to her rags. In front of her was a tambourine in which lay a few quarters and a neatly folded five-dollar bill secured to the tambourine bottom with invisible tape. Sally noticed that underneath the rags the gypsy wore salmon-colored stretch pants and Gucci loafers.

"That's Fidelia," Sid Bloom whispered as they walked along the subway platform. "She runs the gypsy franchise on the West Side. We got her on the payroll. Anything suspicious moves down here, she gives us the word by talking into the lily."

In contrast to the scrubbed walls of the IC hallway, the subway station was a rainbow of polychrome graffiti. The decorations, recently cited by the National Foundation for the Encouragement of Native Arts as an outstanding example of Urban Primitive, covered all surfaces. Mostly these works were free-form blazes of spray can colors and indecipherable jottings in Afro-Spanish. However, here and there a normative or factual message came through with great clarity. On about one hundred feet of wall across the subway tracks someone announced: **De BiGG 50 MUTHas MARCH TooNGH.** On the smashed mirror of a burglarized vending machine another artist proclaimed in purple and green: **UP dE MAYOR.** And on the double doors leading to the Tower an apparently disgruntled consumer had written in a rainbow of colors: **ic SUCKS.**

The picturesque native scene was enlivened occasionally by the passage of gayly colored trains pushing before them great mounds of whirling trash: empty cartons of Cap'n Crunch, Duz, Rice Krispies, and Big Macs; remains of shopping bags from Ohrbach's, Alexander's, and Macy's; wrappers of low-tar cigarettes, unwarrantied birth control devices, and nonaerosol deodorants; a cloud of tattered newspaper pages from the *New York Times, New York News, Screw,* and the *Daily Telegraph* — the detritus of an entire civilization, an anthropologist's dream.

Only a thin crowd shuffled along the trash-littered platform itself. None appeared suspicious, with the possible exception of a red-bearded street violinist who kept surreptitiously looking at Ward and mumbling into a dead carnation. Ward led the group back into the Tower hallway. As he passed Fidelia, he dropped a quarter into her tambourine.

180

"Bless you, kind sir," she said.

Sid Bloom bolted the doors.

"They come this way, we'll get them in the doorway," Trader John said reassuringly. "If we can't hold there, we get them for certain on the escalators."

"Splendid," Ward said.

Their next stop was the fourth basement to check the truck ramp entry normally used for delivery of mail and supplies. The ramp ran from the Street down a long, winding path to a large steel door that was opened electrically by a coded card.

The door was now closed and a shiny, streaked, dark gray substance appeared to have oozed around it on all sides and hardened. It appeared as if the door were holding back a flow of lava. The entire area had a strong smell that was a mixture of rotten eggs and long-dead fish.

"No one gets through here, sah," Trader John said. "Mr. Bloom saw to that."

"Yeah," Sid said, "Trader John first thought we might put about ten of the guard dogs on the ramp, turn out the lights, and let anyone trying to get down have to fight his way through the dogs in the dark. But I figured, what the hell, we do it easier by just closing it up with one of Doc's new products that's still in test. The boys in the lab call it Quikmarble™. All you do is add a little water and it practically explodes. One crate makes enough simulated marble to build the Parthenon. Only problem is you have to move fast before it hardens. And Doc is still working on the smell."

"How much did you use?" Ward asked.

"We threw in about ten crates. I figure they'll have to chop through that marble all the way from the street. In fact, I think it may also be blocking the Street."

"And the beauty of it, suh, is we can use the dogs elsewhere as sort of a bonus," Trader John said.

On the way to the elevator they walked through the communications center. Underneath the bright lights the dozens of printers clacked away unattended. Messages poured in from throughout the world. Reams of unread paper piled up on the floor. Thousands of miles away at the frontiers of corporate empire IC employees were fighting and dying to achieve the highly quantified near-term, midterm, and long-term objectives enshrined in the latest IC Business Plan. The great organization continued to lumber forward around the globe on its daily rounds.

Ward idly sampled what was coming in on the printers.

Dicketydicketydackdack. . .
NEED TRANSFER WEMBLEY TO NON-MOSLEM POST DUE TO RECENT UNPLEASANTNESS JIDDA HILTON INVOLVING EL AL STEWARDESS. PRESENT PLAN MOVE WEMBLEY TEMPORARILY TO OUR REYKJAVIK OFFICE. NEED RESOLVE IF OUR WORKMEN'S COMP PROGRAM COVERS PUBLIC FLOGGING.

Dackdackdicketydicketydickety. . .
MINISTRY COMMERCE CHAD WANTS PURCHASE 500 CARLOADS PURWUL ON BASIS EXCHANGE 200 CARLOADS ASSORTED GIFT ITEMS. PLEASE ADVISE.

Dicketydickety. . .
LOSS OF 50 PERCENT MARKET WEST GERMANY TO POLISH CONSORTIUM OF COURSE REGRETTABLE AS YOU POINT OUT. HOWEVER, STILL ANTICIPATE NO PROBLEM MEETING PROFIT OBJECTIVES THIS QUARTER. EXCELLENT MEETING TODAY WITH PUTZI IN BONN. HE NOW UNDER-STANDS OUR PRICING, QUALITY CONTROL, DELIVERY, AND SERVICE PROBLEMS ARE ONLY TEMPORARY AND PROMISES TO EXPLAIN TO HERR GRUBER. RELATIONS COULDN'T BE BETTER.

Dockdicketydock. .
EFFORTING PLAN MEET OUR U-S AFFIRMATIVE ACTION AND HUMAN RIGHTS GOALS WORLDWIDE.

HAVE HIRED 1,000 ADDITIONAL UBANGIS FOR JOBURG TUNA CANNING FACTORY BUT REGRET MOSTLY MALES.

Dicketydickety. . .
SEND IMMEDIATELY CARE OF CITICORP ISTANBUL DOLLARS ONE MILLION REPEAT DOLLARS PAYABLE IN GOLD FOR RANSOM OUR DISTRICT SALES MANAGER FROM KURDISH TRIBESMEN. SUGGEST STRONGEST TERMS NO PRESS.

As Ward finished reading the last item, Sally handed him another that she had spotted. It was addressed to Tommy.

LIGHTMEADE — NY
CONFIRMING FOR YOU, WIFE, AND THREE DAUGHTERS SUITE AND SINGLE ROOMS FOR SPRING BUSINESS REVIEW PARIS. COUTURIER TICK-ETS OBTAINED FOR YVES ST. LAURENT, LANVIN, AND DIOR. ALSO YOU SET FOR BUYING TRIPS BORDEAUX AND COTE D'OR.
ANSELM — PARIS

The group moved on to the Tower lobby, which looked like an advertisement for IBM. Hundreds of cartons of computer paper rolls were piled into barricades in front of all doors. A second inner line of defense surrounded the elevator banks and a two-story-high, free-form steel sculpture in the center of the front lobby. The statue -- often referred to by IC iconoclasts as the Phallic Propeller -- was officially called *Etruscan Dawn*. Tommy had personally commissioned it for one million dollars from the until-then little-known Tuscan artist and former grape picker, Leonardo Figgi.

About fifty PKs busied themselves about the lobby setting up guns, stacking various munitions, passing out gas masks and extra truncheons. Orange paint had been sprayed on all lobby windows as protection against onlookers. And five banks of independently powered high-beam vapor lights had been arranged to blind anyone trying to force an entry through the doors.

"Actually, we don't expect much action here," Trader John said. "It's too obvious. But we want to be ready."

"Morale seems terrific," Sid Bloom said approvingly. "Ever since the word went out that we really expected an attack these guys have been in great spirits."

"We figure that we can hold off anything but tanks," Trader John said. "Do you think they may have any tanks, sah?"

"I would doubt it," Ward said. "It isn't easy to get them through midtown without attracting a lot of attention."

They began to walk around the inner defense line. Suddenly the fire alarm gong, now converted to an attack alert signal, began to sound. The PKs scrambled to their barricades. The vapor lights blazed on. All other lights went out.

A PK ran up to Trader John and led him and the others to a nearby phone. Trader John listened a few moments on the phone, hung up, and spoke into an electronic bullhorn.

"No apparent immediate attack," his voice boomed. "But hold position. Bandits are reported on the thirtieth floor."

Sid Bloom and Sally retreated back to Wiggy's Tower office. Trader John, Ward, and a half dozen PKs went directly to the thirtieth floor where they were met by two PKs crouching near the elevator.

"Three of them," one PK whispered. "They working on a lot of big green sheets down at the end of the hall. We didn't see no guns but they could be carrying knives."

"I think they getting itchy to make their move," the second PK whispered. "The top cat, he's the fat one with crazy little glasses, keeps coming out of his office and talking about making the run. And the other cats keep asking for a few more minutes to get everything lined up."

"Let's go get 'em," Trader John said and led Ward and the eight PKs silently down the office hall to a suite of lighted rooms. Both Trader John and Ward carried drawn .38s; two PKs carried M--16s; the others carried three-foot weighted truncheons.

They crouched outside the open suite door for a moment. On a signal from Trader John, they burst through the door on the run.

"Move and you're a dead man," Trader John shouted.

Two middle-aged, mousy-looking men who were sitting at a table covered with green accounting spread sheets raised their hands as all blood disappeared from their faces. A very fat man with half glasses came out of an inside office, took in the scene, and said: "Ward, for Christ's sake, what is all this about?"

"Marvin Plotkin," Ward said, disgustedly.

"I'll search the bloody bastard," Trader John growled.

"No need," Ward said. "Put down the guns. These guys are traveling auditors."

"Ward, I want an explanation," the fat man persisted.

"So do I, Marvin," Ward said. "How the hell did you get in here? This building has been closed since yesterday."

"Not to us. We have a job to do. When I saw the signs on the doors this morning, we just went around back and came in through the private door to the IC Executive Athletic Club. I have a key."

"Marvin, I'll give you and your guys ten minutes to get the hell out of here."

"Are you kidding? We have to finish this audit for a meeting first thing tomorrow with Or Boon. We don't have any time to fool around."

"Ten minutes, Marvin."

"Come on, Ward. We're not bothering anyone. You're going to louse up the schedule."

"I'll give you a half hour. After that, these fellows with the clubs will stuff you in the computer."

"Thanks, Ward," Marvin said. "I knew you'd understand."

Ward and Trader John turned and headed back to the elevator. They stopped briefly at Wiggy's office for Ward to issue some special new dispositions and pick up Sid Bloom and Sally. Then they went to the roof to complete their inspection.

The helicopter pad and glass-domed Reception Center were empty. A PK machine gun crew was in place near the Center entrance. It was five o'clock but the late afternoon sunlight made the slight breeze still soft and warm. Ward, still carrying his swagger stick, walked over to the roof railing and looked out at the other buildings poking up through the fluffy smog cover. Sally followed him.

"You're having a goddamn ball, aren't you?" she said.

He turned and looked at her. Her blonde hair was blowing fetchingly across her face just the way it always does, particularly if there are three makeup men standing by with brushes and an electric fan.

"All the world hates a smart ass," Ward said, but he took her arm as they walked back to the Reception Center and the elevators.

*   *

The meeting at IC Temporary World Headquarters had been going on all afternoon.

Wiggy sat at the head of a long, oval table covered with green baize, memos, newspapers, and architectural plans of the IC Tower. Various top IC executives found places around the table's perimeter. Both Randy Dingle and Buzz Malone, scenting disaster, strategically found reasons not to be present. However, among the more important lightweights were Doc Plumb of Research, Quince Harold of International, and Georgie Queen of Natural Materials.

Staff members, as usual, found chairs that they positioned around the room as closely as possible to their respective bosses. Each time another of the top managers summoned from the Greenbrier arrived there was a shifting of position at the table to accommodate rank. At the same time the staff aides rejockeyed their positions, occasionally knocking over smaller tables, dirty coffee cups, and half-filled water glasses.

Cords of newly installed telephones snaked across the room. Three flip charts had been set up behind Wiggy. Two more stood at the ready. A small staff of secretaries clacked typewriters in adjoining bedrooms now converted into offices. A bank of TV sets carried pictures but no sound.

"I have the terrible feeling that we're not progressing," Wiggy said to no one in particular. "What happened to Or?"

"He's talking to the investment bankers," an aide said.

"What about M. Pont?" Wiggy said to Tommy.

"His man, a Colonel Wulf Ernst, should be here any minute."

"How about the press?" Wiggy said to Les Gross, who had arrived only twenty minutes earlier after stopping at his apartment to change his clothes and to try to arrange for some theater tickets for the evening just in case he could break free.

"Coming along just great," Les said. "They had the story all screwed up as usual, but I think we're beginning to turn them around. Let me tell you, when I first started talking to them it was really bad."

"Give me another orange juice," Wiggy said, and an aide handed him a glass of orange-tinted vodka.

Doc Plumb cleared his throat and adjusted some papers.

"Wiggy, if I may, there is something I'd like to bring to your attention while we're all sitting here," Doc said.

Wiggy, whose thoughts had strayed to Aruba, said nothing, which Doc immediately took to mean encouragement.

"You know we currently have fourteen major programs underway at the lab and there has been no increase in our budget allocations in two years."

"I don't think we want to get into discussing an allocation increase today, Doc," Wiggy said vaguely.

"Maybe never."

"No, no. I don't want to," Doc protested. "But when we do increase that allocation, and we are going to have to, you know, I am going to have to do some fast recruiting. Now to do that we need to build up our recognition in the scientific community. And one of the best ways to do that is to start a new award program. I suggest that beginning immediately we start presenting a gold medal to the five American scientists who have made the greatest contributions in their field each year. We could call it the Pratt Award."

"Hell of an idea, Wiggy," Les Gross interjected. "Timing could be perfect."

"Have you worked out the details?" Wiggy asked, his spirits lifting slightly for the first time in hours. Here was something they could get their arms around. "Lot of wrinkles to be worked out in a program like that."

"Glad you asked," Doc said. "I have a few flip charts right here that I brought along just in case this might come up."

In an instant two aides set up a flip chart and Doc was on his feet turning pages. For the next half hour all details of a Pratt Award Program were explored with full participation of everyone present. Georgie Queen was particularly enthusiastic. "What an idea!" he kept saying. "Just great."

"I think you may really have something here," Wiggy said finally. "But I don't know about the name. Maybe we should call it something else."

A chorus of disagreement burst out.

"Absolutely not," Les Gross shouted over the hubbub. "Nothing would be more appropriate."

"Couldn't agree more," Georgie said.

Before they could resolve the question, an aide interrupted to announce the arrival of Colonel Ernst. Wiggy and Tommy immediately adjourned to Wiggy's private office where the colonel was then conducted.

Colonel Wulf Ernst was a short, wiry military officer

clearly of German origin. He had saber scars, a small, well-trimmed mustache, short sandy hair, and very cool green eyes that seemed to keep saying something like: "Take him out and shoot him." He wore civilian clothes but one had the distinct feeling that if he were able to take them off there would be a uniform underneath.

Colonel Ernst was rumored to be one of the few remaining veterans of Nazi Germany's elite Sixth SS Panzer Division; an officer who had distinguished himself from Paris to Moscow, including the final battle of Berlin; a man of great military brilliance who after the war escaped to Paraguay where he began a notable career as a participator for monetary consideration in a score of causes around the world.

Unfortunately for most of the colonel's clients, his greatest strength was in the field of personal packaging. Like so many of his countrymen just after World War II, his opportunities were limited and he was forced by circumstances to choose what came easiest to hand. In 1945 he had been a fourteen-year-old cadet in a school outside Berlin. As the Russian Army closed in for the final kill, Wulf and some of his fellow students were hustled to Tempelhof Airport, where they spent a great deal of time filling sandbags. After five days and nights of this, Wulf heard that he and his fellows were about to be reassigned to the defense of the Reichstag against the encircling Soviet tanks.

Others, when told, cheered. But Wulf gave an immediate and early demonstration of his aptitude at assessing a military situation. An hour after hearing of his opportunity to participate in the thrilling action at the Brandenburg Gate, he managed to board a Junker 52 bound for Stockholm with some Nazi bureaucrats who had felt a sudden need for a little R and R away from the strains of running the thousand-year Reich. From there he made his way to South America where he was amazed to find the market for German war heroes quite brisk.

At first, of course, because of his youth and

inexperience, he put forth relatively modest credentials. But, along with the market for them, his credentials improved with age, even if his military prowess and eagerness to demonstrate it did not. Furthermore, as the expatriated heroes of the Wehrmacht and Luftwaffe became incapacitated with age and good living, Wulf found himself in increasing demand, particularly as he recalled an ever-more-colorful past. Whatever he may have lacked in military ability and zeal for battle could be made up by underlings recruited off the streets. Meantime, he alone could provide the Prussian panache that kept high the price for M. Pont's services.

"So, Herr Pratt, I understand you have a little problem," Colonel Ernst said, and sipped a small cognac. "M. Pont has told me everything. But there is one thing of which I am not clear. How many men do you think they have?"

"We know exactly," Tommy said triumphantly. "We have a man who was one of their prisoners but escaped. He is one of our guards. His name is Manuel."

"Ah, very good," the colonel said, and rubbed his hands. "And how many of these PKs does he report?"

"Not more than twenty. He says he personally saw only four or five, but he suspects more. Twenty would be an outside number."

"Excellent. Excellent. With so big a building, it makes our job very easy. A lightning surgical strike in a variety of places and with overwhelming force we crush them like gnats. The building and the papers will be yours by midnight, I assure you."

"Minimum violence," Wiggy said. "We must have minimum violence."

"Be assured. We will overwhelm them in the first few minutes. I, of course, will personally lead the assault. The whole affair will be handled with the greatest discretion."

"What do you suggest we do about the police?" Tommy asked. "We have told them nothing. We want no police."

"Good. It will be all over before they know what has occurred. Auf Wiedersehen."

The colonel rose, bowed from the waist, and walked stiffly from the room.

'That's our man," Tommy said.

Wiggy shook his head and opened his hands in a gesture of helplessness.

"Poor Ward," he said.

*   *

Colonel Ernst planned what was designed to be a brilliant coordinated attack at four points.

There would be a major assault at the main doors of the Tower. At precisely 2100 hours, one hundred men previously deployed in various restaurants, coffee shops, and hotel bars in the area would congregate in front of the building, remove their matching Burberry trench coats, and, exposing their powder blue security force uniforms for the first time, advance on the Tower's main façade.

Simultaneously, fifty armed men would use Wiggy's personal key to enter unopposed the private door to the Executive Athletic Center; an additional fifteen men would make a diversionary attack on the subway entrance to the Tower; and a Huey helicopter would land the colonel himself, along with twenty armed men, on the Tower roof.

In every case, except at the main doors, the PKs would be overwhelmed in a manner of minutes, if there were any resistance at all. The colonel's other forces would sweep through the building and, arriving at the lobby, catch the main body of Ward's guards in a fatal pincers. It would all be over in half an hour.

Unfortunately, the assault on the main doors was delayed. First there was the problem of paying checks in the various restaurants. Then there were difficulties in assembling on the Avenue of the Americas. Although the crowds had thinned considerably, at least a thousand people still milled on the sidewalks behind the police barricades and the colonel's troops had difficulty forming up without attracting undue attention.

191

Meantime there were additional problems.

The subway assault was totally aborted when the colonel's men boarded an express train at Forty-second Street and found themselves whisked past the Tower station to Ninety-sixth Street. There, when they emerged from the train, they were attacked by the Amsterdam Sevens, a street gang that specialized in the use of tire chains and weighted walking sticks. Only two of the colonel's men survived.

The fifty men with the key to the Athletic Center entered the private door unopposed, slipped down a long flight of stairs, and moved swiftly around the unlighted Olympic-sized swimming pool. Suddenly they were exposed in an explosion of light and, looking up, they found more than a score of PKs with automatic weapons covering them from the balcony bleachers.

"O.K., you mothers," someone shouted wittily, "throw yo weapons into the pool or kiss yo ass goodbye."

None of the colonel's men chose to participate in a farewell scene.

Finally, on the Tower roof, Ward and the machine gun crew watched silently as a Huey rattled out of the night sky and began to descend on the helicopter landing pad. When the awkward machine was only forty feet from the deck, two large banks of lights came on and the machine gun crew loosed a stream of tracers.

The chopper stopped its descent, took evasive action, and suddenly, instead of dashing away, dived toward the Reception Center and the machine gun crew. As the PKs scattered, Ward methodically raised a small metal tube to his shoulder and fired a rocket that totally eliminated the Huey's tail assembly. The big chopper shuddered, slipped sideways, and disappeared over the edge of the roof floating in the general direction of the East River.

By this time the assault on the main doors had finally begun. The colonel's men formed into a long blue line directly in front of the building and advanced as one as the crowd applauded. The advance was greatly aided by the bright lights of the TV crews, which had been assembled by Hobart York.

Even the onlookers who had fought off all comers for their excellent sidewalk positions had, in the end, a very poor view of what happened next. As usual, the best seats were in front of TV sets all over America.

Among those so favored was SR. Wiggy had phoned to him only an hour before to reassure him that everything was under control. Feeling relieved, he had asked Bottle the butler to bring him a Scotch. SR then settled himself in front of a telecast of the *Nutcracker Suite* from the Kennedy Center in Washington, where President Edsel was entertaining a military trade mission from Upper Chad. The mission was reported to be seeking purchase of a mothballed battleship as a tourist attraction. As the prima ballerina began a spectacular pirouette, the program was interrupted by a live newscast from Fifty-fifth Street.

"This is Network Riot Correspondent Joe Garden," Network Riot Correspondent Joe Garden said with barely suppressed glee. "We seem to be watching a small war about to get under way in front of the famed IC Tower in midtown Manhattan."

As he talked the camera began to pan across the long line of one-inch-high soldiers in powder blue uniforms advancing slowly across the Avenue of the Americas. The troops carried shields and long truncheons. Over their faces they wore clear plastic hoods. A good-humored crowd of about one thousand one-inch-high bystanders held back by barricades and a few one-inch-high policemen watched from the sidelines and across the Street.

"The police are trying to find out what this is all about," Garden said. "These men just seemed to appear. There is an unconfirmed report that we are watching an attempt by an Arab consortium to take over IC by force, but these men don't look like Arabs"

The powder blue line had reached the broad open plaza in front of the Tower. Suddenly there were ten bright

193

flashes from Tower windows and large, gray clouds began to engulf the advancing men. In seconds the line broke and the little men began to run in all directions. There was a rattle of automatic weapons fire and tracers streaked over the heads of the fleeing, gasping, coughing men. Finally the front doors opened and several hundred one-inch-high lime green men emerged wearing gas masks and wielding truncheons. They charged the few little powder blue men still trying to advance, clubbed them to the ground, and disappeared back into the Tower.

"This is a real debacle," Garden shouted over the sounds of battle. "And we're bringing it to you live on prime time.'

SR pushed the off button on his remote control TV wand and reached for a phone. He felt a sudden urge to put in some sell orders before the market opened in Europe.

Upstairs in the Tower Executive Suite Jocko Burr opened bottles of champagne and Ward personally poured.

Sally noticed that Ward was still wearing a shirt with powder burns picked up during the attack on the roof. His face shone; he laughed at everything; he was having a wonderful time.

"I haven't had so goddamn much fun since I helped take Frankfurt," he said at one point.

Much later that night, when Sally joined him in the bedroom of the executive apartment with the dome, he said, "See, I told you this would be more entertaining than the Greenbrier."

23

"**THE BATTLE OF FIFTY-FIFTH STREET**" dominated Tuesday morning front pages and TV network news shows throughout the world.

There were brave, exciting pictures of gassed men in powder blue being clubbed by happy men in gas masks and lime green; a photograph of an unmarked helicopter sinking slowly into the East River and a "mysterious Colonel Ernst" being fished from the viscous water and refusing in guttural tones to comment under the rules of the Geneva Convention; a blurry photograph of two unidentified "Arabs" moving rapidly through the lobby of the Waldorf.

The general reports that went with the pictures were less than clear. There apparently was a takeover fight. There was opposition by an unidentified minority shareholder group. There were unspecified charges of financial manipulation. There were unspecified denials. There were rumors about a tanker full of Arab oil money. IC stock, which had been alarmingly volatile, seemed to have stabilized in the mid-30s. The men in powder blue and lime green appeared to have sprung fully armed from the asphalt like mythological Greeks.

Harvey Catoni, investigative reporter, was everywhere. More than eleven hundred Tuesday morning newspapers carried his syndicated column with exclusive fact and even more exclusive fiction on the "Arab grab for IC."

The NBC network *Today* show carried as a special segment "Harvey Catoni Reporter" live from the nation's capital. Harvey's report was dark with hints of international skullduggery and promised numerous new disclosures at any moment.

Advance copies of *Newsweek* appeared throughout the country with an exclusive "As I See It" column. The I, of course, was Harvey. The content was a rehash of his syndicated column plus an indignant plea for a return to the Era of Honesty and Openness in Human Affairs. He did not give the Era's dates.

Finally, he appeared along with a new country music star and a 145-year-old Russian beekeeper as a guest on the *Phil Donahue Show* to discuss his forthcoming book. Its tentative title, *The IC Debacle.*

"I can't disclose the details but I think you'll see red faces from New York to Tokyo," Harvey said good-naturedly.

"How does it all end?" he was asked.

"I don't know. It hasn't happened yet."

The camera panned to an applauding audience that included Helen Palm, who was almost buried in gold chains.

* *

The day also was to be remembered as the Day of the Four News Conferences.

Ward went first. At 9:30 that morning he met with an assorted gaggle of shouting and jostling newsmen in the lobby of the IC Tower. Ward stood on a low platform in front of the towering statue of *Etruscan Dawn* and talked into an array of cameras, blinding lights, and microphones. He wore a clean, blue shirt with epaulets, a red silk foulard ascot, whipcord pinks, gleaming desert boots, and his sidearm. A company of PKs stood at attention on his flanks. Hobart York sat behind him on the platform and kept jotting comments on a large yellow pad, ripping off the pages, and passing them to him.

"We are in a clean, straightforward fight with a foreign power," Ward said. "The current management of IC, with the connivance of a profit-crazed board, is trying to sell this great American company to the Arab oil interests. We, an independent group of self-sacrificing American shareholders and IC employees, vigorously oppose this blatant sellout. It is against the long-range interests of our fellow shareholders and employees, the free enterprise system, human rights, equal opportunity employment, clean air, fast food in every pot, ending the partition of Ireland, a Jewish homeland, sexual freedom for consenting if kinky adults, and the overall security of the United States of America."

"What do you propose as an alternative?" shouted a frizzle-haired woman wearing a fifty-dollar Yves Saint-Laurent necktie and a dirty Burberry trench coat.

"We are petitioning the shareholders," Ward said. "We are suggesting that a more intelligent and enlightened management run the company as a special shareholders' committee. Us, to be specific."

"Would that make you president?" asked a dwarf with a large pad and a cigar.

"Who else?"

"Why does the present management want to sell to the Arabs?" asked a three-hundred-pound woman in a sable-dyed rabbit fur coat and green granny glasses.

"The cupboard is bare. Management is out of cash. Also ideas. Also guts. But not idiocy."

"Who were those gunmen in powder blue?" asked a tall, cadaverous man with pink eyes and a nose to match.

"Agents of an international vendor of armaments," Ward said. "They are dedicated to the suppression of the American way and school busing," he added, after glancing at a new note from Hobart. "Also windmill power."

"They looked mostly like overaged bank guards," Cadaver shot back.

"The mercenary business isn't what it used to be."

"Well who are these creeps in lime green?" shouted Burberry Trench Coat.

"Native American lads from disadvantaged neighborhoods. All of them are enrolled in one of IC's most successful vocational training programs. In every case we have introduced a feeling of usefulness into their previously barren and antisocial lives."

"Do you know a crazy kraut named Colonel Ernst?"

197

asked a pipe-smoking TV anchorman wearing a blue blazer, shirt, and tie along with tennis shorts and sneakers.

"He's a notorious Nazi soldier of fortune reputedly in the pay of IC management," Ward said. Then, referring to a fresh piece of yellow paper, he added: "In Africa he is known as the Slayer of the Sudan. In Asia, as the Butcher of Bangladesh."

"What about this story that you were thrown out of Yemen on a charge of pederasty?" catcalled Fun Coat. "You don't look like the type who goes for little Arab boys."

"That's a boilerplate charge of displeasure with Americans that Yemenites always have made ever since they found out pederasty was illegal in New York. In this case, however, I think you will find that the IC spokesman who issued the statement was engaging in personal wish fulfillment. Any other questions?"

"Yeah, is that cannon on your hip for real?" sneered Dwarf.

"Are you?"

The press circus moved as a group across town to the Waldorf. At eleven o'clock Wiggy, well fortified with Black Label, took his turn before the cameras, lights, and microphones. TV cable snaked across the floor and along the red-flocked walls of the J. P. Morgan Conference Suite. Les Gross stood behind Wiggy with a black looseleaf notebook at the ready. Or Boon, looking sick, and Tommy Lightmeade, looking mad, stood on the sidelines.

"We are witnessing a totally illegal effort by a small group of dangerous malcontents to destroy a great American institution," Wiggy said, carefully working his way through a typewritten statement. "This group is comprised entirely of former IC employees who were discharged for gross incompetence and cheating on their expense accounts. They have made completely fallacious charges; trespassed on company property; stolen company money and files; usurped authority from the legal management of IC; and, in general, have violated the basic rules of good sportsmanship that have made the American free enterprise system the envy and glory of the world."

"Is it true that you are selling IC to Arab interests?" asked TV Anchorman, who had discreetly positioned himself behind a table so that he was visible to the cameras only from the waist up.

"Absolutely not. The Board has approved a proposal by a fine old American company called Yankee Properties to acquire a major position in IC. This company has an excellent business record in such Sunbelt service industries as budget hotels, soft drinks, and waste collection. We feel the folks at Yankee Properties bring excellent management know-how and a splendid balance sheet to IC."

"How about the Arabs?" shouted Dwarf, who was standing on a reproduction Louis XV armoire.

"We understand the Arabs have an investment position in Yankee Properties. They have many investments. But the president of Yankee Properties is Mr. Marvin Ikworth, a native son of this very city, a major benefactor of the United Jewish Appeal as well as the Republican and Democratic Parties, and a well-respected Miami business statesman."

There followed a fusillade of nasty questions as Les Gross shuffled frantically through his black notebook in search of prepared responses; but the questions came too fast to keep up with them.

"Is IC short of cash?" asked Cadaver.

"No comment."

"Are your bank loans being called?" asked Fun Coat.

"No comment."

"Will you put Arabs on the Board?" asked Dwarf.

"No comment."

"Were those men who attacked the IC building last night on your payroll?" asked TV Anchorman.

"No comment."

"What is your next move?" asked Burberry Trench Coat.

"No comment."

"Who is the Butcher of Bangladesh?" asked Dwarf.

"I haven't the slightest idea."

"Do you plan to resign?" asked Fun Coat.

"Certainly not," Wiggy said. "Why would I?"

The newsmen fled for the phones as a group.

"Was that all right?" Wiggy asked no one in particular after the last cameraman packed his gear and departed.

"You were great, chief," Les said. "They never got Mamoud's name out of you."

*   *

The soft sunlight of the Old South filtered lazily through the partly closed blinds of the Oval Office. There in the early afternoon silence it played lazily on the treasures of the past: a Chinese export coffeepot from Washington's dinner service bearing the arms of the Society of the Cincinnati; Roosevelt I's galloping bronze cowboy by Remington; a Fabergé egg sent to Woodrow Wilson by Czar Nicholas II; a painting of Benjamin Franklin by Stuart. With exquisite impartiality, the sunlight also played on the treasures of the present occupant: a polychrome plate depicting the hotels of Atlantic City; a bronze bowling ball from the Knights of Columbus of Secaucus; a key to the city of Sherbrooke, Quebec; a signed photograph of the movie queen Kim Novak.

The present occupant himself, the Commander in Chief of the Free World, Gaston Edsel, was curled fetally on a small, silk-covered Duncan Phyfe couch in the early stage of his normal postluncheon nap. There he might have safely remained causing trouble to no man throughout much of the afternoon when he was abruptly awakened by the pressures of high office. The disturbing influence was Secretary of the Treasury Warren Rasberry, his dark, untrustworthy face awash with concern. As usual, the secretary moved into the Oval Office at the head of a parade of gleaming young men carrying books of computer read-out sheets, flip charts, and calculators— all items that made the President highly nervous. Before Rasberry opened his mouth, Gaston began to work agitatedly on his teeth with the end of a match.

"Mr. President," Rasberry said, "we face a major economic crisis."

"Oh shit, Warren," Gaston said. "We don't need one of them this week. We got those spooks from Africa in town trying to buy an old battleship and everything is going pretty good."

"Mr. President," Rasberry pressed on, ignoring the comment, "you will recall the special rider that we sent to Congress to guarantee the two-billion-dollar loan for our good friends at IC. Well, sir, I am afraid that our efforts have been overtaken by events. Bunkie, brief the President."

Bunkie, a newly minted MBA from Stanford by way of the office of the senior senator from California, jumped to his feet and began flipping multicolored charts.

"Mr. President, as you can see by our first chart, the economy for the last two months has, to put it mildly, been on the ragged edge," Bunkie began, turning to a chart with twenty-seven curve lines in various colors. All jumped up and down across the chart, but the general trend was downward.

"Particularly note the blue curve," Bunkie said in a flat, overeducated tone oozing insufferable superiority. "That's pork bellies, an important leading indicator. Also the orange curve —that's consumer spending on discretionary upward mobility indulgences — the so-called DUMI Curve. And, most important of all, please note that industrial inventories, processed meats, the retail price of Chips Ahoy, and real take-home pay on a nineteen thirty-eight base with a nineteen fifty-two kicker index are paralleling."

"I was making seventy-five cents an hour parking cars in Bayonne in nineteen fifty-two," Gaston said to no one in particular. "I bet this guy doesn't know how to park cars."

"The international macroeconomic picture that we see

evolving is also less than encouraging," Bunkie continued, turning to a new chart with the usual twenty to thirty colored lines. But, in this case, all but one tended upward. "Here is the dollar in green, continuing its free-fall drop. Meanwhile, other currencies such as the D-mark, the Swiss franc, the yen, the zubi have positively bounded upward."

"What the hell's the zubi?" Gaston asked. "I wish Boom Boom could hear this guy."

"The zubi is the major currency of several of the former French colonies in Central Africa," Rasberry explained. "The zubi itself is a small chocolate candy similar to an M and M. Prior to its recent increase in value against the dollar, the zubi was often eaten by the native populace during ceremonial dinners as a substitute for captured enemy warriors. It was a French innovation, of course."

"Here," Bunkie said, pointing to his next chart, "you see the current critical disruption in the labor market. This was caused by the unexpectedly sharp readjustment of the economy to the administration's 'Everyone Gets His' package enacted in the last Congress. The new ten-dollar-an-hour minimum wage; the eight-dollar-an-hour guaranteed income; and the twelve dollar-an-hour unemployment insurance has resulted in an unemployment rate of thirty-three percent. Fortunately, as you can see from the fourteen curves on this overlay, the twenty-five percent increase in Social Security payments and the forty-two percent projected increase in total government employment should ease the impact of what otherwise might be considered an alarming unemployment number. But to do this, we must keep all other factors constant and, as you can see on this next chart, the outlook for that is not good."

Bunkie's next chart showed a series of free-falling lines somewhat resembling a diving demonstration by an Air Force jet acrobatic team.

"Look at pork bellies!" Bunkie said, his voice rising excitedly. "Look at the DUMI curve! Look at Chips Ahoy! All are paralleling the fall in the price of IC stock and the corresponding fall in the Dow Jones Index. Absolutely fascinating! Mr. President, the numbers do not lie. This is not the standard lousy inflated economy that we have learned to live with on a week-to-week basis. We are facing a major economic crisis."

Gaston, who had become increasingly bored as the numbers flooded over him, jumped to his feet in alarm when he again heard, in less than a half hour, the painful words "economic crisis." These were words to stir with panic any red-blooded American office holder.

"Sonofabitch, Warren," Gaston shouted. "What are we gonna do? If we're really gonna have a big goddamn economic crisis, you know the voters are gonna blame all that kind of shit on me."

"That's why we are here, Mr. President," Rasberry said calmly. "We have a plan. Show him, Bunkie."

"As Secretary Rasberry reported, the committee has failed so far to act on our proposed legislation authorizing a mere two-billion-dollar guarantee to IC for private financing," Bunkie said. "Furthermore, as you possibly may appreciate, no bank in its right mind would advance one hundred dollars to IC without such a guarantee at this time. Therefore, it is essential that we force committee action."

Bunkie paused pontifically and turned to the next chart. Gaston nervously relieved an itch somewhere between his legs.

"Here are the essential steps that we feel we must take," Bunkie said, and tapped the chart which had only three words on it.

It said:

- **EDUCATE**
- **DIRECT**
- **SUBORN**

"I don't understand what the Christ he's getting at," Gaston complained.

"Bear with the lad," Rasberry said. "He's our type."

"Our first step should be to call a news conference and inform the nation that Congress, as usual, has failed to act in the national interest in this matter," Bunkie said. "The second step is to inform the committee and the congressional leadership what is required for the common good.

"The third step is to inform members of the committee and other key congressional figures on a confidential basis how you will screw them if they fail to vote for the bill."

"Now there's a program a man can get his mind around," Gaston said, and slapped his knee.

"I knew if you stayed with us you'd like our approach," Rasberry said.

Within twenty-five minutes a news conference was assembled in the Oval Office. Because of the short notice, it included only the White House regulars and a handful of visiting newsmen from the hinterlands and overseas who happened to be drinking in the White House newsroom when the surprise conference was announced.

"I have a brief statement," Gaston said, shuffling some papers in search of the prepared words. "Then we'll take your questions.

"As you may recall, I asked the Congress last week to take emergency action to guarantee loans for one of our great American institutions, the International Coagulants Corporation. We viewed such a move as vital to this great nation's economy and national defense. But so far, despite our repeated requests, Congress has failed to act. As a result, the far-sighted business leaders charged with the management of IC have been forced to seek aid overseas from our gallant allies in the Middle East. Under ordinary circumstances, this would be fully in line with the great principles of free enterprise. Few people are more supportive of our good friends in the Persian Gulf than this Administration, although we certainly have equally good feelings for our fine friends in Israel. But this is a matter of national emergency. IC must remain American. Congress

204

must act to save IC."

Gaston removed his half glasses and blinked out into the room as if he were seeing it for the first time.

"Are there any questions?" he asked.

"What are the chances that Congress will go along with this handout?" asked a well-known liberal columnist noted for his independent thinking and income.

"We are hopeful that Congress will somehow do the right thing."

"Are you still in favor of busing?" asked an editor from *Ebony*.

"Only in Bangor, Maine," Gaston said.

"Do you think the Supreme Court will uphold the Appeals Court decision supporting the rhythm system based on computerized readouts?" asked the correspondent of the *Osservatore Romano*.

"If it's the same computer that handles my American Express card, why not?"

"What is this Administration's definitive position on the partition of Ireland?" asked an editor from the *Boston Herald American*.

"I have never wavered."

"Do you and Mrs. Edsel sleep in the same bed?" asked the correspondent from *Penthouse*.

"I answered that last week," Gaston said.

"Thank you, Mr. President," shouted the man from AP, who had just arrived.

They rushed for the phones.

*   *

The fourth news conference took place two hours later on Capitol Hill.

Senator Jefferson Jennings Bryan stepped before the microphones, lights, and cameras in the hearing room of his Joint Committee on National Oversight at precisely 4:15, a time, as luck would have it, that enabled him to top the statements of the President and preclude anyone else from topping him on the network evening TV news.

The impromptu news conference, carefully planned by J-J's staff for the last two days, attracted all the stars of Washington newsdom. There was Marcia Madonna, witty interviewer of kings ("Do you ever wear your crown around the house?") and popes ("What do you think are the best Northern Italian restaurants in Rome?"); Bink Barton, famous battle correspondent ("War came today to the little people of Ping Pong Nu"); Cecil Twombley, world pundit ("As we watched the Big Eight enter the Hall of Mirrors, we knew that the outcome would mean peace or war or continued stalemate or a situation entirely different in the Fertile Crescent"); and Milton Muck, veteran underdog journalist ("No one can condone cannibalism in Lafayette Park, but neither can we condone the roughing up of suspects by the police"). The imposing presence of these journalistic greats and many more among the scores who crowded the marblette hearing room was made possible by considerate calls from J-J's staff throughout the morning with promises of juicy tidings to come. And all knew that J-J sought never to disappoint.

As he surveyed the assembly, his Canton blue eyes shone beneath the huge mound of white hair that kept falling over his noble pink forehead. Some compared his appearance at such moments to that of a signer of the Declaration seen through the paint of Gilbert Stuart; others, to a happy sheepdog on first beholding dinner. He cleared his throat dramatically and his Louisiana working-on-the-levee voice rolled across the room.

"Seldom in a long career of public service," J-J said, "have I been so shocked as I was today when I heard the President of the United States ask the American people to dig into their jeans to give two billion dollars to the robber barons of a multinational cartel. At the same time, this Administration has suggested that if the Congress does not rubber-stamp this outrageous giveaway of public funds to private greed, the Congress is somehow un-American and failing in its sacred duty.

206

"Shame, shame on those who try to hoodwink the American people in this grievous manner. Shame, shame on those who would seek for political advantage to shore up the small group of ruthless malefactors who hold sway over the international octopus recognized with fear throughout the world as International Coagulants.

"I will not indulge in spreading innuendoes and truth on the record this afternoon. But tomorrow the Joint Committee on National Oversight will begin hearings on this murky affair. And I assure you the world will then see what kind of men the Administration has blindly sought to bail out."

J-J paused for questions and a hundred hands waved wildly for attention.

"The President says that if the money isn't voted, IC will be taken over by the Arabs," shouted Bink Barton over the garble of a half dozen other questions. "Will that affect the balance of power?"

"I do not see how. There are very few Arab votes in Louisiana."

More noise. More flashing lights.

"Would you characterize your statement as a formal break with the leader of your own party?" asked Cecil Twombley.

"That depends on whom I recognize as my party's leader."

"Mr. Chairman, Mr. Chairman," shouted Milton Muck, "can we interpret this to mean you plan to run against the President in the primaries?"

"I have no political ambitions beyond serving the people of the great sovereign state of Louisiana," J-J said, shaking his head modestly. "However, I would never refuse to do my duty."

An explosion of lights and a cacophony of shouts. The chairman waved and disappeared through a private door in the marblette wall. The newsmen surged from the room, trampling a group of Baton Rouge schoolchildren waiting to give the senator a cake baked in the shape of the

Jefferson Memorial.

24

World in Brief— Three
(Wednesday P.M., EST)

French horns. Drum beats. A mushroom cloud of psychedelic color exploding across the screen. The electrifying words, "Your Evening News." And once again, as all America watches, the camera zooms in on the two-inch-high figures of Martin Dasher and Betsy Poke.

"Hi ho there, Betsy. It's a great big beautiful night again here in New York."

"Hi ho to you, Martin. It sho' is, as they say down in Ol' Miss where we'll be going later for the crowning of the Weevil Queen. And y'all know, Martin, tonight we also have an exclusive interview with the first quadriplegic to float from Catalina Island to San Diego to dramatize Employ the Handicapped Week."

"Right on, Betsy. And we have our roving correspondent, Paolo St. John, all the way from Iwo Jima interviewing the last Japanese still holed up there in a cave since those nostalgia-filled days of World War II. And, as always, we have ol' Jim Jump with the weather. And Bo Bang with the big game from L.A. And plenty more."

"But first you have the headlines for us, right, Martin?"

"Right, Betsy. The news this evening is not too good."

Martin's suntanned face broke into a broad grin and he shook his head at the boys-will-be-boys incorrigibility of all mankind.

"In Havana today the United States finally paid a big price in the long negotiations to free from a Cuban prison Sanchez Taco, the Nobel-Prize-winning human rights advocate. In special ceremonies at Ché Guevara International Airport, CIA agents in exchange for Señor Taco turned over Pancho, the satellite spy dog, who was captured when he parachuted into the South Bronx from his crippled spacecraft three years ago. Because the Cubans lacked sophisticated electronics, Pancho had been trained to activate the camera shutter with his paw upon receiving a secret radio signal. Network Prisoner Exchange Correspondent Joe Garden was there for the historic swap." Fade to Joe Garden in front of the terminal building at Guevara International with a small, sixty-three-pound dark man dressed in an ill-fitting KGB-issue black suit. Nearby a gleaming U.S. Air Force transport has just rolled to a stop before the waiting dignitaries.

"Tell me, Señor Taco," shouted Garden over the jet whine, "How does it feel to be free after fifteen years in a Cuban jail?"

"Señor, are we on camera?"

"Everyone in America is watching you, Señor, and they all want to know what are you going to do when you get to Miami.

"First, I send a telegram of muchas gracias to El Gringo Grande in Washington. Then I apply for the stamps for the food."

The band begins to play the Cuban national anthem; the honor guard comes to attention; and the plane's hatch opens. Pancho, a brown and white chihuahua wearing a tiny beret and earphones, steps from the plane, blinks into the sunlight, and runs down the steps with a wild series of happy yaps into the arms of the Premier.

Fade back to Martin Dasher and a picture of the IC Tower guarded by a ring of New York policemen.

"No doubt about it, folks, the big story today continues to be the charges and countercharges over the ailing International Coagulants Corporation. In Washington President Edsel says he wants to help by underwriting a loan of two billion dollars. But Congress, for reasons not clear, isn't in its usual spending mood. And tomorrow Senator Bryan, chairman of the powerful Joint Congressional Committee on National Oversight, promises to tell us why at an exciting new investigation. Meantime, in New York, there was plenty of excitement on Wall Street.

210

Here to tell you about it is Network Entertainment Editor Tucker Boardwalk, standing in for Network Economic Disaster Correspondent Joe Garden."

Fade to the deeply littered floor of the New York Stock Exchange and a trim, dandified figure wearing a red carnation and sunglasses.

"Tucker Boardwalk here on the deeply littered floor of the New York Stock Exchange where knives suitable for slashing wrists have been selling at a premium all day. Heavy dumping of IC stock began with the opening bell, driving the price from a high of thirty-five down to twenty by noon. At the same time, the Dow fell thirty-five points. The floor went wild. Selling pressure eased, while those who could still afford it ate lunch. Finally, when the President called for a two-billion-dollar loan guarantee, the market started to turn around. IC closed at thirty. The Dow made up half of its losses. But there is no joy here tonight, Martin. Millions of sell orders are pouring into brokerage offices as word of the forthcoming congressional investigation spreads. And the big question that Wall Street insiders are asking is, 'Who is doing all the buying?'"

Fade back to the grinning faces of Martin Dasher and Betsy Poke seated before a map of the world.

"Now some news briefs from all over and I warn you, Betsy, the tea leaves don't look so good:

"In Cicero, Illinois, thirty-two tiny skeletons have been found in the attic of a man who has been Santa Claus at one of Chicago's leading department stores for the last fifteen years. Police are investigating.

"In Burbank, California, the nation's first disco funeral home has opened. The reviews are strictly rave.

"In London, the name of terrorist bomber Abdul al-Geez appeared on the Queen's Honors List. Buckingham Palace says it was a clerical error.

"In Washington, a government lab reports that white mice who were injected with massive doses of lobster bisque have developed cancer. In response to a press query, a government spokesman says croutons were not included in the test.

"And finally, in Memphis, the Reverend Bobby Towel of the First Church of Heaven and Earth has revised his forecast of the end of the universe. The Reverend Bobby says not to look for much after about ten o'clock tomorrow.

25

Pushing lines of spectators seeking admission to the IC investigation formed long before ten o'clock in front of the awesome, simulated mahogany doors of the hearing room of the Joint Congressional Committee on National Oversight. Overweight guards barred premature entry. Harried clerks bustled everywhere with huge files. TV cameramen adjusted their lights. Other cameramen took pictures of the TV cameramen.

The hearing room, quite appropriately, was in the new Spiro Agnew Senate Office Building -- the largest and most recent addition to the ever-growing number of gleaming white, classical palaces built on Capitol Hill in the losing struggle to house adequately the nation's overworked legislators.

The Agnew Building was a king-sized adaptation of the summer palace of that well-known bon vivant of the Ancient World, Caligula Caesar. As the architect said, "It's what Caligula would have done if he had had the resources." The approach from the street was up a flight of one hundred marble steps, one for each senator; through a forecourt surrounding a cove-sized fountain; and into a second court featuring potted trees and a twenty-foot statue of the building's namesake. The former Vice President, swathed in a toga, was seated in a Roman curule, his hands on the heads of two portly kneeling men dressed in three-piece business suits. The statue was popularly called *Freeing the Contractors.*

The great building in its entirety accomplished something Washington had needed for some time: It served as a means of celebrating in one central place those elected officials of the federal government whose primary distinguishing characteristic had been betrayal of the public trust. The building was a veritable pantheon to malfeasance, gross ineptitude, self-indulgence (colorful

213

and otherwise), grandiose bumble, and general old-fashioned enrichment at the federal trough. Paintings and statues of qualified officeholders had been brought from government office buildings and museums from throughout the capital for installation in the Agnew Building. Many government buildings were left denuded.

Portraits of congressmen whom constituents had gratefully forgotten more than a century ago were resurrected from storerooms where they had been quietly interred.

The result was most impressive and educational. The building became in a matter of months one of the capital's biggest tourist attractions. Incumbent legislators, inspired by the building's popularity, redoubled their efforts to qualify for inclusion.

Fifteen minutes before the hearing began, the double mahogany-type doors were opened and the crowd swept into the huge marblette chamber. The permanently installed TV lights had already been turned on and bathed the room in Sahara brightness. Committee staff jammed together at the front tables below the raised semicircular committee bench. Newsmen began to crowd each other at long tables on either side. Despite the early hour, several household TV names made entrances and posed for their own cameras. Harvey Catoni looked in and left with two of his better sources, a committee staff aide and a member of the custodial staff. The noise level rose rapidly.

At 9:55, the committee members began to appear through hidden doors in the sweep of marblette wall behind the bench. They entered one at a time, looked briefly in the direction of the TV cameras as if surprised to see them, and moved slowly to their assigned seats where they became immersed in paperwork.

At 9:59, Senator Thurston Everfast of Pennsylvania, ranking minority member of the committee, entered through the main door. Senator Everfast was a short, chubby man with great blond, bushy eyebrows and a boyish smile. As he made his way through the crowd, he shook hands constantly and shouted phrases such as, "You be good, Charlie"; "Hi there, hi there"; "Good you're here"; and, "Don't forget us."

At 10:02, just as the TV anchormen in the network studios were completing their introductory commentary to their special televised programs of the hearing, Senator Jefferson Jennings Bryan stepped through the marblette wall into the full glare of the TV lights. He paused to look directly into the camera lenses, took a professional count of the house, and proceeded to his seat in the center of the bench. There he conferred for a moment with his special committee counsel, Sydney Stick, a birdy-looking man with a balding head and a high, rasping voice; turned in his seat to face the hearings room with a beatific smile on his pink moon face; and rapped for order.

"As chairman of the Joint Congressional Committee on National Oversight, I declare this hearing open for business," Senator J-J intoned. "We are here today on a most serious matter, indeed. As many of you are aware, the President has somehow seen fit to request the Congress to pass enabling legislation that would permit him to guarantee emergency loans of up to two billion dollars to one of America's largest corporations, International Coagulants. Consideration of that request is not the direct responsibility of this committee. However, in conducting the normal business of this committee, certain shocking information has come into our possession that is very much our business to investigate. That information, if proven correct, would have a direct bearing in my opinion on how the Congress may wish to act on the President's request."

Senator J-J paused dramatically, looked toward the press tables, and deliberately winked.

"That is," he said, "should the President still wish to persist in the matter."

A half dozen newsmen ran from the room, an undercurrent of titters welled up, and J-J rapped for order.

"I would remind the spectators that this is serious

business," Senator J-J said with elaborate sternness. "Also, please be aware that we must move along rapidly to finish within the TV time programmed by the networks. I will now ask our special committee counsel, the eminent attorney from Brooklyn, Mr. Sydney Stick, to summon our first witness."

The main doors opened and six armed policemen began to push their way through the crowd to the front of the hearing room. Amid this wedge of moving force walked a short, heavyset man with enormous shoulders. His head was totally covered by a brown paper bag. On the front were two holes for his eyes, two small air holes for his nose, and a square thin slit for his mouth. On the back, in red letters, were the words "Big Dollar Market."

It took Senator J-J a full three minutes to gavel the room into silence after the witness was guided to the center seat at the table in front of the committee. The second team of wire service newsmen rushed from the room; the first team returned. The witness took the oath with one very low mumbled word. He said, "Sure."

"Tell us your name, please," Sydney Stick said in a raspy tone that would make the sentence "God rest ye, merry gentlemen" sound like a nasty remark.

"Smith," the witness said. "Mr. Smith."

"Is that your real name?"

"Naw, that's the name you guys told me to use."

"And why did we tell you to use it?"

"'Cause if I use my real name I ain't ever going to be found again."

Sydney Stick adjusted his glasses with mild displeasure and turned to the official reporters.

"Let the record show that Mr. Smith is appearing here voluntarily incognito for his own personal safety. Is that correct, Mr. Smith?"

"Sure. Like you say."

"Now, Mr. Smith," Sydney Stick said, leaning forward, "tell us where you were on the eighteenth of April, nineteen seventy-six."

216

"To the best of my recollection, as the saying goes, I was in a very tony room in the Dorchester Hotel in London to pick up a package for delivery."

"Do you know what was in the package?"

"Hey, Syd, I don't deliver no packages what I don't know the contents."

"Fine. Please tell us then."

"Hey, that package was in a suitcase with some guy's initials all over it and it had in it one million balloons cash American."

"Do you remember the man's initials?"

"Yeah. L. V. But I never met him."

"All right. Please tell us who gave you the suitcase and what you were told to do with it."

"The guy who gives me the package was a tall, fancy-looking guy who I never met before but I later found out is a big shot from IC called Kennedy but he ain't no relation to those bums from Massachusetts. Anyway, he gives me the package for delivery to a certain general at the Hilton in Teheran who apparently is being helpful in some business deal."

"Then what happened?"

"I left for the airport. Hey, I don't screw around."

Laughter broke out from the less serious in the crowd. J-J rapped for order and again managed to wink at the press.

"Mr. Smith," Sydney Stick continued, "the time is important here. Would you say that your meeting at the Dorchester with Mr. Kennedy took place at about two o'clock?"

"Na, it was later. Maybe more like four, maybe five."

"How can you be so sure?"

"Hey, Syd, I'm a busy guy. I got a schedule. At two o'clock I was working on another job."

"And can you tell us what that was?"

"I guess. You government guys are supposed to be all on the same team. At two o'clock that day I was over at a washroom in the National Portrait Gallery there in London putting a wire around the neck of some KGB guy for a friend of mine in northern Virginia whose organization is supposed to remain nameless."

J-J rapped his gavel and interrupted.

"I appreciate the counsel's flair for pursuing potentially exciting stories, but I don't see the connection with the witness's sensitive activities at the National Portrait Gallery and the subject at hand."

Sydney Stick said warmly, "Mr. Chairman, I think it is important, in establishing the credibility of the witness, to show his excellent references. Now, Mr. Smith, was the delivery of this package the only service that you ever performed for IC or for Mr. Kennedy?"

"Oh, hell no. I did lots of good stuff for them after that."

"So we understand. We will want to hear all about that later. But first I want to ask you to look at this picture which is being projected on the screen behind the chairman so that the TV cameras can pick it up, too. Is this the man whom you met with at the Dorchester in London?"

A projector threw on the screen a full-color photograph of Archibald Kennedy and Wiggy Pratt eating lunch on the terrace of the Beau Rivage Hotel in Lausanne.

"Yeah, yeah," said Mr. Smith. "I never seen that fancy guy with the white hair on the right but the other guy pouring the bottle of wine, that's Archie."

"Very good, Mr. Smith, very good indeed," Senator J-J said. "We will want to get back to the additional assignments that you had for IC, but before that we must move on to some other witnesses if we are to get them all in while we are still on television. Mr. Smith, if you would please, just move over a few seats. Keep the bag over your head. I hope you're not getting too warm."

"Better than having my ass shot off," Mr. Smith said and moved down the table.

"Please bring in the next witness," Sydney Stick said. Two policemen immediately led through the main doors a strikingly beautiful and very tall blonde woman of about thirty. She wore pipe-stem velour trousers, exceedingly

218

high heels, and a gossamer off-white dueling blouse under which she obviously wore nothing but her plentiful self. As she walked with an absolutely deadpan expression she kept shaking her long hair like a nervous pony. She was followed by her lawyer, a man wearing a black silk suit, white patent leather loafers, and many diamond rings.

"For the record, your name please," Sydney Stick said.

"White," she said. "Charlene White. But everyone calls me Snow."

"Miss White," Sydney Stick asked, "do you recall attending a private party in late June of nineteen seventy-six at the Hotel Crillon in Paris?"

"Is that the hotel down the block from Christian Dior?"

"I think you're confused with the Plaza Athénée."

"Is it the hotel up the block from Lanvin?"

"No. That's the Bristol."

"Is it the old one near Chanel?"

"Miss White, the Crillon is located on the Place de la Concorde. It is the famous hotel where Woodrow Wilson stayed."

"I do not know his clothes."

"Regardless, Miss White, do you recall the party? Among others, it was attended by a certain Youf al-Waddi of Yemen."

"Oh, of course," she said, a look of comprehension breaking through her mask for the first time. "The man with the green teeth. A darling little man."

"Precisely. Now will you tell us what you recall happening at the party?"

"Well, Youfy kept offering everyone these green leaves to chew. He had them in a big Hermes shopping bag and he kept saying they had just arrived from the best qat farm in Yemen. After awhile he became very relaxed and he kept inviting me to his room for a quiet chew."

"Did you go?"

"Of course not."

"Why?"

"I didn't know that he owned an oil field."

219

"What else happened?"

"There was a very important American businessman, a Mr. Tommy Lightmeade."

"He and Youfy had a terrible fight. I was about to leave with a friend of mine from Boeing and a customer of his from Air France and I was looking for my sable and I interrupted them."

"Do you recall what they were saying, Miss White? Now think carefully. We want to be fair."

"Well, Youfy kept saying that he couldn't get the prime minister to sell Yemen for all the qat in the world. And Mr. Lightmeade said he expected more than a sack of salad greens for ten million dollars and a villa on Cap Ferrat. And then he really got very angry and threw Youfy's Hermes shopping bag out of the window."

"Then what happened?'

"Boeing, Air France, and I went to Tour d'Argent for dinner."

"One more question, Miss White. Do you recognize the picture of the man on the screen?"

A colored slide flashed on the screen behind the chairman. It was a photograph of the Korean ambassador toasting in champagne a grinning Tommy Lightmeade at a gala Washington garden party.

"Which one?" asked Miss White.

"The American on the left with the smile and the white carnation."

"Oh, hell, that's Tommy."

"Thank you, Miss White. Now, if you would move over a few seats for a little while and sit next to Mr. Smith, we will hear from our next witness."

Again a small group of policemen moved through the main doors in battering-ram formation. Amidst them was a small, fat oriental man in a gray silk suit. He showed many gold teeth when he smiled, which he did constantly.

"Your name, sir?" said Sydney Stick with painful disapproval.

"I am, as you know, K. C. Ting."

"And are you the K. C. Ting who operates a curio shop in Queen's Road in Hong Kong?"

"The very same," he said with a little bow and even broader smile.

"And is it correct that you received between nineteen seventy-two and nineteen seventy-six from the International Coagulants Corporation no less than ten million dollars?"

"Ah, would that it were so. It was more like five."

"What was the nature of the service performed? That's a lot of curios, wouldn't you say?"

Mr. Ting laughed pleasantly.

"No, no, not curios," he said. "That is my tourist business. With IC, I have helped from time to time in many things even more delicate than my fine porcelains."

"Please be specific, Mr. Ting. Give us some examples."

"It would not be good to be too specific, Mr. Stick. But, for example, I was able to be useful to my friends at IC when they established their fine factory to make Purwul in Thailand and also their fine Albeef factory in Singapore. Then there were some unpleasant difficulties that I helped them with in obtaining trading licenses in Indonesia. And another time I helped them obtain five thousand workers in Malaysia. They are really quite satisfactory workers and they work for thirteen cents an hour. You will agree that beats Detroit?"

"Can you enlighten us as to the nature of this help you provide?"

"Talk, Mr. Stick. I have so many friends and we talk."

"I have here a list of public officials in various countries in Asia, Mr. Ting. What would you say they have in common?"

Mr. Ting read the list carefully and looked up with a full smile.

"I would say that they all became very rich because of their wisdom."

"And what was their wisdom?"

"Dealing with me."

"All right. Here is another list. What would you say they have in common?"

Mr. Ting again read the list carefully and looked up, again with a full smile.

"Regrettably, everyone on this list is dead."

"Do you know of what they died?"

"Certainly. They chose not to deal with me and fell among evil companions."

"Thank you, Mr. Ting," Senator J-J said. "I would like to reserve further questions so that we can move along to our next witness while we are still being televised live."

"Just a minute," interrupted Senator Everfast. "As ranking minority member of this committee I have a comment to make on these proceedings so far and I want to make it, of course, while we are still on camera."

"Of course," said Senator J-J. "I yield to my affable and honorable colleague from the great state of Pennsylvania."

"I thank my genial and able colleague from the great state of Louisiana," Senator Everfast said, turning slightly to the left to face directly into the cameras. "I have been most interested in these proceedings because anything proposed by the incumbent in the White House is certain to be grounded in fiscal idiocy. However, I am most distressed to find that these hearings are being used to besmirch the reputation of one of America's great corporate citizens. IC is a corporate name that has stood forth as a shining symbol of fair dealing, clean living, and regular dividends. Against such a shining reputation I can put little confidence in a curious parade of witnesses that so far has included a man with a bag over his head, an underdressed woman named Snow White, and a peddler of Chinese curios."

A burst of applause stimulated by Everfast staff adroitly dispersed about the room was quickly hammered into silence by Senator J-J.

"We appreciate, as always, the admirable loyalties of the kindly and learned senator from Pennsylvania for those who have supported him during his long and distinguished

222

political career," Senator J-J said. "However, I think even he will not challenge the credibility of our next witness -- Mr. J. Wigglesworth Pratt, the distinguished chairman and chief executive officer of International Coagulants."

The doors of the hearing room opened and a wedge of policemen preceded Wiggy into the chamber. Wiggy himself, looking slightly flushed but beautiful in a dark blue suit, was surrounded by a half dozen IC lawyers, a matched set of legal-sized corporate clones. Behind them, carrying a pile of papers and notebooks, came Les Gross and Lloyd Nightingale. Trailing them all was a tall, silver-haired man with sad bloodhound eyes, a ready smile, and an even readier hand. Everyone immediately recognized Harold "Big Hal" Trott, former Speaker of the House and currently president of Insider Associates, the priciest public affairs consulting firm in Washington.

The entrance of the IC group created a general disturbance. Various teams of newsmen rushed from the room while others took their place. Standing spectators pressed forward. Mr. Ting, seeking to move out of the way, stumbled over Snow White and fell against Mr. Smith. He, in turn, unable to see very well and misunderstanding what was happening, thought he was being attacked and pulled from his coat what some said later looked like a handgun of alarming proportions. However, before anything truly unpleasant occurred, Mr. Ting deftly struck Mr. Smith's arm with a karate chop, causing Mr. Smith to drop whatever it was he was trying to show Mr. Ting. By this time the police reached them and diplomatically escorted them back to their seats.

Meantime Big Hal moved through the crowd shaking hands and waving. Even after Wiggy and his IC associates sat down, Big Hal proceeded to the front of the chamber and walked along the committee bench, shaking hands and chatting with the committee members. Then he did the press tables. Finally he rejoined Wiggy and, sitting down at his side, squeezed his arm encouragingly and gave him a semipublic wink.

"Mr. Pratt," Senator J-J said, repeatedly pounding his gavel. "Mr. Pratt. We welcome so distinguished a business statesman as yourself and appreciate your interrupting what I understand is a very busy schedule to appear here today. Before we ask you any questions, I believe that you have a statement that you wish to make."

"Mr. Chairman, I do have a statement," Wiggy said, filling a plastic mug from a quart-sized stainless steel Thermos bottle helpfully placed at his side by Lloyd Nightingale. "However, it is quite brief. My associates suggest that such a statement fits in best with this kind of TV programming."

"Excellent, excellent," Senator J-J said. "Please proceed."

Wiggy took a long swallow from his plastic mug and cleared his throat.

"We have followed with interest the charges made by this committee and others," he said. "We also have followed various statements made by your witnesses. Our reaction can be summed up in four words: We didn't do it."

Wiggy sat back, closed the notebook in front of him, and folded his hands on the table.

"That is your statement?" Sydney Stick sneered, interrupting what was becoming an awkward silence.

"You have it in its entirety."

"You have to admit that that is not very responsive."

"I admit nothing."

"So you said."

"But we will be happy to cooperate with you in every way that we can."

"Very good of you," Sydney Stick snarled openly into the cameras. "Perhaps then you can tell us about *this* photograph."

A colored picture appeared on the screen showing Wiggy, Lydia Pratt, and Mr. Ting sitting together in the bar of the Peninsula Hotel in Hong Kong. Wiggy seemed to be handing Mr. Ting a fat envelope.

Wiggy huddled with his lawyers, Big Hal, and Les

Gross, who was trying to find something in his black notebook. Then Wiggy started to speak; stopped; huddled again; took a sip from his plastic mug; and again faced the committee.

"That picture would appear to have been taken on my last trip to the Far East," Wiggy said. "My wife is an avid collector of Canton Fitzhugh garden seats. Mr. Ting, who as you know is a well-known antiquarian, seems to have an endless supply of them. Whenever we are in Hong Kong, Lydia never fails to buy at least a pair."

"That is all you have to say about that picture?"

"Well, I would commend your photographer. That bar is truly very dark. He must have an extraordinary camera. Do you know what shutter speed he used? I take pictures myself and I could never get anything as good as that."

General laughter. Much gaveling.

"Mr. Pratt," Sydney Stick growled. "Possibly you will find the photography in this picture equally arresting."

A picture appeared on the screen showing three closely typewritten lists of names of foreign political leaders. Next to each name someone had penciled a number or the letters "NA." Sydney Stick leaned forward like a tiger preparing to pounce.

"I want to state for the record," he said, "that this document was found in the briefcase of an IC executive who had checked it in a West End massage parlor in London on Boxing Day last year. What do you think those numbers represent, Mr. Pratt?"

"I find it unbelievable."

"What do you find unbelievable?"

"That one of our executives would be in a West End massage parlor on Boxing Day. Most unsuitable."

"What about the numbers? What do they mean?"

"I can't imagine. Possibly they show the number of visits made to the massage parlor."

More laughter. More gaveling. Senator J-J impatiently waved away Sydney Stick.

"Mr. Pratt, I want to ask you one final question before

we run out of TV time," the senator said, his voice oozing good fellowship and snake oil. "We have heard considerable testimony and we have extensive evidence in our files that, from time to time, IC executives have indeed given large bribes to various government officials around the world. Do you really deny this?"

"Mr. Chairman, as far as I know, there is no truth in it. If there were, I, as chief executive officer of IC, would know it."

"How?"

"Because of our strict policy. Four times a year we make every executive of the company sign our Policy Sixty-nine form. That form asks two questions: 'Did you bribe anyone in the last three months?' and 'If yes, whom?' We have all of those completed forms in our files and I can assure you that they all are negative."

"You are a company of Boy Scouts then?"

"Precisely."

Before anyone could comment further, one of the TV producers signaled to the chairman by drawing his forefinger across his throat. There was only one minute to go of live TV time.

"Well," Senator J-J said, turning fully to the cameras, "I guess that wraps up our hearing for today. We especially want to thank our witnesses -- Mr. Smith, the man with the bag, Snow White, Mr. Ting, and, of course, our special guest, Mr. J. Wigglesworth Pratt. You were a swell, swell group. We'll be back again in the next few days with Senator Everfast and Syd Strike and all the gang here. Until then, this is Senator J-J Bryan of the Joint Congressional Committee on National Oversight saying, Let's make democracy work. Have a good day."

Wiggy took a long drink from his plastic mug. Big Hal gave his arm an encouraging squeeze and simultaneously winked and waved at the chairman who was gaveling adjournment.

"You were great," Les Gross whispered to Wiggy. "Just great."

226

26

"And now what happens, old boy? Can we expect something quickly?"

Major Mamoud sat comfortably in the library of Wiggy's Park Avenue duplex and smiled in the general direction of Tommy Lightmeade. Wiggy personally poured generous shots of Scotch over ice in three glasses and passed them around.

"I have just come from the White House," Tommy said, enjoying the sound of every word. "I have been assured -- let's put it that way — by the highest authority. We have the administration's support."

"But, you know," the major persisted, "we need it very quickly. In this recent bidding for the stock, the price is up to fifty. We have increased our tender offer twice. It seems to make no difference. There are few sellers. And no one will tender to us any more than they have unless they can be assured that we will not be blocked by the government. I have already had several unpleasant conversations with His Highness, the sheik. He is saying very crude things." The major sighed and sipped his Scotch. "All of these Bedouins are alike, I am afraid. The veneer of civilization is still terribly thin."

"Be assured," Tommy said again. "I was with our friends only three hours ago. We are all set. I have their word."

"Well, good-oh, then. It's so wonderful to be dealing with first-team people like yourselves. But tell me, do you think this chap, Senator J-J, is going to have any effect on the situation? Regular dog's breakfast that hearing, what? I thought that you personally came off quite well, Wiggy. Cheers to you and all that."

"Thanks," Wiggy said. "Apparently my wife Lydia didn't agree. She left for our place in Aruba right after lunch."

"How extraordinary. What did she say, if I may inquire?"

"She just left a note that said: 'If you can't join me, I'll bake you a cake.'"

*   *

Ten blocks downtown at the Sherry-Netherland Hotel, Ricky de Salida carefully placed on the reception desk his ostrich hide attaché case bearing the initials "AGD" and asked to be announced.

"My name is Arthur G. Detroit," he said distinctly so that anyone in the small ornate lobby could overhear him. "Mr. Rosenberg is expecting me. I am with Citicorp."

Master of disguise! Salida was wearing a neatly clipped blond wig and an equally neatly clipped mustache. Casually he looked about the lobby. Other than the doorman there was only a small, elderly woman with three Lhasa apsos and a small bag of Godiva chocolates. He was not fooled for a moment. The woman obviously was on stakeout; the chocolates undoubtedly were filled with cyanide; and the dogs clearly had miniature microphones concealed under their long hair.

"Please go right up, Mr. Detroit," the concierge said.

"Thank you," Ricky said loudly. "If someone from Citicorp should call, you know where I can be reached."

Technique! Good technique! Control would be proud! One had to keep working constantly.

Bottle, the butler, the shape of his gun clearly visible under his tailcoat, opened the door and ushered Ricky into the living room where SR was waiting.

"Ah, Mr. Detroit," the old man said, "please sit down. That is how you wished to be addressed?"

"Not at all," Ricky said. "Not necessary. You can call me by my real name, André Lamont."

"Very good, Mr. Lamont. And now perhaps you would explain a little more the nature of this unusual visit. You say you represent certain investors who seem to have

228

acquired a considerable position in IC and now may be interested in private sale or purchase. Do tell me more."

*　　*

That gleaming symbol of French hubris and financial jocularity, the Concorde, swept from the runway at JFK International Airport on the daily flight to Paris. Archibald Kennedy sat comfortably in seat 4B, savored a flinty cold martini, and debated with himself whether he would lunch on saumon a la d'Artois or sole Ambassade. Across the narrow aisle two Arabs in robes drank screwdrivers and studied copies of *Penthouse* and *Hustler*.

The occupant of seat 4A next to him, an elegantly dressed man who looked like a cocker spaniel wearing smoky glasses, had plunged immediately into an attaché case before takeoff, removed a fat financial report, and immersed himself in it.

Surely it was a bad time, indeed. Archibald felt that IC faced imminent disintegration, dismemberment, or worse. Regardless of what happened, he estimated that his chances of survival in his present salubrious position were small. Accordingly, he had slipped away early from the mounting chaos at the Greenbrier and was hurrying back to Europe to explore alternate career opportunities. Also, before company funds were frozen or totally disappeared, he wanted to make as many long-term advance payments as possible on such things as his club dues in a half dozen cities, car leases, legal services, vacation home rent, and season tickets. With any luck he might even be able to authorize for himself a couple of sizable cash advances.

Archibald sighed heavily over the misery of living in an uncertain world and again reviewed the luncheon menu. He decided against both the saumon and the sole in favor of the truite Impérial and idly let his eyes wander to the financial report next to him. The numbers were impressively large. Then, as the Cocker Spaniel turned a page and adjusted the report in his hands, Archibald noticed that he was wearing 18-karat-gold Patek Phillippe wristwatches on both his right and left wrists: one had New York time; the other, Paris time. Archibald's mental electronic calculator flashed in his head: $10,000. As Archibald's eyes dropped momentarily to the floor, he examined more carefully the cocker spaniel's attaché case. The thin, black leather box was from Dunhill. The metal fittings were obviously gold. The readout on Archibald's mental calculator flashed: $2,000. It was all very reassuring. This was Archibald's type of guy. Within ten minutes he had him engaged in conversation.

"J. Blaire Flair," the Cocker Spaniel said, introducing himself. "I'm president of IAM, the International Art Mutual Fund. You people at IC are having quite a time these days."

"All blown up by the media," Archibald said with a little laugh and a shrug. "Tell me more about IAM."

"Booming, absolutely booming," J. Blaire said. "Biggest game in town. We started only last fall and we can't get our money working fast enough it's coming in so fast. We passed the five-hundred-million-dollar mark last month."

"Most impressive," Archibald said encouragingly and began nibbling a bit of foie gras. "How does it work? I assume you're buying things like French impressionists and American primitives.

"No, no. That stuff is appreciating at only about twenty percent a year, barely ahead of inflation. We go strictly for the big ride -- minimum is double our money annually. Our art experts and art market analysts determine what will be hot next year; then we go into all of the big auctions and make our investments. Currently we've been buying Balkan Renaissance icons, nineteenth-century Greek frescoes, and nineteen-thirty Japanese ceramics. We also are into blue chips like Rembrandt and Picasso when we pick them privately at the right prices. That's a little sticky, of course, because usually when we do that the folks at Interpol are looking for the same items."

"What do you do with all the stuff you buy?"

230

"That's the beautiful thing," J. Blaire said. "Some of it we keep in our warehouses in Chicago and London. But most of it we lease for extra current revenue. For example, we do a particularly big leasing business with UN representatives of Third World countries in New York. After all, what do they know about art?"

"How about the downside?"

"Oh well, I don't pretend we're always right. We took a pretty big bath only last month on a carload of Florentine school genre prints. We just missed the turn in the market. But two days later we made it all back with two Dufys. Dufys, you know, are now selling at a multiple that makes IBM look like Penn Central. If you're not into Dufy now, of course, you're too late. However, if you want a little flutter, take a look at Ingres."

"Are you headquartered in Paris?"

"Actually, we're a Liechtenstein corporation; however, that's just a mailbox. I've been dividing my time between our New York office and our Paris office, but now our sales have been so big in Europe that we're going to have to have a full-time man to head up our European operations. You wouldn't happen to know of someone?"

"I just might," Archibald said, and took a sip of the Montrachet '75.

*   *

At the Greenbrier, the World Management Meeting of International Coagulants lumbered forward determinedly through its last fifteen hundred slides, and the IC managers still present began to disperse to their offices around the globe. Cookie personally wrote the closing message from Wiggy, who read it to the assembled managers from a phone booth at National Airport.

"There is no reason for concern," Wiggy said in a blurred, tinny voice further obscured by the roar of planes taking off. "Our momentary problems are being overcome. Our company will emerge stronger than ever. We know

231

what we're doing. . ."

There were several other sentences, but the phone call was interrupted at that point by an operator asking for more change.

Both Harmon "Buzz" Malone, vice president of the Peace Products Division, and Randall Dingle, vice president of the Goodtimes Division, missed the final message of inspiration entirely. They were upstairs in their suites working on more urgent projects.

Buzz sat at a small desk and tapped his silver-tipped swagger stick against a closed notebook marked "Top Secret" as he talked on the phone with Ward Read in New York.

"Listen, Ward, these guys have gone crazy," Buzz said. "I really didn't find out what was going on until this week and I just want you to know Ward that I'm with you. When the old chipperinos are down, I've always liked your style."

Within the next ten minutes, Buzz also called, in the long-range interest of his creditors, two top headhunters and the executive vice president of a large aerospace and outdoor living products conglomerate. In every case, he said, "Just checking in. No urgency."

Meantime, one floor down, Randy Dingle lay on his bed talking on the phone while his wife Kim packed.

"Eddy," he said cautiously to one of Wall Street's leading investment bankers, "you alone?"

"Watch yourself, Wormy," Kim said, using an old college nickname as she passed the bed with an armful of dirty laundry.

"Eddy," Randy said, giving Kim a pained look, "remember what you and I talked about a couple of weeks ago? Well, you tell Mr. Rosenberg that if he is really looking for someone to pull this place together that I'm his boy."

Randy also made three other phone calls. One was to a top executive headhunter in Los Angeles. One was to the president of a fast-food chain called The Erogenous Egg Roll. And one was to Wiggy's office at the Waldorf, where Or Boon answered the phone.

"Hi, Or," Randy said, "Just checking in. How's everything going?"

*   *

Or Boon himself had already made two decisive moves.

First, he took what turned out to be a final look at IC's books. He did not have to look very long. He knew. They were a total disaster.

Second, he telephoned his wife, Eleanor, from his temporary office at the Waldorf.

"I think that we should go away for a little vacation," he said "How does that sound to you?"

"Orrin, I couldn't possibly leave now. My Ban Nuclear Power Now Association is having a most important meeting next week. And the Committee for a Decent Breakfast for Hispanics is holding a meeting at the Pierre on Friday."

"What if I told you that it is very important to me to take a vacation right away?" he asked, and his voice took on an unusual tone of pleading.

"Well, it's just absurd. Impossible! Why do you always do these things at the wrong time? Orrin, I wish you would appreciate how important it is that someone worry about something besides IC."

"Eleanor, you are just going to have to trust me. I feel that a vacation out of the country just now is urgent. I'll probably leave this afternoon and I'll call you."

"Orrin," she suddenly screamed, as the enormity of what he was saying impinged on her. "Where the hell are you going?"

Orrin paused. Until that moment he truly had not decided. Now he did.

"I think I'll go to Milano," he said. "I like northern Italy at this time of year and I want to look into investing in a movie.

233

*   *

Without even resorting to entrails or the flights of birds, Mayhew Stark went into a mystic trance and reported cryptically in the *Specialist's Insider:*

Maybe big oil can still save IC in the end. If so, the stock would not be overvalued at 75.

Mayhew Stark would be the last to ignore the full implications of his own advice. He instructed his broker to sell IC from his personal account when the stock hit 70. Mayhew spent the rest of the afternoon shopping for a Sung dynasty incense burner.

*   *

In the IC Tower, Ward decided a minor celebration was called for and ordered dinner to be brought over from "21."

During the morning everyone had gathered in Wiggy's office to watch the hearings. Despite Wiggy's testimony personally absolving himself of any culpability, they immediately issued a new demand for his resignation along with their attack on the Arab deal. A rising air of victory began to pervade the building.

Throughout the afternoon they felt the situation continued to improve. Three more injunctions against the Yankee Properties deal were granted. A State Appeals Court judge upheld Ward's demand for a proxy vote on election of a new IC Board. The press was having a picnic with the hearings. Everything appeared to be moving in the right direction.

At 7:30 two waiters and dinner arrived from "21" and were escorted to the IC Executive Dining Room by four armed PKs.

"Don't we get to order our own dinners?" asked Square Root.

"We're all having venison," Jocko said.

"Ah, not again," Hobart York said.

"Best looking take-out dinner you've ever seen for eleven hundred dollars," Jocko said.

Dinner was increasingly bibulous and the diners began to try to outdo each other with horror stories from the business wars.

"Do you remember how we sold the key IC patents on the paper copier because Wiggy insisted that business would never go anywhere?" Square Root said. "That's when Wiggy headed up the Office Products Division and their principal product was carbon paper."

"That was just before Tommy Lightmeade and Wiggy went to Europe and paid top dollar for the wine conglomerate," Jocko said. "They planned to introduce modern production methods and make a killing by reducing costs. Then they found out that the companies they bought had already reduced their costs to about a dime a bottle by not using grapes. They made the wine in an old Fiat paint factory in Turino and shipped it to Burgundy for bottling in the chateaux."

"As I recall," Hobart York said, "Tommy blamed the whole thing on our French managers because their English was so lousy."

"How about the deal to use our excess plastic production to break into the toy market with the Big Boy Build-Yourself-a-TV-Kit?" Buddy Jones, the computer expert, said. "That was a Wiggy program until we were hit with the sterilization suits and he promoted Georgie Queen to division manager and shuffleboarded the program under him."

"Yeah, but you still have to give Wiggy some credit there for bail-out," Ward said. "Remember we unloaded all of our inventory of Big Boy Kits on the government as part of the economic aid program to India. We figured that the Indians would never be able to assemble the kits in the first place, but even if they did the results would be a major contribution to their birth control problems."

"That was you, you smart bastard," Hobart said. "Wiggy never would have thought of that. I remember handling the press. Also a magnificent job, I might add."

"Your final contribution, I believe," Ward said.

"Sure. Right after the Big Boy Kit giveaway, that S.O.B. Gross cut me off at the pass with Tommy and Wiggy."

"Not really," Ward said. "Your problem, my friend, was that as the company's top PR professional you kept going in to Wiggy and talking about the real world and what he ought to do about it. Wiggy hates that kind of conversation. Finally he just asked to find someone who wouldn't do that. Tommy looked round for a first-class jerk and Les Gross won the competition hands down."

It went on for two hours.

"Oh shit, oh dear, how in hell do we survive?" Jocko finally asked, wiping tears of laughter from his eyes.

"Simple," Ward said. "Everyone else is so much worse." Sally Laurence stood up and proposed a toast

"To American management know-how," she said. Everyone cheered.

"To Management by Objective," Square Root said. More cheers.

"To Mr. Smith, Snow White, and Mr. Ting," Jocko said. Wild applause.

At 10:45, the party broke up and everyone wandered unsteadily from the dining room. At 11:00, Ward and Sally turned on the TV in the executive apartment with the dome and heard Cecil Twombley in Washington say, oracularly:

"To coin a phrase, the political fat is really in the fire. Senator Bryan promises more disclosures tomorrow in the growing IC investigation. Among other things, the senator says he is looking into direct links between the Administration of President Edsel and big campaign pay-offs."

The phone rang. It was the Secretary of the Treasury.

"I'm calling for the President," Rasberry said. "The President often remarks that the principal reason for the world's troubles is that people just don't sit down together and talk. I think that's pretty neat, don't you? Now, unfortunately, the President has to meet with a fellow from

Atlantic City named Luigi 'Big Pig' Puccino tomorrow about the sale of a battleship from the mothballed fleet. Big Pig wants to convert it into a casino. It would be a good dual-purpose buy for him considering his security problems. Anyway, the President wants me to come up to New York in his place and sit down with you and Wiggy and see if we can come up with something."

"Have you talked to Wiggy?" Ward asked coldly.

"Just a few minutes ago. He'll be delighted to attend."

"I'll bet. Here in the Tower; otherwise, no meeting."

"Anything you say. We have Wiggy highly motivated now to reach a settlement. Let's meet at ten. Oh, incidentally, I'll be bringing with me Sydney Stick from the National Oversight Committee and Harvey Catoni."

"Bull shit you are. I don't want them near this place."

"I don't either, but they seem to have reason to be there. See you tomorrow."

Ward slammed down the receiver and sat at the desk staring at his hand. Sally walked over to him, brushed her hair past his face, and kissed his ear.

"Let's go tour the apartment," she said.

27

In the newsroom of the *Washington Post,* Maurice, a fat seventeen-year-old office boy in dirty jogging shoes, methodically explored his nose and wandered somnambulistically through an acre of desks for the fourth time in twenty minutes with press releases marked "Urgent." They said:

NEWS FROM THE OFFICE OF SEN. J. J. BRYAN
FOR IMMEDIATE RELEASE
Washington — Sen. Jefferson Jennings Bryan (D-La.), chairman of the Joint Congressional Committee on National Oversight, called on the Administration today to renounce "its disastrous proposal to shore up International Coagulants Inc. with taxpayers' dollars."

The Senator, known for his fair-mindedness and patriotism, said testimony before his committee this morning "clearly showed the Administration's catastrophic lack of judgment through its support of an international ring of criminal business interests."

[Etc.]

NEWS FROM THE OFFICE OF SEN. THURSTON EVERFAST
FOR IMMEDIATE RELEASE
Washington — Sen. Thurston Everfast (R-Pa.), ranking minority member of the Joint Committee on National Oversight, today charged congressional leaders and the Administration with "conspiring to destroy the credibility of American business."

Senator Everfast said, following testimony before his committee, that he had "new evidence clearly indicating a plot to so confuse the American public regarding monetary difficulties of International Coagulants Inc. that nationalization would become the only solution."

He went on to say that "the free enterprise system and the company that brought the world such American bywords as House of Buns, Limogeware, Purwul, and Albeef must be preserved."

[Etc.]

NEWS FROM SACCO & VANZETTI ASSOCIATES
For: Yankee Properties
Contact: J. Cabot (617—725—4000)
FOR IMMEDIATE RELEASE
Miami — A top executive of Yankee Properties Inc. charged today that "anti-Semitic forces" were seeking to block a tender offer by YPI for control of International Coagulants.

YPI President Marvin Ikworth said, "The signs are unmistakable if you know where to look."

Mr. Ikworth announced that he was leaving for New York immediately to address the UN Committee on Human Rights.

[Etc.]

NEWS FROM INTERNATIONAL COAGULANTS
FOR IMMEDIATE RELEASE
Occupied IC Headquarters — Ward W. Read, chairman of International Coagulants Shareholders United Committee (ICSUC), today issued the following statement:

"If the Arabs want this company, they are going to have to come and get us."

#

In the Washington studios of BBC, Harvey Catoni prepared to telecast live to London by satellite for the U.K. evening shows. Nearby, in the observation booth, Helen Palm ate a late lunch of paté and sliced fruit while talking on the phone to Hollywood.

"Yes, Sweetie-pie," she said just as Harvey was given the one-minute sign. "We have oodles more and you can

240

be first in the pool if you get off your ass and write us a check."

"*This*. . . is the capital of the Free World," Harvey began, as he always did in his exclusive international telecasts. "We've had plenty of action here today in the breaking government/business scandal over International Coagulants. It is sending political leaders for cover throughout the world. Shocking testimony before the powerful Joint Committee on National Oversight barely scratched the surface. The Administration of Gaston Edsel is in greater disarray than usual. International Coagulants World Headquarters is under siege. The Arab oil interests and big money forces still unidentified are scrambling for IC stock. Wall Street is in shambles. The economy is crumbling. And there is plenty, plenty more to come. I can tell you exclusively now that Gretchen Smolinski, former Mouseketeer and two times Miss Jersey City, was the IC link with playboy Sheik al-Dubi and Premier.
[Etc.]

A few blocks away in the Oval Office the Master of the Capital of the Free World was confronting the crisis in an ill humor.
He had been only twenty minutes into his post-luncheon nap when he was interrupted by an unscheduled visit from the International Leisure Snack Food Association. Sitting up grumpily on the Duncan Phyfe sofa, he listened to complaints of how thousands of Americans were being put out of work by government bleeding hearts who kept bad-mouthing the idea that snack foods could provide starving Third World populations with 85 percent of their daily vitamin and mineral requirements. The Snack Food Association then presented him with "The Chip," a 14-karat-gold paperweight in the form of a potato chip given annually by the association to the individual making the greatest contribution to improved nutrition.
No sooner had the good folks from the Snack Food

Association departed and Gaston had again curled up on the sofa when Treasury Secretary Rasberry arrived along with a group of worried assistants. He also had with him Tommy Lightmeade.

"This better be pretty goddamn hot," Gaston said petulantly. "We just can't have all this unscheduled stuff all the time, Warren. I'm President of the United States. I got a busy day."

'Mr. President," Rasberry said, "I assure you this is of the greatest urgency. This country, the economy of the Free World, this Administration are in peril."

"Oh shit," Gaston said and collapsed into the Johnson-Kennedy rocker. "I guess we better take a look at it then. There goes another afternoon."

"Bunkie," Rasberry said, to his top and most eager assistant, "Brief the President."

Bunkie, who surreptitiously had been buffing his Gucci loafers with a pocket handkerchief, jumped up from his seat and stood in front of a flip chart that two other aides had already set up in front of the rocker where all crisis briefings took place.

"Mr. President, here is the situation," Bunkie began importantly, and flipped to the first chart. It said: **THE SITUATION.**

"As we have reviewed it," Bunkie said, "the hearing this morning before the National Oversight Committee has all but closed off the option to grant IC a federal loan guarantee. True or not, disclosures made at the hearing would create for us high dissatisfaction impacts among key segments of the electorate if we should press for the loan guarantee at this time. Furthermore we can anticipate continued pressure from Senator Bryan on this issue."

"That bastard is running for President," Gaston interrupted.

"You got it," Rasberry said.

"Meanwhile, as Mr. Lightmeade advises us, the IC situation is continuing to deteriorate," Bunkie proceeded. "This has a continuing adverse effect on the world economy and your standing in the polls. Here, for example, are the latest figures that we received just before lunch."

Bunkie flipped the page and revealed a blur of numbers in a six-dimensional matrix.

"You can see immediately the pattern. In a sample of one thousand voters, accepting a variance of less than point zero zero six percent from the standard, we find that when asked 'Do you think the President is doing a good job?' only two said yes. Now that is somewhat alarming. Even more disturbing is that that is down from four on last week's survey and from five two weeks ago. The trend is definitely unfavorable. Moreover, the current score has the distinction of being the lowest in American history."

"O.K.," Rasberry said encouragingly, "that's the bad news. Now, Bunkie, give us the options."

"Yes, sir," Bunkie said. "Here we go." He flipped to the next chart, which said:

- **YPI**
- **ICSUC**
- **OTHER**

"We all agree that it is essential that IC be saved. The question is what is the effective way of doing it in the best interests of the American people, the free enterprise system, and the President's forthcoming campaign for reelection. There are three options."

He paused and tapped the flip chart tutorially with a collapsible metal pointer. Gaston slouched in the rocker, sighed audibly, and began to explore a back tooth with the little finger of his left hand.

"First, there is the tender bid by Yankee Properties or YPI. Our understanding from Mr. Lightmeade," and Bunkie nodded toward Tommy, who sat with a fixed smile on his face next to Warren Rasberry, "our understanding is that this fine company, backed to some degroo by desirable foreign investors, has by now acquired or has been tendered about thirty-five percent of outstanding IC stock.

YPI, however, despite the support of the IC Board, is having some difficulty in obtaining the remaining shares needed for control. Second, there is the group that calls itself the IC Shareholders United Committee or ICSUC. This is the group that, in an unusual gesture of protest, has occupied IC headquarters in New York and, as a result, has received considerable notice in the news media. This group also has attracted some major media attention through issuing a series of colorful charges of mismanagement and financial irregularities." He paused and nodded sympathetically at Tommy, but Tommy, smile still fixed, was staring out the window. "Third, there are other groups that have been buying heavily in the Market in the last few days. Some are arbitragers looking for quick gains. But the most active of the buyers is a Texas holding company called Alamo Enterprises. They may have more serious intent."

"O.K., O.K.," Gaston interrupted, and looked at his wristwatch, a gift from the grateful people of Newark. "So what do we do?"

"The way we see it, Mr. President, the choice is obvious," Rasberry said. "We have to come down in support of one of these groups to make certain that IC will survive intact. Moreover, I think the choice is obvious. Politically speaking only -- and, of course, that can't be our only consideration -- the ICSUC people have some attraction because their leader, a former Army tank commander, seems to have attracted by his unduly flashy nature some public favor. But, other than that and some apparent management competence, they do not have much going for them. Furthermore, as Tommy rightly points out, we would in supporting ICSUC be encouraging competent managers to take over our great private corporations just because current management is inept. There is no telling where that kind of thinking could lead."

"Yeah, screw that," Gaston said. "We don't need any of that."

"I couldn't have phrased it better," Tommy said.

"Now, as for Alamo Enterprises," Rasberry continued, "we know very little about them other than that they appear to be well financed and own an Indian antique basket and jewelry factory outside of El Paso."

"Nothing wrong with being well financed," Gaston said.

"Yes, of course," Rasberry said. "But we can find so far no history of demonstrable loyalty to the political campaigns of any party. Texans are not noted for niggardliness when it comes to patriotic support of the candidates of their choice, but these people seem to be the exception. As treasurer of your forthcoming campaign, I see nothing there that looks promising. That, of course, leaves our third option -- Yankee Properties. On balance, we recommend supporting them in the best interests of the nation. To do so, all that is required is to let the financial community know that we see no problem with an acquisition involving some foreign interests because in this case the foreigners are only our fine friends and allies on the Persian Gulf."

"What about my fine friends and supporters in New York? I just made a lot of good voters happy there by coming out in. favor of Israeli control of Cyprus. I don't want people to start saying I'm going pro-Arab."

"Not to worry," Rasberry said, and winked broadly. "Mr. Ikworth, president of Yankee Properties, is already working on the problem. And there's something else to keep in mind. Tommy definitely advises me that IC management and Mr. Ikworth will not forget who helped them in their hour of need. That's why you wanted to be here today personally, right, Tommy?"

"Absolutely," Tommy said. "And in view of what Senator Bryan was saying this morning, Mr. President, you're going to need plenty of patriotic help as soon as possible."

"You can bet your sweet patooti on that," Gaston said, demonstrating his celebrated flair for regional patois.

"Can we assume, then, Mr. President, that we have your Administration's support?" Tommy said.

245

"Oh, sure. We'll give it a whirl. Just don't forget what they always used to say in church when I was a kid."

"What was that, Mr. President?"

"The Lord loves a generous giver."

Tommy left immediately to fly to New York. Warren Rasberry and his entourage left three minutes later for their offices next door at Treasury to begin spreading the word that the Administration would not move to block the Arab deal. But within an hour Rasberry was summoned to return immediately.

It took his limousine twenty minutes to drive the one block that separates Treasury from the White House. Soldiers and police filled Lafayette Square. Pedestrians had been crowded behind barricades. Cars were stopped and checked every thirty feet. The city seemed to be frozen in a paroxysm of fear and national crisis.

Inside the White House there was near panic. Secretaries and aides and assistants and assistant assistants ran in every direction through the corridors. Police, marines, and secret servicemen stumbled over each other at every door. All telephones were in use. Warren Rasberry could barely make his way to the Oval Office.

Finally there, he found he had to edge his way into the crowded room. Along with more than a dozen assorted spear carriers, he saw the Secretaries of State and Defense; the Director of the CIA; the Joint Chiefs of Staff; the Attorney General; and the Speaker of the House. All appeared ashen. All were silent, forming a historic tableau around the great oak desk of the President. Sitting at the desk was Gaston, his face grayer than all others, his small, pink eyes darting with open terror, his hand frozen on the phone.

"Jesus," Rasberry said to Boom Boom Kelly, who was leaning against the wall near the door with an open can of Budweiser in each hand. "What's happening?"

"The Kremlin's calling," Boom Boom said. "Would you like a beer? I got this for Gaston but he has to wait for the call."

No one said anything more. The phone had already begun to ring. Gaston, the hysteria in his eyes rising steadily, paused a moment more; then he picked up the receiver. All the world stood still. Comets fell. The earth opened in many places. Some said the dead walked. Others saw a great flaming sword in the sky over Iowa. The air was filled with beating wings. Gregori Nickolaievitch Ilnyetoff, Emperor of the East, and Gaston Henry Edsel, Emperor of the West, were about to talk on the hot line.

'Hi," Gaston said "What's up?"

"Tovarisch! This is Ilnyetoff! What are you doing?"

"Well, Mr. Premier, we were just sitting around talking and thinking about having a cold one when we heard you were calling."

"Da, da, but what are you doing with these Arabs and International Coagulants? I hear you are going to help the Arabs grab that company. That is dumb, Tovarisch! Very dumb!"

"Why do you say that, Mr. Premier? Who cares who owns a company that makes breakfast rolls out of plastic and dog food out of garbage?"

"Gaston Henriovitch, my friend, does not that company also make the warheads that go on your missiles? And does that not suggest something to you? This year they get the warheads, next year they get the missiles, and the next year you and I, Tovarisch, get both the warheads and the missiles on our heads."

"My guys, Mr. Premier, say that would not be possible. My guys say that even if we gave them the missiles it would take the Arabs twenty years to figure out how to open the crates. My guys say not to worry."

"Listen, Gastonilla, my little cup of vodka, don't be a *durachok*. You tell your guys that these are Arabs — not Poles. And something else: These are not sensible people like you and me whom we are talking about. We are talking about crazy people. They don't just worry about getting two

247

cars in every dacha and who's on first. They worry about God and the Jews and how many times a day you pray! They will blow us all up over whether some woman flashed her ankle on a bus in Beirut. Gastonilla, how would you like a Palestinian Arab to hand-carry a nuclear bomb in a cardboard suitcase to Bloomingdale's because some Israeli policeman took away his orange pop on his way to pray at the Dome of the Rock?"

"Mr. Premier, I appreciate your concern but I have my problems, too. I have to keep IC from going down the tubes or I'm going to be back driving a fork-lift truck."

"The Soviet Union does not interfere in the internal affairs of independent nations. That is a well-known fact throughout the world. I could tell you that here in the great Soviet Union we have a special gulag for yo-yoski managers like that crowd from IC, but that is your affair. On the other hand, I, Gregori Nickolaievitch, also tell you that we will not stand by while you turn over a nuclear warhead factory to those yo-yoski camel drivers."

"Mr. Premier, is that a threat? I am shocked. Anyway what can you do? We have detente. We have nuclear stalemate."

"Gastonilla, my little bowl of borscht, let me put it this way: Your missiles point at the Spassky Tower. My missiles point at the Washington Monument. But how would you like twenty Red Army divisions in Ryadh? Gaston Henriovitch, I do not threaten. Let me just say the electric light bill will no longer be a problem."

"Mr. Premier, I think we have reached an understanding."

'Tovarisch, I knew we could! Some of my generals said: 'Nyet. They will not understand. First we overrun the oil fields. Then you call. Then they will understand.' But I said: 'Do not be impetuous. Sooner or later, we get the oil fields anyway through good old American bumble -- a fine trait picked up from the British. Why risk lives? Why cause problems? I will call Gaston. He will understand.' I thank you for allowing me to show my yo-yoski generals the better way. Someday perhaps I can do something for you."

"Well, as a matter of fact, Mr. Premier, you could do something for me right now. I'm sure everyone around here will be going bananas wondering how you learned so quickly what we agreed to about IC only a couple of hours ago. Tell me how you did that?"

"Tovarisch, why not? We are friends. I can give a little. That rocker you sit in to make all the big decisions. Tovarisch, if you do not want me to know what is going on, do not rock while you are talking. That activates the microphones. *Das veedahnya*, Gastonilla. And sleep well!"

[28]

They met in the IC Board Room.

Ward sat at the head of the great, oval teak table. He had changed from his paramilitary costume to a dark blue suit and striped tie, but he wore his pilot's glasses and he had spent twenty minutes under a sunlamp earlier in the morning. Wiggy, appearing somewhat used up and at least momentarily shaken by being escorted to the Board Room by a half dozen armed PKs, sat on Ward's right. On his left sat Warren Rasberry and his aide, Bunkie.

Behind them two full walls of glass opened the room to a view of the entire smog cover over Manhattan, the Outer Harbor, and New Jersey. The other two walls were paneled and hung with portraits of such IC worthies as Wingate Cotton, Heinrich Volksblatt, SR, and Wiggy.

From where the portraits hung, IC's worthies could gaze anytime the smog happened to lift at what was one of the world's great panoramas — the mighty towers of Corporate America, the fabulous gateway to Golconda, the Statue of Liberty with her upthrust welcoming beacon, the open Atlantic causeway from the Old World to the New. Regrettably, the smog today was a particularly thick field of dirty yellow gauze. Only the tops of the World Trade Center and the Chrysler and Empire State buildings were visible, along with a small plane hauling a streamer. It said: **SAVE ENERGY — EAT BEFORE SUNDOWN.** As the plane neared the IC Tower, the pilot waved, but suddenly his propeller stopped turning and the plane plunged dramatically into the smog.

"Sydney Stick and Harvey Catoni are expected to arrive within the hour," Rasberry said, in an opening statement designed to show he was running the meeting even if he had been seated on the floor. "I thought it best that we go over some matters first. Bunkie, brief us."

Bunkie jumped up, removed a small table easel from a

candy-striped carrying case, and propped some large cards on it.

"Let's start with a look at the situation," he said and turned the first card. It said: **SITUATION.**

"We all understand that something must be done quickly to save this company," he said. "The question is not so much what is to be done. I think it is agreed that what is needed immediately is a massive transfusion of dollars. The question is who will insert the needle."

"A little less color, Bunkie," Rasberry said. "Just go on."

"Yes, well, as I said, who will do the job is the question. Let's look at our options."

Bunkie turned a card. It said:

OPTIONS
- **W. PRATT**
- **W. READ**
- **ALAMO ENTERPRISES**

"Now Mr. Pratt might obtain the money from the banks with a government-guaranteed loan. But the President, in view of Senator Bryan's hearings, no longer feels that this is a happy idea. Mr. Pratt also might obtain the money from a merger with Yankee Properties and their good supporters on the Persian Gulf. But that no longer can be permitted because the President has an aversion to war with the Russians. Mr. Pratt also may have a new alternative, but on the basis of Mr. Read's charges and information in the hands of the committee, Mr. Pratt could spend the next one hundred and thirty-four years in jail and therefore, from a practical viewpoint, he would not be able to pursue an alternative course no matter how promising. This eliminates our first option."

Bunkie picked up a red marker and drew a line through Wiggy's name. Wiggy looked pained. Bunkie proceeded.

"Our information indicates that Mr. Read would indeed be able to attract any new bank support he might need if he can win a proxy vote to oust the present Board, elect a

252

new one, elect himself as president, generally clean house, and institute a new era of superb management for this great company. That, of course, is precisely what should happen under our free enterprise system and if there is any justice in the world at all. As our Secretary of the Treasury himself often says to me during our frequent discussions about my insulting level of compensation, 'Bunkie, don't worry. The true professional always rises to the top.' But, unfortunately, we have some special circumstances. Because of the occupation of this building, there are enough charges against Mr. Read to send him away for life. We simply don't have that kind of time. Furthermore, let's face it; no President of the United States, let alone the leaders of American business, can allow gross incompetence to become a valid reason for dismissal of top management. That, gentlemen, is a matter of national policy. In sum, option two is eliminated."

Bunkie picked up his marker and drew a line through Ward's name. Ward looked pained.

"Happily, we have a confluence of random factors that could make our third option attractive," Bunkie said, brightening. "During the last few days a fine Texas firm called Alamo Enterprises has acquired almost a third of the outstanding common shares of International Coagulants. Furthermore, we were informed only last night that Alamo Enterprises has reached an agreement with a private group of investors headed by the noted financier, Mr. Solomon Rosenberg, by which they have voting control of an additional twenty-five percent. In brief, they have majority control. Now, as it turns out, such a takeover would have the support of Senator Bryan who, it seems, has long been familiar with the fine folks at Alamo and appreciates their continuing support of his many campaigns. The President, in turn, would also find Alamo acceptable since that would solve the IC problem and at least for the present get Senator Bryan off his back. Therefore, Option Three is the best for all concerned."

Bunkle drew a circle around Alamo Enterprises, sat

down, and looked toward Warren Rasberry to continue. But, before Rasberry could say anything, Ward slammed his hand on the table.

"Damn it, Wiggy, are you going to sit there and let this happen?" Ward shouted. "These bastards are trying to steal our company. It's one thing for me to kick you out on your ungrateful ass, but I'm not going to sit here and let this happen and I expect to get your support."

"I don't think we have a lot of choice," Wiggy said vaguely.

"If we're smart and slippery enough, there's always a way," Ward said. "You know that better than anyone."

"Gentlemen, please," Rasberry said. "We don't wish to discommode anyone. I think when you hear the total package you will see that the best interests of all have been taken into consideration."

"O.K., I'm listening," Ward said and folded his arms over his chest. "So far, I don't like a damn thing I've heard."

Rasberry stagily took some papers from his attaché case and adjusted his half glasses. This seemed to double the normally untrustworthy impression he projected.

"We all recognize the need for accommodation," Rasberry began. "After all, the motto of this Administration is *Everybody Gets His* and the President is a stickler for keeping his campaign promises. Bunkie has outlined to you the realities of the options we face. Alamo Industries does have majority control. Both the President and Senator Bryan have agreed for the reasons outlined that acquisition by Alamo would be best for the country. However, both also recognize that the efforts of others must be rewarded to assure a smooth transition. Therefore, Senator Bryan has agreed to stop his hearings and find all charges against Mr. Pratt, IC, and, most of all, the President to be inconclusive hearsay and vicious rumor. Mr. Pratt, in turn, will seek immediate early retirement from IC and make himself as invisible as possible."

Rasberry paused and tried to look over his glasses at

254

Ward in what he hoped was an ingratiating manner.

"Now in your case, Mr. Read, we would hope that you would drop your charges against Mr. Pratt and his associates and withdraw the fifty-two legal actions that you currently have pending across the country. In return the government will not prosecute any charges against you and your associates for such things as illegal entry, trespassing, embezzlement, kidnapping, and inciting to riot. As the President often says, let bygones be bygones. Moreover, in recognition of your obvious talents and good sportsmanship, the President is willing to appoint you as ambassador to NATO, director of the CIA, or special advisor on Far Eastern Economic Affairs, depending on where you prefer to live."

Rasberry again paused and a momentary meaningful smile appeared.

"I hardly need to add to businessmen of your astuteness and statesmanlike outlook that neither you nor your associates will be exactly hurting because of the Alamo Enterprises takeover," he said. "IC stock opened this morning at seventy-four. I believe all of your options, Mr. Read, are under thirty. And, of course, all of yours, Mr. Pratt, are under ten. Well, there you have it, fellows. What do you say? Do we have a deal?"

"I already have my tickets to Aruba," Wiggy said. "Tommy is on his own."

Ward shrugged and winked at Wiggy.

"I have never learned to enjoy rape no matter how inevitable, but I do know when to resign myself to it," Ward said. "Furthermore, under the happy circumstances that you outline, Mr. Secretary, I think government service could be most exciting -- particularly as an alternative to jail."

"Good," Rasberry said. "Then there is one more thing that you must know. We have something of a little problem with Harvey Catoni. It seems that he has accumulated a great deal of information, but, in the interests of the nation and his media contracts, he is ready to be most helpful.

Bunkie, Mr. Catoni should be outside. Please show him in."

Harvey Catoni entered the room, followed by Sydney Stick and Helen Palm. Harvey, wearing a rumpled blue blazer and rope-soled earth shoes, appeared in high spirits and walked around the room shaking hands. Sydney Stick was as bleak as ever. Helen Palm, towering over Harvey, jangled as she did a brief inspection of the windows; then cascaded like a slot machine jackpot into one of the big conference room chairs next to Wiggy.

"I thought it a good idea for my agent, Helen Palm, to join us," Harvey said, nodding in Helen's direction. "She can add a lot to a meeting like this."

"I'm sure that she can," Rasberry said. "Now, Sydney, you and the good senator will be happy to know we are all agreed. Therefore, Mr. Pratt and Mr. Ward need some reassurances from you.

"You have them," Sydney said in his rottenest tone. "For the record, and in Mr. Catoni's presence, we at the committee, of course, have no idea of the substance of the agreement. However, the senator asked me to say bon voyage to Mr. Pratt and to tell Mr. Read that should he ever be appointed to anything the senator would support the nomination."

"Excellent," Rasberry said. "And now, Mr. Catoni, you had a small favor to ask."

"You bet," Harvey said. "As you know, I have enough in my files to blow everybody out of the water. However, my agent, Ms. Palm, has suggested that if much of this information can be held on an exclusive basis for the next month I will have time to fulfill contracts for two more books, a movie, a four-part TV series, and at least ten speaking engagements. Accordingly, strictly in the national interest, I am willing to forget about certain outrageous tidbits if I can be assured of a clear first shot."

"You, sir, are a patriot," Rasberry said convivially. "All those in favor of Mr. Catoni's noble gesture, so signify."

Wiggy, Ward, Sydney, and Warren held up their hands.

"You're all a bunch of sweetie-pies," Helen Palm said.

"Don't forget, when you get around to writing your own books on this, I can get you a better deal than anyone in the biz."

"Ward, do one last favor for me," Wiggy said. "Unless your fellows drank it, I think you'll find some Scotch over there in the safe behind SR's portrait. How about a little pick-me-up all around?"

*   *

Shortly after 3 P.M., with absolute precision, the main doors of the IC Tower opened and, under the command of Trader John, more than one hundred PKs deployed into the street. The PKs swiftly swept pedestrians from the sidewalk and formed a human square blocking off the plaza in front of the building. TV crews, alerted within the hour, along with their bosses, who were preparing the prime-time evening newscasts, were already set up. A large crowd of newsmen waited in position in the lobby in front of *Etruscan Dawn,* where microphones and a platform were in place.

Sirens wailed from a long way off; then grew increasingly louder. Finally the motorcade approached, up the Avenue of the Americas: a half dozen motorcycle police riding abreast; two black Mercedes 600s; another half dozen motorcycle policemen riding as flankers on either side. City police joined the PKs in holding back thousands of onlookers as the motorcade approached in the dim, smog-filtered light. On a signal the PK square opened to permit the motorcade to enter; then closed ranks. The two enormous limousines pulled to the curb. President Gaston Edsel and Senator Jefferson Jennings Bryan, both having arrived minutes earlier by helicopter from Washington, landed on the Tower roof and walked together from the Tower to meet the cars.

There was a pause to allow cameramen to close in on the scene. Then a uniformed chauffeur jumped from the lead car and opened the rear door. The man who emerged

257

was heavyset, of medium height, with ebony hair and eyes, mahogany skin, and a huge hawk nose that broke in three places as if it had been carved from basalt. He was dressed gorgeously in a melon-colored Pierre Cardin silk suit. On his right wrist he wore an ashtray-sized gold wristwatch with four dials and a calculator. On his left wrist he wore a five-pound gold identification bracelet. It said: **JOE THE X.**

As he shook hands with the President and the Senator, the door of the second car opened and two men emerged. One was a very tall, weatherbeaten man in cowboy boots and a ten-gallon hat. The crowd recognized him and applauded wildly. It was Billy Bowie, the famous movie star. The other man was Tommy Lightmeade. He drew no applause.

The official party now moved back across the plaza into the Tower and mounted the platform where Warren Rasberry was waiting with the press. As soon as Joe the X was seated, with the President on his right and Senator J-J on his left, Warren opened the proceedings.

"The Administration," he said, "with the full cooperation of the great senator from Louisiana has saved this major corporation from being swallowed up by foreign Arab sheiks glutted with ill-gotten oil profits. Only in the nick of time did we uncover the plot, thanks to able staff work by the Treasury Department and the Committee on National Oversight. Fortunately, we also have been able to bring about within the normal processes of the free enterprise market the acquisition of International Coagulants by a truly all-American company that can bring to IC the capital resources and fresh management capability needed to continue its great role in American industry, national defense, and world trade. That company is Alamo Enterprises of Houston, Texas, headed by none other than Billy Bowie, star of no less than fifty stirring sagas of the Old West. Moreover, the principal shareholder of Alamo Industries is another great American in the broadest sense of the word. Let me introduce you now to Mr. Joseph

Xypaxtyxl, philanthropist. . . friend of the American Indian .
. . and, best of all, Mexican oil billionaire."

Joe the X read a brief statement:

"Señor Pratt is retired. Señor Lightmeade is chairman.
He will be headquartered in New York. Señor Arthur Drake
is president and chief executive officer. He will be at a new
second headquarters to be established on my estate at
Cuernavaca. Employees take heart. No other changes are
planned today. Señor Lightmeade will answer any
questions. He talks good."

Joe the X left immediately. As the Mercedes 600 pulled
away, Ricky de Salida, dressed in a chauffeur's uniform at
the wheel of the car, watched through the rearview mirror
the changing of the Tower flags. The flag of the United
States and the battle flag of the Third Army came down. In
their place, unfurled to April's breeze, were the flags of the
Republics of Texas and Mexico.

Technique! Master of disguise! Control would have
been proud!

JUST OFF the Faubourg St.-Honoré, in an ancient and elegant *hôtel particulier,* the American Ambassador to NATO maintained a small Parisian hideaway where he and his wife Sally fled when they wearied of the depressing atmosphere of Brussels.

More than a year after the acquisition of IC by Alamo Enterprises their old friend Jocko Burr visited them there one evening in time for cocktails. It was not a purely social call.

Sally, beautiful as ever, had significantly improved her overall appearance as one can only do with the aid of excellent taste, a half dozen couturiers, and a ready supply of francs (Swiss). Ward was unchanged. No matter what he wore he looked as if he were in uniform. His appearance was increasingly distinguished in the Kennedy School of Great Perpetually Boyish Profiles. But he had a problem and it made him testy.

"I need your help, goddamn it," he said for the fourth time. "Everywhere I look, we're screwing things up."

Jocko stared into the bottom of his empty glass as if astonished that the four ounces of gin that Sally had poured into it three times had disappeared so quickly.

"I don't know what I can do," Jocko said. "I've only been with Senator Everfast for six months. I don't think he'll listen to me."

"He'll listen to you. Don't underrate yourself. Tell him you've been talking to me. Tell him I said he doesn't have a chance of beating J-J for President and J-J, once elected, couldn't manage a whorehouse in Baton Rouge. Tell him if we're going to save the country and the free enterprise system, we damn well better put a top manager in the White House. And tell him I'm available and I'm going to do it one way or another."

"Oh shit, oh dear," Jocko said. "Oh shit, oh dear."

ABOUT THE AUTHOR

James Baar is a writer, international communications consultant, journalist, corporate communications software developer, and business executive and college lecturer. His latest book, *The Careful Voter's Dictionary of Language Pollution (Understanding Willietalk and Other Spinspeak)*, is available from 1stBooks Library as an electronic book and in softcover; also from booksellers throughout the world.   In addition to *The Great Free Enterprise Gambit,* Baar is also the author of four non-fiction books on politics and technology. He lives in Providence, RI.